From This Time Forth

June Masters Bacher

HARVEST HOUSE PUBLISHERS
Eugene, Oregon 97402

FROM THIS TIME FORTH

Copyright © 1991 by Harvest House Publishers
Eugene, Oregon 97402

Bacher, June Masters.
    From this time forth / by June Masters Bacher.
    ISBN 0-89081-891-6
    I. Title.
    PS3552.A257F76   1991   91-11226
    813'.54—dc20   CIP

Printed in the United States of America.

Dedicated to:

Med Cody Barnard
Carol Campbell
Jan Henderson
Marjorie Johnson
John Leykom
Lucke Miller

In appreciation for their faithfulness
in sharing my work with others.

I always thank God for you
(1 Corinthians 1:4 NIV)

Contents

"*Look down, ye gods, on this and on this couple drop a blessed crown.*"

—Shakespeare

We will bless the Lord from this time forth and forevermore.

—Psalm 115:18

1

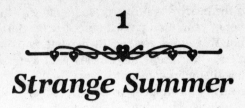

Strange Summer

Rachel jumped when the urgent knock sounded at the door. No sound-of-mind person would brave such a storm!

Or was it a *person*? Opening the drape a crack, she saw what looked more like a raven sent from Noah's ark in search of carrion. The hooded black slicker, peaking to cover the face, and the black rubber boots created the illusion, of course. Nevertheless, it was impossible to control memories of those early-day superstitions when such scavengers, searching for prey, sailed over Blue Bucket Mine. They portended danger—which came ... changing their lives forever.

"Open up! Lordsburg's drowning!"

Yolanda.

Quickly Rachel Lord Jones opened the door against the unexpected storm and ushered in Yolanda Lee Killjoy. Without waiting for an invitation, the always-welcome guest began stripping off her rain gear and hanging it on the hall tree, hung her umbrella on the hook beside it, then expertly positioned the heel of her left foot in the V of the homemade bootjack and yanked her foot free. Both feet released from captivity, she padded in her stockinged feet from the entrance hall into the dimness of the lamplit parlor.

"Turn up the wicks. Yo, while I warm up the coffee. You don't have to tell me you have a problem. Well, so do I, darling. We'll talk."

Yolanda's face, turned toward the window, looked tired—and, Rachel realized with a jolt, so much older than even a year ago.

Reflected in the nearby oval mirror suddenly was the face of a stranger. A lot of years had passed since the Lee family left the East for what Yolanda described in her letters as "God's rose garden" because "He keeps the bushes well-watered the year 'round so they'll stay in constant bloom."

Lordsburg truly *did* appear to be drowning. It was easy to believe on a day like this, Rachel thought wryly as she placed small teatime napkins on the silver tray. Or were both of them *looking* for an excuse to drown along with the city?

Yolanda did not look up when Rachel pushed the tea cart before her. "That coffee could walk," she promised as lightly as possible. "Shall we—"

It was no use. Yolanda wasn't listening. Her long fingers, as expressive as her eyes, were now twisting and knotting her handkerchief, and the eyes were confused, concerned—those of a lost little girl. Even her hair was different, Rachel realized. Usually so neat, dressed in a thick, rich swirl on top of her head, Yolanda's hair now hung dank with the damp of the day to rest on the wilted lace surrounding the lower-cut neckline of her summer blouse. Both women had a need to talk. But now?

Rachel inhaled deeply. Then she, too, turned to watch the storm.

Rain struck against the windowpanes sharply...steadily... insistently. Each drop paused as if to peer inside inquisitively. Then, as if satisfied with what it saw, it joined the other raindrops to form a hazy pattern and flowed lazily to earth.

What the eyes of the rain saw in one of Lordsburg's oldest dwellings were the pale faces of two lifelong friends, perplexed by life's problems and attributing them to the rain. It was true that such weather belonged with the preceding months as a part of the muddy rites of spring—not to mid-June! This was the time for weddings....

Weddings! Rachel stiffened. Was that what started it all?

Only moments ago Estrellita had stood here in the gloom of this very room—so young, so beautiful, and so mystery-filled— once so uncertain, now so in control. Or was it only an illusion that painted the dark eyes so fiercely and set the rounded jaw with such defiance? Certainly, it was no illusion that caused the musical chimes of her voice to hush, changing her somehow from child to woman. Star, her little Star, was growing up.

"I must make my own decisions!" In Rachel's ears, the words stabbed the air.

Tears that matched the rain formed in Rachel's eyes. Her daughter might as well have said: "Who are *you* to tell me what the Lord would have me do? In reality, by what authority do you tell me *anything*?"

The words hung between them unspoken. Star was too thoughtful, too polite, to speak in such a manner. But this child of mystery who had appeared from the vast nowhere along the Oregon Trail left as much unexplained now as then. The truth was that Rachel had stood in awe of her, viewed her as a miracle child, a child of the spirit who was by the Creator Himself stamped "Handle with Care."

"I've done a good job," Rachel had thought a little defensively, only to regret the thought immediately. "I never learned to deal with the child of the flesh—to tumble and tease the way Cole did, to listen and learn as Buck does." How then was she to know— really *know*—what was in the heart of this dark-eyed beauty who had known so much tragedy in her 16 years? The sadness in the baby face remained. Shouldn't she have been able to erase it— bring the gift of Star's seldom-seen sunlit smile more often?

Right then, why did she feel awkward? Because of what Star had said—or was it something left *unsaid*?

Well, give her credit for trying. Tongue-tied, Rachel reached out uncertainly to touch the cream-bisque satin of the tapering fingers, so obviously those of an artist. Was it by accident that Star pulled her hands away, laced the fingers, and drifted into her private world, closing the door behind her—a door Rachel had never been able to open? In fact, she hadn't known or wanted to face what suddenly widened the gulf between them until something in Yolanda's voice...

Yolanda! Rachel had forgotten her presence. She must speak. *Now.*

"Haven't we watched the storm long enough?" This time her attempt at lightness was more successful. "'Rain, rain, go away; come again some other day'—remember our little jingle, Yo? Shall I warm our coffee?"

"Yes—and no. Yes, I remember. No, the coffee's all right—"

Rachel pretended to stir her own. "What is the big secret? I mean, who's being married Sunday? Remember telling me—or starting to?"

Yolanda jumped, spilling coffee in her lap. "See why I preferred it cold?" She tried to smile as she wiped at the small spot. "It—it was mention of the word *marriage*." Yolanda kept her face averted.

Rachel nodded, although moments before it would have been she who was startled. "Don't ask me how, but I knew. Go ahead, Yo."

"It's Callie," Yolanda blurted, strengthened by the friend who always understood. "I promised Ma—uh, my mother—on her deathbed—" Yolanda's voice broke before she was able to continue, "I'd look after Callie—and now—"

"Wasn't Callie old enough to look out for herself?"

"Yes, and a lot smarter than I am. But I'm guessing my parents always wanted their youngest to avoid the mistakes of their oldest. It's a way for me to make up for the suffering I caused them. A promise is a sacred thing and, oh Rachel, a promise *is* a sacred thing, and I—I can't handle it. I'm about to fail them again."

And this time I can't help you. Our problems are too similar.

"Maybe you're being too hard on yourself." Was she speaking to Yolanda or herself? "Tell me the problem, Yo."

Yolanda drained the remains of the cold coffee. "We were never very close. I'd like to blame it on the age difference, but deep down I know it was because I was too involved in my own problems. Still," she said, straightening, "at least, I'm not jealous, like she called me."

"What brought it about?"

Callie was the girl of the mystery pair to be married. No, Yolanda's sister did not tell her, she just *knew*. And to *him*. Oh, Yolanda could not bear that, so they had a fight—a terrible one, without ever really *truly* nailing down the reason. It was stupid, but Yolanda realized too late it was because she had never been the "big sister" she should have been—never talked, never told Callie how beautiful she was or how smart. And, most of all, never told her how much she loved her. "Even when we were screaming at each other, Rachel, I loved her—wanted to reach out and take her in my arms. Oh, I must go!"

"Not before we pray!" *And I tell you my story*, she wanted to add.

"It's going to be a strange summer—maybe heartbreaking," Yolanda said.

Rachel nodded, and they dropped to their knees.

2

A Searching Heart

The rain had blown away with a single puff of the north wind. The big clock chimed six. But pale-blue shadows lingered in the fragrant garden to match the long muslin dress into which Rachel had changed. Would she never grow accustomed to the long summer twilights of the Oregon Country? By sun-time or clock-time, however, six o'clock announced evening. By *dinner-time*, six chimes meant gathering of the family (she smiled), a time for Buck to call out words of the old poem: "Are all the children in? The night is falling; The dark clouds gather in the threatening West...."

The clouds were not arriving, but the family should be. Rachel's depression had receded like the clouds as she hurried to freshen for her husband's homecoming, but now anxiety came to replace it. Why the delay? Of course, their children—Mary Cole and the twins—were at camp meeting for a week. But Buck had made no mention of tardiness. Yet it was foolish to be concerned about him. It was only a few minutes past the hour. But Star—where was Star? Bible classes ended at four, and she usually hurried home to share events of the day. *I didn't dream this morning or put more significance to it than it rated*, Rachel told herself one moment. The next moment her imagination ran wild. The scene was ugly. She *must* talk to Buck, feel his arms around her. *Now!*

Without thought of preparation of the evening meal, Rachel hurried out the door, forgetting to lock it in her haste. "Be still," she commanded her heart. "Any moment now my prince will come." Yes, her prince—just an ordinary man, lacking the shining armor, and afoot instead of riding the fairy-tale white charger. But in the eyes of a loving mate, a prince. Sir Buckley. The thought brought a smile which worked magic. It erased two-score-and-more years between maturity and maidenhood. And it brought her husband.

"Hello, my prince!" she greeted and rushed into his arms.

Clowning, he hesitated then spread his fingers wide in laughing surrender before returning her embrace. There was a strength and vitality in him which sent an electric current through her veins that rivaled that which passed through Ben Franklin's key. "Have mercy, my lady," Buck begged, pretending to gasp. "What have I done to earn this?"

When she released him with suddenness from her embrace, Buck caught one of her hands and stroked it gently in concentration. "I guess I should be asking what you have been up to." His words fell short of wit.

Events of the day returned in a single flashback. It was then Rachel realized that she had expected Star to be with him. Estrellita, their dainty, appealing dynamo of unspent strength—what could have changed her so suddenly, so completely? Unless Rachel was right....

Robins twittered. A light mist rose from the river, took its toll of fragrance from the pines which an invisible breeze set aquiver. Rachel fought against the headiness threatening to steal away her senses and told Buck of Yolanda's visit, including their conversation.

He listened quietly. He understood, she was sure. How wrong she was.

"So?" was all he said.

"You don't understand at all, do you?" There was accusation in her voice.

Buck's chuckle was indulgent. "No. You and Yolanda have a language only the two of you understand. I neither understand her problem nor why it should upset *you*. You're prettier when you smile—"

"Stop trying to change the subject!"

Buck took her arm, turning her around, his face now sober. "You shouldn't be out alone, Rachel—and you *did* remember to lock up."

"I'm not afraid—"

"You *should* be. You know very well that all the thieves and robbers have not been rounded up. And until they are—"

Yes, she knew. She knew, too, that she was behaving like a child. But knowing did not erase concern for their child. Without thinking, Rachel blurted out, "Where is she?"

"Who?"

"Star—" she all but whispered in the gathering dusk.

"Oh, Star. She's often this late, darling—and not alone. Always with Patrick. Surely you feel our daughter is safe with a couple of ministers. Reverend Luke is almost always with them."

Buck's hand tightened on her arm, giving her little choice in the matter. They were going home. "Shouldn't we look for them? I mean, you said yourself that there's danger. And besides, what on earth do the three of them find to talk about?"

"The Lord."

He was right, Rachel realized, feeling a little ashamed. But did that excuse Star's defiance, her near-rudeness?

"Buck, are you sure, really sure," Rachel said slowly, "that it *is* the Lord's work they spend so much time with? Star has changed so much—is so defensive. We have drifted apart—much farther apart than I realized until she declared her independence this morning in a way that tore at my heart." Rachel paused, realizing for the first time that she was angry, had been all day, and (defensively) she had every right to be. The thought came with a jolt: *Were we both wrestling with wounded pride?*

"So that's it, a mother-daughter conflict?" Buck asked gently as they rounded the curve in the trail leading to that bothersome unlocked door. "I wish you had told me, but there's no time like the present."

Rachel explained in quick, jerky sentences. Her husband did not interrupt. When she stopped, he said, "I think I understand. In my mind, she's not the ingrate you may think her to be, Rachel. But you had every right to remind Star of her manners. Why didn't you reprimand her then and there?"

"I was afraid—"

"Of losing her love? Nonsense."

"Not that," she said in a voice that went with the size she saw herself as being. "I-I suspect she and Patrick are considering marriage. Not that I would object at the proper time. Girls *do* marry—"

Buck circled her waist with a force that almost swept her off her feet and stooped to brush his lips against her ear. "Keep walking. Say nothing. Just look straight ahead—"

Danger! She had learned to sense it. Buck was right. The city was yet unsafe. The realization stripped away her fat complacency. Barbarians, drifters, a stream of no-goods—often posing as solid citizens—restless...rootless...lawless...they looted, killed, raped, stopping at nothing to take what solid citizens and their ancestors had died for. Then, tailing them, came the cowardly hyenas to feed on another's catch. Of course! There would be no end to the ruthlessness until the legendary treasure of Julius Doogan was unearthed.

The nearby crackle of brush stopped them in their tracks. Any movement could place their lives in jeopardy, make them the new target. Bears maybe. Bears! *That* thought should be consoling? Hadn't they better bolt for the house *now*, while there was still flesh on their bones? She was ready to signal Buck with a touch of her hand when a sudden arrow of shame pierced her heart. What had happened to her courage? She was noted for her strength. And here she was with knees ready to buckle, heart pounding like a tom-tom, and hands shaking as if she were afflicted with palsy—all at the snap of a twig.

Still in shock over the flaw she had discovered in herself, Rachel found that the sound of human voices afforded relief. The danger was over. She wanted to laugh, call out a welcome in relief. Buck's whisper stopped her, restored her sanity. "Listen—"

"—but the problem is just how much we should reveal—if anything at all. You *haven't*. Engagements should not be secret, but you haven't—"

"Not a soul. I—I almost spoke of the matter to my mother this morning. But circumstances were wrong and, oh Patrick, the things I said were most dreadful. I hurt Mother Mine because of Callie."

Star, her darling Star. Eyes brimming with tears, Rachel longed to race out, take the child in her arms, say everything was all right.

Only it wasn't. Here she and Buck were, eavesdropping on a once-in-a-lifetime moment. Well, she had learned. And God would help her, give her another chance. He always forgave and strengthened the faulty heart. Now she would know what to say to Yolanda concerning Callie.

Rachel's thoughts were, in biblical terms, "rent in twain." How uncanny that Star should be speaking of Callie now, saying something about a problem which would break her heart. But yes, she must know, else would proceed with the marriage plans. Marriage? *Callie?* Not Star. Then—?

The countless low-hung stars above whirled senselessly about a world so still that surely the tempestuous beating of her heart had to be audible even to Star who was saying, "We will find a way. God gifted Daddy-Buck, Mother Mine, and me each with a searching heart...." Rachel and Buck managed to slip away noiselessly on the leaf-padded path.

—♥—♥—♥—

Buck moved quickly to light the lamps, flooding the house with a warm, welcoming glow. Rachel understood. He wanted everything as natural and normal as Star had always found it. "Relax, sweetheart."

Relax when she was filled with self-loathing? "Oh, what am I going to do or say to make things right?"

Buck paused, holding a match in his hand until it burned dangerously low before blowing it out. The match, reduced to ashes, fluttered into nothingness. "Shucks," he grinned irrelevantly, "there should have been more ash. Supposed to keep moths from the carpets."

Rachel laughed in spite of herself, then felt color creep to her face under his relentless gaze—so loving...so serene...so patient.

"That's my girl," he said and went back to the lamps. "Now, to answer your question. Why say anything? You're very wise, remember? Only, we didn't hear that conversation. Let things happen—"

Rachel inhaled deeply. "It's hard being a mother."

"It's hard being an anything that's worthwhile. Just be yourself."

"Oh Buck, isn't it wonderful how love works? A minute ago I was a cowering quitter. Now you make me feel like racing a bee to its hive and forcing the stinging critter to share honey with us!"

"Not a bad idea. Flapjacks suddenly sound just right. I'll tell you what. We'll invite Patrick in with Star, make them comfortable—"

Yes, and they would be here any minute. Quickly, Rachel burst out, "It was Bonaparte Bixby they meant, wasn't it? Yolanda only said *he*—so—"

Buck sobered. "I found out today the teacher's a traitor. Sh-h-h!"

3

Searching the Soul Comes First

Rachel inhaled gratefully, her eyes closed to hide a senti-mental tear. What would she do without Aunt Em? A year had made no noticeable change, unless one considered the pinch-on glasses. But it was the gingerbready odor that clung to her which made her different from any other human being. When asked her qualifications to enter heaven's door, Emmaline Galloway would say, "Silver and gold have I none . . ." then her "I will give you such as I have" would translate into spicy, still-warm gingerbread plucked from the roomy pockets of her Mother Hubbard apron.

"What's wrong, dearie? Looks like you're in another world."

"Sort of," Rachel, coming out of her reverie, said. "I—I—"

Aunt Em smiled knowingly. "You was tryin' t'fix th' world, less'n I miss my guess. It's about Bixby. I knew Buck'd be first t'git th' word then clamp his mouth shut 'ceptin' fer you. Course Miss Annie here was questioned by Sheriff Brimmerton 'n Davey-Love over there. *Come on out, my good man, 'n git t'grindin' th' nutmeg. Us wimmen can talk louder'n th' pestle 'n mortar noise.* Like now," returning to Rachel, "he had his good ear t'th' keyhole."

"Sure did," the self-styled country preacher admitted shame-lessly as he propelled himself forward in the reed, rubber-wheeled invalid chair by pushing his better foot against the shining lino-leum floor, the withered leg falling limply on the footrest. "How Callie ever come t'choosin' that grinnin' skull messes up my mind. Agree, wife?"

"Well now—gimme th' nutmeg, Davey-Love—I'm admittin' he ain't a heap t'look at. Nutmeg, please."

As Aunt Em took the small amount of spice from her husband, Rachel's mind raced back to the Ichabod Crane replica, saw Bixby's dark hair zigzagged to a comical point on his low forehead, his right eye which tended to drift left, and his drooping shoulders. Suppressing a smile, she forced herself to remember that Cal Merriweather's scissors took care of the comical haircut of Bonaparte Bixby. And Miss Annie took care of the rest. However, the children's reports and the man's unstable behavior always made him a question mark in her mind. First he was an enemy, then a friend, his actions seeming to shift like the drifting eye. But Miss Annie? Why had the sheriff confided in her? True, the woman was a dedicated headmistress, a good judge of character (still in her maidenhood at that time) whose only interest in life was the proper education of children. But none of that explained her involvement at this point. Married...no longer in school...

"Wonderin' why th' lawman confided in Miss Annie? More'n likely, she worked a lot closer'n we knew in helpin' round up them criminals—leastwise, some uv 'em—'n th' woman's uh downright perfectionist."

"Yep—hit's true," Brother Davey broke in above the noise of his own grinding and pounding. "She's done measured th' gates uv heaven t'see iffen she kin git through. S'pose she made it? Hard t'git through as uh needle's eye, th' Good Book sez, 'n she's downright fleshy—"

"Now, now, Davey-Love, that ain't th' lit'ral meanin' 'n you know it! Anyways, all us wives—them that care, that is—*do* know it's lit'ral true that th' way t'git t'our men's hearts is through their stummicks." She blew at a graying strand of hair which had fallen from her pulled-back hair. "Dunno rightly why 'tiz thet *we're* th' ones that gain th' weight. But Miss Annie's happy with the Reverend, so—"

Rachel tensed, realizing there was an added presence in the room before Miss Annie herself called out a businesslike greeting. How long had she been standing there? The Galloways obviously wondered, too. Both muttered clumsy apologies; but the sober-faced lady, her voice as tightly controlled as her buxom body was corseted, disposed of their words as if they were potato peelings to be tossed to the birds.

"What you say is true. I found it somewhat strange that Mr. Brimmerton would seek advice from my husband (lifting her double chin most proudly) and I would be so honored." She frowned. "But I *do* know more about the strange Mr. Bixby—if that's his name—than one would expect others to know. I am not too surprised after all his wishy-washy ways. But you might as well know the entire story. Not only did the man shift sides again, he's disappeared again—found once—"

"*Disappeared!*" the three listeners gasped in unison. "They found him?"

Brother Davey dropped the mortar, sending the raw nutmeg balls bounding to hit the mopboard on all four sides of the kitchen.

Aunt Em muttered something akin to a prayer: "Lord, have mercy!"

Rachel felt as if her heart were squeezed into a ball no larger than the pungent nutmeg seed. But her mind was clearer than it had been for days. Here was something she could deal with objectively.

"Somebody must tell Yolanda, and then there's Callie—"

Miss Annie suddenly took on the characteristics of a human being. She was, Rachel decided, in a strange sort of way a little pleased to have been the one who exploded the cannonball. Her face betrayed her only a moment. Then she said briskly, "We must do some soul-searching. That comes first. What doth the Lord require but obedience to His will?"

Was there a moment's quiet or did Rachel speak immediately? She was to wonder later. "I will talk with them. I'm the logical one. Yes, it is my job." Details of precisely what Bixby had done could wait.

Everything could wait, in fact. What could take priority over being a *mother*? The Burlsons had found it necessary to come home from camp meeting after settling their brood. And with them came a welcome note from her three, away for the first time. Busy as she was, Rachel could not dismiss the aching gnaw of emptiness in her heart. Mary Cole wrote first:

Dearest Mother, Daddy, Star, and Scot:

Camp is fun. Next time all the family should come. We are learning so much about everything in life. I never thought of being alive as a *gift* before. And what *we* do is our gift to *God*. I'm giving Him my heart—it's the best part of me. Sometimes I wonder about these brothers of mine though....

There her message ended abruptly, causing Rachel to smile through her tears. The wrinkled page obviously had been snatched from beneath her pencil by Saul. Little mischief-maker that he was, he loved looking over his older sister's shoulder to read whatever she wrote.

...And we're wondering about *her*. The Reverend says we're not sposed (I will never ask her to spell again—*again*?) to judge each other—and look at her judging all over the place. Anyway, she's not growing one bit. Me? Daddy'll have to make a new notch. Well, that's all the news, only it seems funny away from home. Love to Scot, and to you, too.

David, the more serious of the two, added only one line. It was enough to lift Rachel's concerns about the ugliness around her:

Mail time, but I want you to know that I may become a minister or doctor, whichever God tells me.

Love, D.J.

4

Why Must Life Be So Complicated

Rachel inserted the key in the lock and smiled as she felt it yield. Such a small matter, but remembering to lock the house as she left this morning added to the feeling of being back in charge of her life. Last night had been wonderful, just "letting things happen," as Buck suggested. She had never realized before what fun it would be for the four of them: Star, Patrick (a first-time guest), Buck, and herself. Life need not be so complicated. It was she who jumped to conclusions—conclusions which proved to be wrong. Star faced the problem of growing up, proving herself *to* herself. She needed her mother more than ever, in a new way. It was up to Rachel to keep the doors of her heart open. And that was possible only if she kept in mind that it was God, not Rachel Lord Jones, who was in charge. And everything would turn out all right!

Right now, her heart bubble-light, Rachel paused, wanting to hug herself, wanting to dance around the room. Energized, she felt a need to open the doors and let the world inside—only that would let out the smells of last night's pancakes, stealing away the beautiful memory of Star's laughter as she and Patrick sparred to see which could flip one golden-brown cake higher than the other. "Flip-jacks," they renamed them and asked Buck to serve as judge.

Judge. There was an intangible ring to the word which served to sober her immediately, acting as a spark to the realization of what lay before her this day. The memory exploded into a larger one—one which led her down the trail to remembrance of all the court cases she had thought behind...ended...finished. And now it was to start anew.

She would talk with Yolanda first. Only she had waited too long, she realized, when there was a sudden rap at the door.

"Rachel, Rachel! It's Callie. Please—I *must* talk to you!"

Caught off guard, Rachel hurried to usher her in. There had been no time to plan her strategy. "What's wrong, darling? *What is wrong?*" Rachel repeated, noting the transparent skin was drained of color. "Who has been battering your heart around? Nobody has a right to make such a sweet young thing look so stricken!"

"How much do you know?" Callie's voice was suddenly suspicious.

"Very little—for sure. I believe you were the one needing to talk."

Callie closed her eyes as if to blot out some intolerable vision. "I never want to feel this sad again."

"About what?"

"About life. About growing up. It's all so complicated." The girl all but fell onto the nearest couch without invitation, knowing she was welcome. "Only I *am* grown up—at least I should be. But the test came and—and I failed it."

"Test?" Rachel eased into the corner of the couch opposite her best friend's younger sister. "It's hard to imagine your failing at *anything.*"

"That's a compliment, I guess—an open invitation to try and justify my behavior—"

Rachel looked straight into Callie's sober eyes marveling at the striking likeness between her and Yolanda. The same wide-openness of their steady gaze, the same heavy mane of blue-black hair, the same *everything* as far as appearance. But there it ended. Callie and Yo (though the only two daughters began and ended a family of 14) were what one could call a generation apart. Callie was a still-waters person while Yolanda was a storm-at-sea, always at high or low tide.

"I'm unable to help unless you come to the point, Callie," Rachel urged gently. "As for growing up, well, it's a lifelong process. And yes, it is complicated. So—?"

"I was never sought out by a swarm of suitors, never had anybody who loved me for what I am, *who* I am—whatever the words are—until circumstances brought a man into my life. And I guess I love him—"

Rachel sat erect. "You *guess*? For goodness' sake, Callie, you're going to be married Sunday and you *guess* you love the man?"

"You *did* know." The words were an accusation, followed by a quick apology. "I'm sorry, and it doesn't matter. I only kept it secret because he asked me to."

"Why?"

"Why what? Oh, about our plans. I don't know the answer."

"Let's get something straight. The radiantly happy bridegroom-to-be is entitled to a name other than 'he.' And the bride is entitled to know something about her own wedding. Then I'm wondering why you are less than aglow when your dream has come true. Any answers?"

The girl dropped her head. "You know it's Bonaparte."

"I could have guessed by the process of elimination—your saying that you had no wooers. But why, Callie, *why*? You obviously aren't in love. You've discussed this with Yolanda—right? I can't believe you have her blessing. In fact, let's be honest. She told me."

There was silence. It was Callie who broke it. "Was it a breach of promise—telling me, I mean? Did Yolanda want it secret?"

"She made no mention. She was too upset to make sense, actually—not so much at you as at herself. Yolanda has always been one to wear a yoke of guilt. And she feels that she has failed you."

Callie jumped. "Strange—that's how I feel about *her*. But then I broke a promise—the one I made to my parents. That's the test I told you about—"

Rachel was beginning to understand. "Let me guess, Callie. You were to look after your older sister when your older sister *should* be looking after *you*. In fact, she made the same promise. Before you say anything more, let me tell you that your mother didn't want you to snarl up your love-life the way Yolanda did. That may be hard for you to understand. Just bear in mind that Yolanda loves you dearly."

"And I love *her*. Why do you suppose I had to prove something to her—make her think I was sought after the way she was? And how can I make it up to her—apologize without surrendering my pride? And," actual fear twisted her beautiful face, "how am I to crawl out of this stupid engagement? Oh, I am ashamed!" She began to sob softly, desperately—the way one sobs who is unaccustomed to tears as a solution.

Rachel slid to cover the short distance between them. "Don't cry, darling. Here," she said, drawing the girl's head against her shoulder. "Let me assure your little heart that your problem is not as unique or insolvable as you think. Let me tell you a story."

Quickly, she covered the events of yesterday: how she felt, the heated exchange of words between herself and Star, and then the happy ending. "You see, I'm going to offer the same advice to you, sweetheart, that Buck gave me: 'Just let it happen.'"

"Oh, thank you, Rachel! You're wonderful! But—" hesitating, "that won't solve the problem with *him*—I mean, Bonaparte," she gulped.

Rachel smiled. "Dry your eyes. Without knowing, you have helped *me*, Callie. Come on, we're going to your sister's together. You see, I have something to share with you both. It will resolve your problem with the man. But I must warn you that the news creates a whole new set of problems. But everything will turn out all right if we let God in on it, *today*. We are commanded to pray! Let's get at it!"

Both the Lee sisters took the news of Bonaparte Bixby's disappearance with sighs of relief, then immediately recognized the seriousness of it. Must they dodge him as they had dodged Julius Doogan all those years? Rachel was unable to answer their questions, admitting that she did not know what the charges were or how this betrayal had given him away. She did know, however, that at the request of Sheriff Brimmerton, Buck, as mayor, had called an emergency meeting of the city council. Secret? Yes, this time. But the ladies must double their guard again. This would bring them back together once more. When Callie's face paled, Yolanda took her rightful place as the older sister. Why wait until she knew the reason for Bixby's advances?

"You have no need for embarrassment, Callie. There was to be a wedding Sunday. But nobody knew who, remember? I *do* wonder who'll be the lucky recipients of all those lovely quilts Aunt Em made."

"Time will tell," Rachel promised, a sense of triumph stealing over her body. She gave the situation another push. "I am so happy that all of us have learned that we do not hate each other." Now, sensing that the sisters needed to be alone, she said briefly, "Let's pray, blow our noses, and prepare for the challenges ahead. Just search your own souls."

Rachel's prayer was brief, during which Callie and Yolanda held hands. How could God answer so quickly? As if unaware of another's presence, Callie's muffled voice, little more than a whisper, said between sobs, "I'll get my grip—never have I shed so many tears."

Rachel tiptoed out.

5

New Facts, New Fears—New Hopes

Lordsburg was abuzz with news. "Might as well uv had one o'them city talkaphones (Aunt Em quietly substituted "telephones"), yeah, telephones like they got in th' city fer carryin' news. 'Course wimmen's tongues does as good a job—bet thet's whur thet Bell feller got his idee." Brother Davey was enjoying his knowledge, *his* news.

No matter how the news was transmitted, the meetinghouse was surrounded by swarms of people demanding to be allowed inside long before the appointed hour. Buck and Judge Hathaway had planned their strategy well in advance. Members of the council would meet, hold a closed meeting, then admit by way of the back door those who were working undercover. Their service would be of no further value when their identities were revealed. The only people allowed inside were the attorneys, government men, and Sheriff Brimmerton and his deputies (called "Robin Hood and his merry men" by Brian Ames). Rachel had laughed and reminded the doctor's son that it was the Sheriff of Nottingham who was the letter-of-the-law law enforcement officer. But Brian had preferred his own version—else how could there be a righthand man like Little John, referred to by some witless people as "Brother Davey"? The child would always be a dreamer.

So "Little John," who long ago had been appointed sergeant at arms, proudly took over. As such, it was his responsibility to turn others away, the wheelchair serving as no handicap. There was muttering and grumbling among the townspeople, which only served to further his feeling of importance.

In relating events of the evening to Rachel, Buck seemed at ease. Nothing appeared to have changed much to her ears. She interrupted him frequently with trivial questions, but details were important. They were the ingredients which made the entire situation real. Somehow, although she had never had any particular liking for Bixby, it was still difficult for her to understand how he was smart enough to "outfox" (Brother Davey's word) the city, only to trap himself.

But the sequence of the events must come first. Then the truly big questions: *What did Bixby do?* and *How was he found out?*

"Judge Hathaway seemed to harbor some secret from the moment he brought the gavel down," Buck grinned. "But that's just to keep your interest high—"

"Buck! I want to know *now*. You know I'm afraid of the dark, and that's just what you're doing, keeping me there—"

"No wheedling, Mrs. Jones. Say, that coffee's great. Think I'll pour myself another cup."

"Go ahead. You won't sleep a wink at the rate you're going, anyway."

Buck's face sobered. "I guess I'm stalling, but why should I?"

He stirred the second cup of the amber beverage. Rachel waited.

"They were all there," he began slowly. But the story unfolded rapidly after that, in spite of his wife's interruptions.

Yes, the judge looked and behaved the same: dignified, attentive. Seemed to Buck that he removed his glasses a little more often, wiping away some imagined speck. And with or without the glasses, there was that little gleam—well, more about that later. Good-looking man for his age (small wonder) but (with a grin) he must stick with his account.

Rachel made a face at him but said nothing. Let him get on with it.

Did she remember Britches? Oh yes, the gangling boy who had taken Willie Mead's place when Willie teamed up with Doogan's gang. He was still the telegrapher . . . took some mail-order coursework . . . and had "grown in wisdom and stature." James Haute was there—not sure why. And yes, he looked the same—much like a field mouse with that twitching waxed moustache ("And matching question marks he calls *hair* on his forehead," Rachel had giggled). The doctors...Mrs. Maxton...Miz Lily. Rachel kept nodding. Yes, these were the people she would expect but—

What was this her husband was saying? "Now darling, grab yourself a skyhook and hang on for dear life. What I am about to tell you sweeps away the laws of gravity."

Rachel's heart began working overtime. She felt unable to breathe. Buck's face was ashen. She should have known that his report had been too lightly given—that he was trying to condition her, that his tone was the forerunner of shocking news. Only it wasn't news. Deep down, she had known. "Star—it's about Star, isn't it?"

Buck had taken her into his arms—arms she did not feel. "Tell me."

"It isn't so bad, Rachel. It is only that she and Patrick were there, ready to make a report, and," Buck brightened as he continued, "that solves the question as to why she was so belligerent. She was uncertain—in need of reassurance—"

"And I failed her—"

"Rachel!" Buck took her by the shoulders and shook her gently. "Didn't we settle those differences and show our support with our pancake banquet? Everybody forgave everybody and put it all aside. I think the Lord would be displeased if we asked His forgiveness then went back to the sackcloth-and-ashes bit. And don't tell me this is different!"

Rachel nodded. Buck was right as usual. Bad? His report was good—dangerous but helpful. She began to feel again, her first feeling being one of pride. Who but this child of mystery and the dedicated young minister would have worked patiently, quietly, wordlessly until they found the trail leading to the discovery of Bonaparte Bixby's evil nature—*and* his hideout?

A million questions whirled like a runaway carousel's drunken spin. Which horse to take as they sped past made no difference. She knew only that there was little time for selection. Likewise, any question would do. "Did our daughter reveal which direction, where the man has fled to? That would be dangerous—risky. Does he know she has tracked him down? Oh Buck—"

"I know, I know," Buck smoothed the truant curls which had strayed from Rachel's chestnut crown of braided hair. "But no, she refused—saying that she preferred to confide only with her parents. Judge Hathaway had every right to cite her on contempt except that he understands Star's nature and, well, as I said, he was preoccupied—"

"Oh Buck, somehow I want to cry, but (squaring her shoulders) I'll reserve tears for Yolanda. We're the town criers, you know."

"There's my girl. I feel happy, too, so I'd understand tears of joy." Buck inhaled deeply. "But we must be prepared to stand by our daughter and Patrick. Star was right in withholding the whereabouts of the man. He's dangerous and would stop at nothing to protect his treasure."

"Treasure?"

"Yes, it seems that Bixby has discovered the ill-gained fortune Julius Doogan stashed away from the train robbery. It's no legend. Bixby told Julius's secret to his aunt, fully expecting her support—"

"Miz Lily? And she reported? Oh bless her, she's a jewel. And does Mrs. Maxton know? Being a sister means he's her nephew—"

"Obviously." Rachel wondered why he smiled. What was he holding back? "She knows now, if not before. She's a secret agent, remember. I wonder how Howard Ames and his nephew make out without her—" Buck bit his lip and switched subjects. "Rachel, I needn't caution you that we're back where we started, not knowing who the enemy is. It's a good idea that you ladies plan to gather again. But darling, we must play mum when our brave young detectives confide. Now more took place, of course; that can wait until the open meeting. We need the entire community's support. But here's a shocker!"

"Go on—give me new hope."

"Hope? You'd better believe!" Rachel had not heard him laugh that deep, mellow laugh for (she was tempted to use Brother Davey's phrase "a coon's age") a long time. "The news has spread now like wildfire or I'll eat my hat," Buck went on tantalizingly.

"Your hat's new. Save it—and *tell* me, Mr. Jones!"

"Well, Judge Hathaway declared the meeting adjourned and Brother Davey pronounced the benediction. And then the unbelievable! The judge rose, removed his robe, and declared himself off-duty—free to make the announcement he had withheld for this moment."

Rachel held her breath. When Buck decided he had teased her long enough, he would end his fun. And somehow Rachel felt that hers would begin. She was right.

"'Ladies and gentlemen,' the judge began," Buck described, "first with dignity then became completely tongue-tied. 'I—er—have an, well, announcement—nothing to do with judicial matters—personal—and—and—I'm not sure I can handle it alone. I should have remembered it's the lady's privilege—'"

It was strange, Buck grinned, seeing the self-possessed gentleman so moved. But not for long. Up marched "Cappy" Maxton—yes, that was the judge's title of address. "I've consented to be Mrs. Hathaway."

Rachel gasped. "Oh, wait till I tell Callie and Yo!"

6

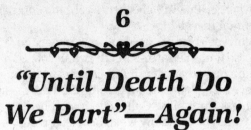

"Until Death Do We Part"—Again!

Buck was right. News of Sunday's wedding plans spread like his predicted "wild fire." Don't need no talkaphone (all right "*telephone*"). Them wimmen could talk louder'n 'n faster'n any machine, Brother Davey declared. No need fer his ding-batten earphone fer thet matter with them magpies all twitterin'. No need—

"—fer men's complainin' when they could be makin' theirselves useful," Aunt Em said in a dangerously low voice. "So much t'do at th' church, so much we need be knowin' yuh whittlin' men could be listenen' fer—" Aunt Em stopped and gave her husband a probing look.

The little man cringed. 'Twasn't often his Emmy-Gal stood up to him. And he didn't like balls uv fire where her eyes oughta be.

"Whut—what's wrong? I gotta funny feelin' hit's in regard t'me."

Hands on her hips, Emmaline Galloway faced her husband squarely. "Has it occurred t'th' likes uv you who th' preacher may be? *You*, that's who—"

"By jimminy, could be—jest could be. Best I prepare anyways."

Shortly, Aunt Em was to find she was right. Miz Lily knocked at the door just as Aunt Em was frosting a mile-high cake and trying to think ahead for a quick lunch for her Saturday customers. Thank goodness they'd be less inclined to eat her out of

33

house and home. Playing checkers, gabbing, and spitting required less fuel than labor.

"I thought you'd be in need of an extra hand." The pink-cheeked nurse with the satin-soft silver hair looked as immaculate and undisturbed as ever. But there was something different about her eyes. They sparkled with a million stars—sure sign of a secret, unless Emmaline Galloway missed her guess. Well, of course she would be all aglow when her sister would be pledging her troth to a man as high-standing as Judge Hathaway. 'Twas a mystery how them two had pulled it off so quietlike. She'd known there was to be some pairing off—women felt such things in their bones—so had prepared accordingly. But those two?

Miz Lily had rolled up her sleeves and, giving a fine imitation of emulating submarines (if there were such things and she guessed there must be) going to harbor, she pushed heavy chairs to the corners.

"We don't need interference—either from furniture or men," she grinned in an uncharacteristic manner. "We have the edge—some knowing, others guessing—about the 'secret wedding' and sort of preparing. You know, this party we're putting together may be the best evidence yet that it's a miracle indeed that women can share this small planet with men and still refrain from slapping them silly when they treat us incapable of voting."

Aunt Em laughed. "Never thought uv it thet way. Better put on thet apron yonder—'n yuh are uh answer t'prayer. Here, scratch my nose. I don't wanta be sneezin' in th' frostin'. Then check on th' hams. Put two in th' oven at onct—one fer th' horde crowdin' Aunt Em's Eatery on th' stroke o'twelve. Hungry er not, they start in salivatin'."

The two of them were working like a whirlwind when Rachel arrived. Yes indeed, they could use another hand—and thank goodness she knew the kitchen and the routine so would need no instructions. She nodded and began setting up the tables for feeding the men, listening without comment while Miz Lily and Aunt Em went on with their conversation.

"Aunt Em, I should speak with Brother Davey. My sister has asked Reverend Elmo and Miss Annie to stand up with them. Your husband needs to be spared a struggle with his Christian conscience regarding—well, what may trouble him—a man's taking for himself a spouse when she has a living husband."

Aunt Em stopped kneading the dough for yeast-rising bread. "Mrs. Hathaway," she mumbled as if tasting the words, "thet 'un slipped up on me. I jest never troubled my brain with th' name. Allus thought uv yer sister as a widder—"

"Which she isn't."

"Yuh be meanin' she sure 'nuff has uh livin' husband? Oh, my sakes, whadda you mean my Davey-Love's got no cause fer worry? Thet man takes th' Good Book by whut hit sez. He ain't no mealy-mouthed preacher who goes tamperin' with th' Word. Fact is," she hesitated, looking confused, "he sez he'd believe hit even if 'twern't so! Tell me onct more, Miz Lily. This woman's got 'erse'f uh breathin' *husband*?"

Rachel stopped, gasping at the thickness of the slices of ham. Why, she was cutting wedges. That came from wondering: *What is the answer to be—and the outcome?*

Suddenly Miz Lily bent double with laughter. *Has the woman gone stark raving crazy?* Aunt Em's eyes asked Rachel. Rachel, knife still in hand, turned her palms up. Certainly, something was in the wind.

"Then Mrs. Maxton ain't all she pretends t'be. There's a customer—"

A gaunt middle-aged man was running in this heat! Coatless, hatless, hair blowing to the four corners of the earth, he rushed in as if pursued by demons, but not to dine. The jumping-jack man gasped out a message: "Town meetin' tonight—urgent! Spread th' word t'all!" And he was off again. "Who was *he*? A stranger, wasn't he?" Rachel wondered aloud.

Aunt Em shrugged. There was no need to ask, "What's up?" The three in this room knew. What they didn't know was what Miz Lily was withholding—and enjoying it! "Proceed!" Aunt Em ordered. "What's goin' on?"

"Back to your question. Yes, my sister's all she seems—and more. And before you tear me apart, give me a chance to identify her husband. Cappy—yes, that's her husband's pet name for her—is married to the judge."

"What?" Aunt Em dropped a pan that took its time rolling around the kitchen. And Rachel Jones almost dropped the clove-spiked ham—the second one reserved for tomorrow's feast—with a *plop* on the cooktable.

"It all happened a long time ago." Miz Lily's eyes misted over with tears. "Never have I seen a couple so completely in love. If ever a marriage was made in heaven, they were *radiantly* happy. Cappy and I are close, but not close enough for her to tell me what happened. She only said they thought they were first with each other and when she found out differently—well, they parted just *days* later. But neither ever asked for papers of divorcement."

"But the name?" Rachel spoke for the first time.

Miz Lily did not glance up as she went back to slicing red-cheeked June apples for the pies. "Cappy worked undercover, remember? That, I suspect, is why the judge was never able to find her. I guess," she sighed, "it's true that something good comes from everything, even the bloodshed caused by my nephew—I blush to admit the kin—and his gang. It brought my sister here. Even then they had to see each other secretly lest she blow her cover. Oh, you're wondering why the ceremony? They want to renew their vows, make a home, and *mean* the until-death part."

"These pesky onions," Aunt Em said and blew her nose, "strong enough t'walk—got me all red-eyed. And I see they've got both uv you in th' same fix!"

David Saul Galloway peddled in, his own eyes filled with friendly serenity. His wife looked at him with a smile and said indulgently, "Yuh heard ever' single word—had thet ear trumpet pressed t'th' keyhole!"

Her husband did not deny it.

The wedding was beautiful, a real tear-jerker (bad as them onions Aunt Em said). *Very* beautiful, so reports went. Rachel missed it, but felt no real remorse. Buck said they must follow Star and Patrick's lead. Folks were riled up at the open meeting—dangerously so. Best go while they were at the wedding.

7

Beyond the Grave

Rachel lost her bearings completely as she and Buck picked their way slowly and silently through the maze of wild grapevines and blackberry brambles which tore at their clothes, their skin, and their scalps. They could be anywhere. Wherever they were, she shuddered, it had to be the Land of Total Darkness. How on earth did Star and Patrick find their way? She realized then that Scot was in the lead. The little Scotty was sniffing his way along what may have been an old Indian pathway—quietly, ever *so* quietly, as if he had been warned about danger.

When it became impossible to do battle with the tightening mass of vines any longer, somehow Buck received the message from the young leaders that they must crawl. She dropped to her knees, her heart pounding, nature's way of warning the human body to prepare for who-knew-what. Did she imagine the strange odor, or was it some sort of incense? Incense *here*? Rachel was ready to dismiss the idea when her face smashed against the seat of her husband's pants. She repressed a nervous giggle at the chain reaction as they fell forward, domino fashion. Surely her neck was broken, and the perfumed smoke was rendering her incapable of breathing. *Oh please, Lord, don't let me cough!* her heart begged.

Her reeling senses came back when a cold, wet nose met hers. Scot! Their little hero whined softly as if announcing the end of their journey. And with it came a warning to be quiet—a caution as clear as a road warning: "Danger Ahead." Who said animals couldn't talk?

There was a low humming which grew louder, louder, *deafening*—a thousand bards, each singing his own song, and each in his own tongue. There was a tiny spark. Fanned by an invisible wind, the spark grew into a little flame which exploded into a conflagration of destructive, all-consuming fire—the kind that produced evil and reduced all that was pure and good to ashes.

By the light of the swift-burning fire, Rachel was able to make out the creatures (surely not human!) draped in white, dancing wildly in circles, round and round the fire. The garb must have been bedsheets tossed overhead, tied around their throats, with holes gouged out as if—oh, good heavens!—their eyes had been whacked out in the torturous blow. Each mad creature threw a handful of powder into the fire, causing it, momentarily, to turn every color in the spectrum in an unholy way that gave the feeling of having consumed the rainbow with fire, as if God's promise to a sinful world was gone. Obviously, this was some kind of religious ritual. But why on earth would Star and Patrick have brought them here in search of Bonaparte Bixby? The pair was not *searching*, she reminded herself.

The light had dimmed. But the great bed of hungry-looking red coals formed an eerie glow. Rachel felt rather than saw a sheet of paper thrust into her hand. Straining her eyes, she was able to make out the stick-figure man Star had sketched. Held high above the single-circle head was a four-legged animal. A cat? Yes, a cat. And with her recognition came the awful truth. The stick-figure represented Bixby and he—oh, dear God, no!—was about to make a live-animal sacrifice. Was the man mad? And where was Scot? He might be next. In fact, such a godless gathering, now in a frenzied state, was capable of anything—including *human* sacrifice. "Scot," she whispered and felt his presence. Grabbing the little dog and hugging his warm, furry body to her breast, she retched and was sick all over his fur.

Buck, without allowing his eyes to leave the bloody orgy, reached a hand understandingly to hold her head. And undoubtedly to remind her that come what may, there must be no noise. Rachel squeezed her eyes shut against the revolting scene. But there was no way to close out the sounds of an eviscerated animal's death cry as its carcass was cast into the coals. Oh, she mustn't be sick again. *Please, Lord....*

In an effort to gain control of her body, Rachel raised her eyes, remembering the azure of the sky the four of them had watched blacken into night had been sprinkled with stars as they listened to Star's instructions. Her warnings had seemed foolish at the time. Imagine the indignity of asking Rachel if she was certain she was up to this! After all she had gone through on the Oregon Trail . . . and the explosion of the mine which robbed her of her first husband. But the question no longer seemed foolish. It was a different kind of trial, and from it would come strength to carry on, do what must be done to capture this demon, this cannibalistic mocker of God.

This she knew when the voice spoke. No attempt to disguise it worked. It definitely was Bixby's singsonging in scorn: "Drink ye all of it!" Nobody need tell her that they were drinking the animal's blood. She gulped and looked upward. The once-brilliant stars, all but invisible in the haze of smoke, now looked flat, brittle, and mocking. But Rachel was in control. Even when the stench of the heavy air tried to turn her stomach upside down, she was in control. And, in control, she could listen:

"Rise up from the grave—you are beyond it. Isn't this proof?" Bixby picked up a tailless black cat which, he explained in a hollow otherworldly voice, had risen, filled with psychic energy. "Spiritualists like us are able to walk and talk with the dead— even bring them back after being purified by fire. Come forth now and receive this healing by the laying on of hands!"

Bixby had raised his right hand. On the middle finger was a stone, obviously a diamond, as big as a marshmallow. "Make haste—wait, I hear the Great Voice from Beyond—yes, yes, I hear you, thou Almighty in the bowels of the earth. You are inviting your chosen ones for your Kingdom!" He turned back to the mesmerized ghouls in white. "Our Ruler has selected only a few—oh, lucky ones you are! So come quickly, those of you who helped me rebury the lost treasure. We are to share it after your purification—"

Rachel understood now. They were instructed to locate and report this man's whereabouts, then wait for instructions by the city council. *Wait?* That meant the slaughter of all the men who were pushing forward. Oh, they must do something. *Now!*

Patrick did not hesitate. Grabbing a rock and without taking aim, he hurled it with all his might. The rock landed on his intended target: smack-dab (as Brother Davey would say) in the middle of the dying embers. Surely it was by the grace of God that they sprang to new life with an explosion of sparks flying in all directions. And with wild, bewildered screams, the crazed men, released from their hypnotic spell, lost no time in dispersing.

Only one man was detained. His hood caught in a low-hanging branch and he was compelled to tear it off, exposing his face. Star was quick to make a crude drawing. Then the four of them, too, escaped, led by a happily barking Scottie. Nobody took time to shush him.

Rachel had forgotten to lock the door again, and Buck wasted no time in scolding. They rushed inside, bolted the door and, as a precaution, drew the drapes before lighting a candle. Then, white-faced, they looked at one another before they all burst out talking at once.

"Are you all right, Rachel?"

"Oh, Mother Mine, forgive me—never was it so bad!"

"What shall we do first?"

And then Buck's steady voice, *"Pray!"*

And pray they did, at first silently and fervently. Then Buck lifted his voice: "And in closing, blessed God, we thank You that Mary Cole, David, and Saul are away and in Your hands. Keep them from all harm and bring them home safely...."

His voice broke. It was Rachel who whispered, *"Amen."*

8

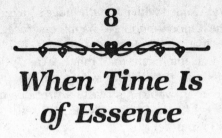

When Time Is
of Essence

Rachel closed her eyes to the intolerable vision of what she, Buck, Star, and Patrick had witnessed the night before. If only she could close it out of her mind as easily. Buck had been right in calling an emergency meeting—right, too, in allowing so few to be present when the four of them reported the barbaric scene. Judge Hathaway had responded immediately. And here they were, the bare bones of the city council.

Although the group, so tension-filled, appeared to have hands on the triggers of firearms, rigid and leaning forward in anticipation as they were, they seemed to recognize a need to do something—*anything*—to calm those about to report. With an unusual attempt at nonchalance, Attorney Haute fingered his upcurling moustache and said jovially, "Well, judge, before you bring that gavel down, tell us a bit about the bliss of matrimony."

Without a moment's hesitation, the judge's eyes blazed with obvious pleasure. The blaze turned quickly to blue-gray ashes, and he was all business. "Just what would you like to know?"

"What your plans are—" Haute, no longer certain of himself, mumbled.

"Well, we do not plan to start a family right away!"

There was a ripple of laughter. *Right away?* The idea of a man his age starting a family at *any* time was preposterous. One day they would come to see that it was not so preposterous as one might think, and Rachel would remember this moment. But for right now, the banter provided a light touch which steadied her.

Her heart quickened with joy at the judge's having reached for and caught the rainbow-bubble of happiness, recognizing that it could well be his last. Time was of essence. Life's candle was burning low. But, intelligent man that he was, Judge Hathaway knew that this was the stage at which the candle's glow was brightest. The man would not waste a precious minute. This, somehow, Rachel knew. So already he had settled contentedly into a domestic routine.

It did not surprise her when he said, "All of you will appreciate knowing that Cappy—er, Mrs. Hathaway—has invited the ladies of the city to gather at the church. I'm afraid my bachelor's quarters would be too small to accommodate the crowd she anticipates. It takes little imagination to envision the organization called The Women's Corps. They'll march into action without a drum and fife—"

"Yeah, bless 'em! An' like as not, it'll be our wimmen'll be the ones that end up capturin' them mindless marauders. What've them vermin done nohow?"

The attorneys exchanged glances. Haute, his waxed moustache twitching, lifted a well-manicured forefinger and made a gesture of slitting his throat. Brother Davey's jaws clamped shut. Mutterings, mostly in monosyllables, circled the room. James Haute hiked up his tight-fitting britches with a pinch of the tweedy fabric just above the knees, stood, and (with characteristic arrogance) addressed His Honor J. Quentin Hathaway: "If it please the court, may we proceed?"

Was there such a thing as "jumping out of one's skin"? If so, Rachel was certain that she did just that when His Honor, with deadly force, smashed the aging gavel against the scarred tabletop.

"You are out of order! What pleases the court is for spectators to remain seated, bridle their tongues, and *listen* to each detail."

Judge Hathaway, in spite of the capacious belly which made believable his oft-repeated claim that he was hungry enough to eat a horse, could not be called comical. He was too dignified. Added to that, a remnant of his Georgian accent remained, just enough to reveal the congenial, warm inner man hidden behind a frontal pouch which no human backbone could support with comfort.

Rachel loved him for being so understanding of her darling Star, so sympathetic with her present plight. Leaning as far as his bulging middle would allow, Judge Hathaway spoke in sorghum-syrup tones (which did nothing to destroy one's faith in his sincerity) to Star.

"Feel like telling us the story, my child?"

Oh, please no, Rachel willed. Her eyes sought Patrick's. But Patrick's eyes were focused on the hobnail scarred floor, his mind pitched deep in thought. When her glance locked with Buck's, he smiled tenderly, and in his eyes was the usual optimistic glow—a promise really. She wished his mood were contagious. Usually it rubbed off on her. Today, of all days, why must she be immune?

Her mind had wandered, Rachel realized. Star had obeyed the judge's summons and approached the bench. Standing before the great man seemingly reduced her from the tall, willowy young lady she had become to the diminutive creature she was such a short while back. And the dainty pale-green nainsook, three-tiered dress added to the illusion. She looked like a wee-small wood nymph. *Poor little innocent...*

But what was this? Star dared suggest to the judge that he disarm the men? And imagine the powerful man being receptive!

"All of you carrying firearms will bring them to me. *Now!*"

Would anybody be so foolish as to bring a gun here? Surely not.

How wrong Rachel was! But who were these men? Lordsburg was growing by leaps and bounds, but these men were supposedly to be numbered with the decision-makers—well, weren't they? Or were they imposters? Apparently not. The judge addressed them by name.

The man who limped forward first Judge Hathaway acknowledged by saying, "Thank you, Simpson. Give Kingman there beside you a nudge so we can get on with this hearing."

When Kingman hesitated, Simpson, forgetting the gag-rule (something Patrick had *not* forgotten, Rachel realized, remembering that she had expected him to ask that Star be excused), demanded: "Which have you lost, man—your hearing or your senses?"

By whatever name, this man had no business in a group like this. Rachel would tell her husband her suspicions tonight. He could be another Bixby. But that would never happen she was to realize within moments. The judge took care of the problem for her.

The scrawny little man called Kingman was obviously a coward. The supposedly concealed weapon bulged out, conspicuously drawing his unbuttoned coat almost to his backbone—if he had one. Without the gun he would be a dwarf—a dwarf with a turkey neck—instead of the fearless giant he fancied himself to be. Suddenly a dark cloud covered the sun causing vines at the windows to cast sinister shadows across his colorless face. Aha! A chance to tighten his grip on the weapon and draw. Not sure which way to point, he swung the barrel from right to left threateningly. With shaking hands! Poor spineless creature. But maybe this was where the danger lay. A wounded animal was to be feared. And how many times had she heard Buck say the same of a cowardly man?

Rachel grasped Buck's hand, her heart two-stepping as she looked at Star standing there like a Joan of Arc in her unselfish singleness of purpose. But this was not required. The judge must do something to stop this madness. It was one thing for Rachel herself to make the supreme sacrifice, but when it came to her children—

Rachel cast a pleading look at the judge, hoping to make eye contact. But his eyes—blazing again, this time in fury—focused on this man who dared defy the court. How dare him challenge, mock the American system—*goad*, actually! Not that he was compelled to pay homage to the robe or the person wearing it, but just to pay respect to what it stood for. His eyes narrowed. This man was a traitor!

There was a tenseness about the judge that Rachel had never seen before, exhibited in a white line drawn tightly about his mouth. He looked as if he were about to spring on the still-defiant Kingman.

"Drop that gun. *Drop it!* You are denied the privilege of bringing it up yourself!"

Eyes glued to the judge's face, Kingman eased the gun to the floor, a telltale sign that it was loaded.

"Brother Davey, as sergeant at arms, will you bring it to me? Use caution. Keep it pointed at the floor until I can examine it."

Brother Davey wheeled forward with expertise never before demonstrated, his eyes filled with dippers of stars. This was the greatest moment of his life—no doubt about it. "If there's a-gonna be gun-play, me 'n th' judge here'll do it. I been suspectin' somethin' queer 'bout you since you outright threw thet fightin' cock in my face, laughin' all th' time he spurred me—"

Kingman examined the toes of his books, face a Congo-red. "Nothing but a scratch—"

"Shut up you—you—" Brother Davey sputtered.

The judge cleared his throat. "Sorry, Your Honor, sir!"

Moments later Judge Hathaway was examining the weapon with meticulous care. He emptied the magazine and said, "This is the newest of firearms. Where did it come from, and what group are you representing?"

Head still down, the stranger mumbled something in mumbo jumbo into the open collar of his shirt. Either he knew nothing or was sly as a fox. *"Brimmerton!"* J. Quentin Hathaway bellowed.

"Escort him to the door, or have your deputies do so. You, I would like a word with." The sheriff, with an air of importance, ordered his men to "get Kingman out of here" then hurried to stand before the judge to receive his orders. He kept nodding in the brief exchange of words. "Yessiree! I'll have a man on his tail 24 hours a day. You can depend on it. He'll take us to his leader."

"And now, under the circumstances, I think it is proper to dismiss the audience. I would like to see only the four actual witnesses alone in my private chambers 'for a privy council."

Brother Davey, who had remained after delivering the gun in order to make sure he missed nary a word, gasped. *"Privy council!* Sometimes my hearin' ain't so good but—*ahem*—yuh be thinkin' thet's a 'propriate place—lackin' space—'n your bench lackin' dignity with them two—uh, holes—and kinda impure—"

For one hysterical moment Rachel had the senseless desire to burst into laughter. The vision flashing before her eyes was too, too funny! The judge, gathering his papers (and she could have vowed repressing a look of amusement), handled the matter with dignity. "Privy" was an old term, he explained, dating back to an English monarch's private meeting with subjects of the Crown. And then, rightly suspecting that Mr. Galloway was hinting that he be included, invited the "statesman" to join them.

The small lean-to on back of the large hall was little larger than Brother Davey's misplaced concept. Construction of a new one was soon to begin, if ever this feverish treasure hunt could be disposed of and the city could be declared safe. Rachel admired the men who put safety of the city's women and children at the top of their priority list. Not that they could accomplish it alone, she smiled inwardly. That was obvious—but a motion broke her trend of thought.

"What—or I should say *who*—was that?" Rachel had not intended to speak aloud.

The judge stopped in his tracks, looking at the single pane of glass serving as a window. Buck took her hand. "What did you see, darling?"

Patrick had rushed outside and was back now. "Not a trace of anything or anybody. What did you see, Mrs. Jones?"

Rachel, feeling foolish, said it was probably nothing—just her imagination working overtime. It had been a stressful day. But deep inside was the niggling conviction that a face had peered into the window—yes, of course it did! And the face was vaguely familiar. But who?

"You are all tired—exhausted," Judge Hathaway said kindly, then informally asked if it would be all right to remove his robe. Peeling it off and tossing it aside impatiently, he mumbled something about the unbearable stuffiness, ending with "so let's go through this quickly."

The interrogation Rachel had dreaded went smoothly. Star told her story quickly and well. "Patrick and I have done much studying and searching, both of the land and within our hearts. When we were most sure of where the evil man was in hiding, he and I were willing to have my parents come with us. They saw. They understood. They were most heroic. I am proud of them— my wonderful, beloved parents. Do not cry, Mother Mine—"

"We were no heroes," Rachel denied, trying to restrain her tears. "If there were heroes, they would have been those young people. I came to see them in a new light," she said slowly, realizing that she had come to grips with truth. "That special spirit within my daughter has matured and—and—Patrick—"

"—was the real hero," Buck declared firmly, proceeding to relate his brave act before the leader—yes, he was sure it was Bixby—took the lives of those misguided, superstitious people under his evil spell.

"Why, may I ask, would he wish to take the lives of his followers?"

"To destroy those who know about his terrible deeds and could testify against him," Patrick answered in a voice both strong and clear. "Yes, we four can identify him now. But bear in mind that he has no idea that we were there. Somehow, sooner or later, word will leak out. Just look at what happened tonight. And then, Your Honor, we, too, will be in danger."

"Very true," the judge answered quickly. "We must apprehend these people. You say they know where Bixby hid the treasure?"

When they all nodded, His Honor rose and repeated: "Time is of essence."

The door opened a crack to admit one tiny dog. "Oh Scot, you are safe, my brave one. It is *el perro* who is the real hero. It is he who led us to the den of Satan. My brave Scot made not a sound when the smell of death surrounded us. It was he who led us away from the gates of hell. *Oh, Almighty God, we offer praise to Thee!*"

"Amen, *amen*, AMEN!" Brother Davey said with fervor, having held his tongue while others talked for the first time in his life undoubtedly.

"Amen," whispered Judge J. Quentin Hathaway, then blew his nose with a mighty snort.

—♥—♥—♥—

Outside, the six people found a knot of faithfuls—men of God and country whose integrity Buck would stake his life on. In a small huddle, they outlined a plan of action and named a time and place.

Rachel heard nothing. Her arms were about her daughter who was clinging to her as she did when they found the little lost waif, alone and frightened, along the trail to Oregon.

9

What Matters Most

If only she and Buck could have had the remainder of the evening together, things would have been far different, Rachel was to pine later. But the precious time alone was denied them.

Cappy Hathaway appeared out of nowhere to announce that refreshments were awaiting at the church—as was the entire community, the small group was to discover. But for the moment, Rachel was too taken aback for anything else to matter. Her first reaction was one of great disappointment. She needed to talk, all cuddled up in his arms, feel the reassurance that the warmth of Buck's tender embrace always brought and, well, just have some coveted time without an audience.

Before she could think that through (for one did not refuse invitations here without "just cause," which was hard to prove!), another matter pushed her thinking to some back burner of her mind. The woman she had known as Mrs. Maxton for so long had gone through a total metamorphosis since revealing that she and the judge were husband and wife, business partners, and more since, in some ways, their professions must remain secret. But what mattered most was their private relationship. And it showed from her poufed-out hair (with an artificial rosebud tucked cunningly on top) to the tassel-soft leather boots. Rachel hoped Judge Hathaway did not see her own mouth fly open. He didn't. He had eyes only for his Cappy.

Then, of course, there was the unexpected mob of Lordsburg citizenry, everybody asking questions at once. Unfortunately, it was Brother Davey who made the expected announcement—and over a megaphone, his most recent purchase (since he was deaf, he presumed all others to be.) "Qui-*et!*" he yelled. "Want th' whole world a-known' whut hasta be kept se-krit 'twixt us?"

The result was shocking. Total silence. All ears turned toward him. This was his finest hour. Aunt Em was trying her best to elbow her way to her husband, mumbling, "Le'me pass afore thet man spills his insides." But the crowd only tightened, some linking elbows to guarantee "freedom of speech."

"We gonna brang civilization back t'this pesthole these low-lives 're a-tryin' to make hit—'n thet includes un-unre-unregen'rate drunks, tryin' t'lure others t'drown their troubles 'long with them thet's plum retired from sober-ity—"

"What? Who? How'd they git here?" Questions came like a hail storm on a tin roof.

"Hit ain't a-comin' free. Hit'll take money, men—pots 'n pots—"

Men were throwing their hats to the man whose tongue surely had loosened at both ends. "Pass th' hat, boys!" Some of the men Rachel had been unable to identify pushed forward and, unable to break the human chains, fired a single shot into the ceiling and, in the white-faced silence, rushed up to usher Brian's "Little John" outside.

The judge's face was livid. Shaking his head, he growled to his wife, "And to think, I am at fault. I trusted him—and here he is blustering away after being sworn to secrecy. Why, why that—"

"Now, now," Cappy consoled. "Watch your blood pressure and your language as well. Makes you want to shake him. But analyze it, my dear, and I believe you'll come to realize that he's said nothing damaging. It just could be that it's best to get people a bit stirred up—"

J. Quentin sniffed in disdain then managed a lopsided grin. "Brilliant mind you have, Mrs. Hathaway. You could think better three-quarters drunk if you were one of his unregenerate drunks than most who never touch the stuff. Too bad you have to hide that brilliant head beneath a bushel—"

"Why, thank you, *Mr.* Hathaway, Your Honor, but," she said, sobering, "you know it's essential that I appear less than I am. My job demands it."

Buck, whose presence Rachel had forgotten during the strange turn of events, reached out to lace his warm fingers through her cold ones. She smiled up at him and squeezed. He squeezed back—*harder*.

And suddenly order was restored. Rachel was never sure how. It was enough to see that somehow a new kind of togetherness had been created from chaos, that people were eating hungrily and soon it would be necessary to make another pot of this bracing coffee....

—♥—♥—♥—

The smell of coffee awakened Rachel the next morning, but Buck was gone—as he was the next morning...and the next. She began to feel locked out, useless. And, like a malignant growth, the feeling spread, almost undetected (certainly undiagnosed by its victim) until it struck her heart. When full recognition reached the brain, Rachel's head jerked back as if she'd been whacked across the back. *I am back to where I started from... alone...a wife-in-waiting.* Understanding—but not understanding at all. When the showdown came, both husbands had chosen. City or wife? No contest. It always came up *city*.

"Stop it, Rachel Lord Jones!" she commanded herself. "It's your city, too. I saw that it was dedicated to the Lord Himself and am just as determined to snuff out crime. The robbers, thieves, makers of strong drink—be wary too of the Johnny-come-latelies who try worming their way in to plunder. And, for that matter, we have had no need for fast-talking, greased-moustache peddlers whose fat fingers were too laden with fake diamonds to shake hands—"

She always stopped at that point, aware that missing was the real problem: money, the root of all evil, and (she shuddered) devil worship. For want of something better to do, Rachel volunteered to help the new Mrs. Hathaway pack her belongings in readiness to move into the close confines of the judge's quarters. Soon this would all be over. Buck would be home. And she could only hope that the newlyweds would be as happy as the Jones family! At least, as happy as she yearned to believe they would be. But she found herself clinging to her doubts. Yolanda, Callie, and Star were right: All of them had remembering hearts. And oh, how she herself remembered loneliness.

"You must get involved in the ladies' group," Cappy Hathaway said as they were tying a well-packed cardboard box one day.

Rachel examined the older woman's face for a hidden meaning but saw no expression whatsoever. "They've assessed what they know about the entire situation, organized into squads—military-like—and—" she smiled, "they're making another quilt. Unfortunately, I must be gone awhile. Can you take my place?"

Well, of course she could. There was no need for this silly state of idleness, thinking dark thoughts, mooning around. Rachel stopped in mid-thought and, speaking without thinking, asked Mrs. Hathaway where she was going. Surely, she concluded, not alone. "Why, you're still honeymooning. Oh, forgive me, I am meddling."

The judge's wife indulged in a rare smile. "My husband understands. Lack of understanding kept us apart a long time ago. We were deaf, dumb, and blind to reason—each accusing the other of being stubborn as an ox. Every time I made mention of being my own woman, he came up with that silliness about a woman's place, which was like waving a red flag in my face, and he did it once too often. I flew off the handle, reminding him that there were women *judges* in the Bible just as capable as the men. J. Quentin took it personally," she paused to sigh, "which I guess I meant it. Called me childish, should be bearing him a son."

An unshed tear rimmed Cappy's eye as Rachel sat waiting in actual fear that the woman wouldn't continue. She was seeing a new woman, a stranger—a part of herself reflected.

"Please, *please* go on," she whispered when the salty taste of blood told her that she had bitten into her lower lip.

One glance at Rachel must have told Cappy Hathaway something. "The childbearing part hit home, made me crazy with pain. You see, I'd never revealed that a fall from a horse had crushed my pelvis, rendered me incapable of bearing children. Oh, I know it was wrong, my harboring the secret, hoping and praying for the impossible. But I was too hurt, too furious, and (sadly) too young. I could have made things right even then. Instead, I went into a rage, told him he'd married the wrong woman, told him what he was looking for was a weakling with no brains—a mindless female who nodded her empty head 24 hours a day without questioning her royal master's orders because (a taste of the old bitterness tainted her speech which she spat out in words, 'Get thee behind me, Satan!')—because the king could do no wrong!"

To hide her own tears, Rachel looked down at her forefinger which was caught in the string the dowager-bride had asked her to hold as they tied the knot. In telling her story, Cappy had drawn the string tighter and tighter. Now Rachel's finger was bloodless. "Can't I remove my finger?" she whispered.

Together they laughed. That broke the tension. But as she massaged her finger, Rachel whispered: "Get thee behind me, Satan!"

Mrs. Hathaway looked confused. But Rachel would never be able to admit the awful truth—the fact that the devil had been struggling to gain control of her soul....

Rachel recognized the sound of her husband's footsteps even before she spotted him. Her heart began to hammer. *Buck is home...Buck is...Buck—*

But the rhythm stopped as quickly as it had begun, then sagged in her chest at the sight of him. His clothing looked slept-in. For how long had he been tardy or, the thought came to her suddenly, was it possible that he hadn't come home at all? He was limping; one boot was minus a heel. His torn shirt and wrinkled trousers were layered in dust. But nothing conveyed failure as much as his drawn face which spelled defeat. It said more plainly than words, "I gave my all and failed."

"Buck—oh Buck, my darling—"

"Hello, Rachel."

Rachel? No word of endearment. No reaching out to her.

And then she saw that his right hand was bound tightly with a dirty handkerchief—and was that blood oozing through? Yes, of course it was. The dried blood about the bright red told the story. It was not a recent wound. No doubt where he'd been. But what infected the wound?

"Your hand must have attention—"

Buck waved away her fears. "Two doctors were with us. But we ran out of supplies, and we were too busy to come home. We failed, Rachel. We *failed!*"

"How long has it been since you ate? Get inside so we can get the hand soaking in Epsom salts while I prepare soup and coffee."

Buck toyed with his food, his mind obviously back at the horrible inhuman scene they had witnessed along with Star and Patrick. "Don't tell anybody—at least until we know more."

"What is there to tell? You've told me nothing so far. Hand me that spoon. You have to eat." Rachel doubted that he heard. Picking up the spoon herself, she forced some of the nourishing liquid between his tight lips. "Swallow! Good boy. Now, tell me," she commanded.

Once started, Buck gulped the soup hungrily, then picked up the mug of coffee on his own. "Awkward—eating with one hand—" he gulped.

Rachel breathed a wordless prayer of thankfulness as the color began returning to his face. His voice strengthened as he related the happenings of the past two weeks. The government agents picked their men for the stakeout, swore them to secrecy, and took turns watching for a repeat performance. None came. They became more and more certain that meant that they had to be on the wrong trail. Sheriff Brimmerton lost track of Bixby, so the government men couldn't help wondering. (Here Buck had stopped, looked straight at her for the first time, then continued—different though, in a lighter tone.) Oh, there was a brighter side, he said. Star and Patrick, there earlier, saw where the box was buried hurriedly as two unrecognizable men made a quick getaway.

"The money from the train robbery?"

"We can assume as much. But no amount of digging turned it up."

That explained the blistered, infected hand. It did not explain another matter. "Buck, what was it that the government men couldn't help worrying about?"

Buck groaned. "Oh, Rachel—Rachel darling. I—I—don't want to—"

"Tell me? Buckley Jones, I am your partner—and your *wife*."

He reached out for her then. Lips against her hair, he whispered, "It's the wife part that matters most—giving me courage to go on, to know that we *can* go on. What changed my mind? You, wonderful you. Now put your arms around me, hold tight! What I am about to tell you is ghoulish—"

It was.

10

The Importance of Believing

Rachel swallowed hard, then swallowed again in an effort to dislodge the lump in her throat. Otherwise, she would choke. "You see, doctor," she could hear herself saying, "it began when Buck told me about—about, well, you know. You were there when your men unearthed the terrible remnants of the fire. Help me! It's growing bigger all the time! *I can't breathe!*" Air—or she'd be sick again.

In desperation, she forced herself to look upward at the colorful glory of the sky where the early-morning mists had fluffed clouds into dainty meringues. A remnant of the waning moon, barely visible in the sun-bright morning, a mother-of-pearl cradle, paused its swinging momentarily, suspended as it was in the fir trees at the point where they brushed the sky.

"Oh Lord, my God, how great Thou art," she whispered, feeling small indeed in the midst of the majesty His fingers had created. The lump receded and she was able to inhale the healing power of sap the warming sun sucked from the needled branches surrounding her. The loving Lord had created a heaven-on-earth for mankind. And look what stragglers like Bonaparte Bixby had done to destroy it.

Straightening her shoulders, Rachel promised herself anew that she would reveal nothing her husband had told her. She must put it out of her mind, he cautioned. That she was unable to do— particularly today when meeting for the first time with the ladies' now-militant group. They had agreed, she recalled Cappy

Hathaway's saying, to reveal all their findings. Wouldn't she be placed in an awkward position?

But Buck insisted that she join the group. Being absent could create suspicion. Rachel had agreed if her husband would get some much-needed rest. He agreed after telling her that was resorting to bribery.

And now she was on her way to Aunt Em's.

The "squads" in the cinnamon-scented kitchen stopped reporting when Rachel entered, and rushed forward to greet her warmly. Oh, it was good to be back with them all. There was such a crowd—newcomers, early settlers. She paused in her survey to wave to Elsa O'Grady, Mandy Burnside, and Opal Sanders—fellow travelers in the long trek to the Oregon Territory so many years ago—Miz Lily, of course, and happily, Yolanda! Rachel wondered fleetingly about Callie. Then, with a smile, she said, "I mustn't hold up the meeting. So 'As you were, ladies.' Isn't that how the military officers say it?"

Those familiar with the phrase laughed appreciatively. "Sure is, dearie. You sit here, which if my countin' ain't off makes you next in line. Ready to share yore findin's?" Aunt Em queried.

So soon? Rachel glanced around the room nervously.

Miz Lily must have noticed. She covered the situation by saying, "Let Rachel catch her breath. We should fill her in on—well, first, let's explain the absences of some of our members. Yolanda—"

Yolanda smiled. "Callie? I am happy to share that my baby sister is to be a full-time teacher next year, having passed the state teachers' exam." She paused until the applause stopped. "And I guess I'd be foolish not to be proud, in spite of the unhappy circumstances."

"Don't you be frettin'—ain't your fault," Elsa O'Grady soothed. "Ain't hers either. We needed rid uv that Bixby man. He wuz uh—"

"Two-legged jack—uh, rear end uv uh donkey!"

"Brother David Saul Galloway, don't you know you're goin' 'gainst rules? Th' sign says 'Women Only.' So be gettin' yore noodle out!"

Brother Davey, with a hangdog expression, peddled out, mumbling to his usually agreeable Emmy-Gal about bossy females, his being a chosen one to keep a watchful eye on anything looking suspicious, and he wuzn't 'zackly sure 'bout this buncha wimmen 'n their secret meetin's. Looking over his shoulder as if suspecting his wife in hot pursuit, he picked up speed. "Iffen you ladies'll 'scuse me," he bluffed, "I jest 'membered I gotta meetin', too. Jest be watchin' yore step—not thet *I* be uh talker—"

He peddled even harder when Aunt Em, having spotted a fly, reached for the broom.

Everybody began talking at once at that point. There were rumors, they said, of hootch being bootlegged in. Imagine the nerve, this being a "dry" city by vote of the men, since local option allowed the alternative. Ladies were not allowed to vote, but (after a roar of *boos*) they surely did the next best thing: up and warned their mates against voting "yes" on the "rot gut 'lowed hereabouts." So, "Woe be unto him what be found guilty just afiddling with the sinful firewater." The ladies added to their search for Bonaparte Bixby and his gang, and, of course, the buried treasure. *Everybody* was a suspect—guilty until proven innocent—the way they interpreted the intent of the law. . . .

"Ready, Rachel?" The question came from Miss Annie (as the spinster teacher continued to be called even after her marriage to the Reverend).

Choosing her words carefully, Rachel repeated what most of them knew already. "As you know," she concluded, "Star asked the judge's permission that her immediate family be allowed to view what she and the young minister had discovered. So we followed through—"

And then the horror came back—remembrance of the hooded men and their bloody ritual. Sickened, she stopped.

The women's faces bleached of all color. But was there more? Not that she saw, Rachel said truthfully. But she knew more? Not that she could share. "Oh please—please don't tempt me. I—I'm sworn to secrecy—"

There was sudden silence. Rachel was unaware of suspicious looks cast her direction. She was too locked into the scene as Buck described it—a scene so real in her mind that she might as well have been there . . . not a sound . . . not a sign of life . . . a *graveyard*. The men, having waited and watched so long, began hallucinating. Suffering from fatigue, hunger, and dehydration, they granted license to their imagination. All the forest creatures united against them . . . hooting . . . howling . . . screaming . . . the din deafening . . . until exhaustion overcame them. Did they doze? Or were the white creatures floating overhead real, their moanings and groanings a pleading for them to turn back... allowing the spirits to return to their graves? Finally, the men must have dozed....

How strange that all the weakened team should awaken at once. There must have been a sound, they whispered among themselves. But for now there was a ghostly silence. Unnatural, chilling, causing the exhausted few to fashion fears and problems. "As if we didn't have enough to contend with without borrowing trouble, contriving problems, letting our imaginations lead us into who knows what," Dr. Killjoy decided. "I prefer patients with a pulse—not the living dead."

"That's when we decided to sift through the ashes," Buck had told Rachel, his voice hollow with recollection of the satanic fire, the sardonic grin of death—it spoke without words.

Rachel knew by the great beads of sweat on her husband's forehead the story would end in a heart-stopping discovery. "Tell me," she whispered. "What—what did you—f-find?"

"Bones—countless bones—of sacrificed animals. And oh, my darling (Buck's head had dropped into his hands and his voice was a groan), I wish I could spare you this, but among the bones we found a full skeleton of—"

A human being! Rachel knew before he told her.

The bones were now collected, bagged, and would be examined by a committee of medical men to make sure the bones *were* human, and to identify the skeleton, if possible. Little hope, of course. Classified information, to be guarded. One small leak could make the case null and void....

Yolanda's voice jolted Rachel back to the here and now. "Don't push her," Yo said. "I understand. You see, my husband was among those who helped find some evidence—so important that they must keep details from everyone. And that includes wives."

"Right. It has nothing to do with doubting one another. That's the last thing in the world we should allow to happen. We *must* keep believing in one another. I, too, am involved—and understand. Surely you have all noted the absence of my sister. What am I able to tell you other than that she is away on a secret mission— secret even from her own husband. Can you imagine that— withholding information from the judge himself? But then, her being a secret agent—" Miz Lily said.

"Oh, I get it! Clear as uh bell now why Judge Hathaway calls his wife Cappy, ain't it now? Her bein' such uh great officer. My husband sez th' great lady's uh captain—Cappy, get it?"

All nodded. Yes, they "got it."

"And now, please, may we talk about other matters? I—I need to get back to normal." Rachel realized she was almost pleading.

"Sure can, dearie," Aunt Em said before anyone else could "butt in." "I'd uh-thunk yuh all'ud been asking 'bout th' new quilts! Ain't yuh jest uh teeny-weeny bit curious?"

When they all called excited yeses, Emmaline Galloway grinned slyly, obviously pleased with herself. "Well, you ain't a-gonna know! I got me myself some secrets, too! Now, I *will* tell yuh we gonna have fresh-ground coffee 'n Mississippi Mud cake!"

As they stitched and dined, all seemingly "at ease" now, Aunt Em reminded the group that, important as the search for the Bixby scoundrel was (imagine his hiding right here before their noses and who could have guessed that such a devil-worshiping ground even existed!), the squads had other duties—one being to keep Lordsburg sober. "I double-dog dare even one drop t'be toted in here. We'll dry 'im out in uh hurry. Right, ladies?"

In practiced synchrony, near-uncivilized yells went up in a dare.

Opportunity was to come sooner than expected. But for the moment, Rachel turned her head away to hide her smile of amusement, suddenly very glad that she had attended. These wonderful friends were so sincere.

It was then that she caught sight of a stranger—a man standing dangerously near the sagging porch of Aunt Em's Eatery. With all doors and windows open to invite what little breeze might pass by on this stuffy late-summer day, it would be easy to hear every word said, particularly if a person was bound on eavesdropping. Something said he was.

There was something familiar about the man. But where and when could she have seen him? "Anybody know that man?" Rachel queried, pitching her voice down to keep it casual.

The quilters stilled their needles. All heads turned in the direction of the street where Rachel pointed. But the man was gone.

Yolanda was right in her prophecy. It had been a strange summer.

The sun in the heavens, like a fire in its grate, burned itself from flaming coals to the mellowing glow of late afternoon. The men would be expecting their evening meal. Aunt Em raised the quilt frames with a skillful jerk of the ropes suspending them from the ceiling. "Join me," she said.

"We believe in the Holy Scriptures . . . the Trinity—Father, Son, and Holy Spirit . . . the deity of our Lord Jesus Christ and His virgin birth . . . the forgiveness of sin *only* by the blood of Jesus . . . in salvation by grace through faith . . . guidance of the Holy Spirit . . . return of Jesus Christ . . . and, Lord, we add faith in each other—our believin'!"

11

Eye of the Storm

The change must have come slowly. But most of the women of
Lordsburg were too busy jelling, jamming, and "putting up"
remains of the fall gardens to take note. There was sewing to do
in preparation for the opening of school. Then there were the all-
important meetings and sharing. But over the city and all its
surrounding valleys hung a cloud of mystery made up of threads
of the weaving together from rumors and facts, with bits of
suspicion woven in. The pattern enlarged into a design of downright fear—fear which nobody talked about.

Reverend Elmo refused to believe any evil amid his beloved
flock. The trouble came from outside. But yes, indeed, he would
cooperate. Doogan's gang had been an isolated incident. Even so,
he frowned, the authorities who came to investigate must have
had just cause. So thinking, he told Mayor Jones that he would
cooperate in order to prove the ugly rumors false, their suspicions
unfounded. It wasn't possible that this area could be a port of
entry for contraband. And there had been no evidence of rum-
running since the Doogan mess. The legendary treasure was just
that—a legend. And as for the so-called "healers" (suspected of
cannibalism and devil-worshipping), "Poof!"—just a bunch of
pranksters.

"Of course, there's no stopping Brimmerton. You know that.
The sheriff is suspicious of every stranger who enters this county,
and the barber shop keeps his imagination well-nourished. Cal

Merriweather's no spreader of gossip, but he's addicted to listening," Buck had said in response to Rachel's report on the ladies' meeting. "It seems as if by plan that the barber's use of lathering and shaving somehow loosens men's tongues at both ends. Too bad that women can't be seen in such places. Sounds to me as if you ladies could put an end to some of their prattle—" Rachel knew how he felt.

"And yet, you men call *us* the gossips!" Rachel teased. Then, sobering immediately, she said slowly, "I—I hesitate to so much as refer to—to that horrible scene—"

Buck had jerked erect. "Nobody else knows—you're sure?"

"Quite sure. They do know about the ritualistic dances and claims to heal. But nobody knows more. We are the only ones who know that the rumors are, in reality, truths. Trust me to say nothing, darling. I *wouldn't*—"

"Oh sweetheart, don't you think I know that? You're a little goose." Buck reached out to grab at her skirt. Rachel dodged.

"Not now, my darling. *Please.* I didn't finish my question."

"I know what it is but was trying to spare you. You're wondering if proof lies in the remains. Yes, and I was in touch with doctors in Portland while you were attending the meeting. Those of us witnessing it all are, in the judge's opinion, the only ones who can be trusted completely. And I guess you know who's designated to make the delivery."

"Oh Buck, *no!*" Rachel gasped in horror. But there was no use in pleading. Buck would do his duty as he saw it—and would she wish it otherwise? "When?" her voice slid to a whisper.

Buck inhaled deeply. "Trust me, Rachel. I don't know. And when I do know—"

"You will be unable to tell me." Her voice was dead.

"Let me hold you now."

Rachel had crawled into his lap, curling into a little fetal ball. A broken heart did not mean that a woman had to cry....

—♥—♥—♥—

There were several opportunities for Rachel and Star to talk in the fleeting weeks to come. The time together drew them closer than ever before. All wounds healed so completely, they left not a single scar. "Human hands could not have accomplished this,

Mother Mine—only the Great Physician whose laying-on-of-hands takes place spiritually."

"That is true, my darling," Rachel agreed. "The Bible tells us that the only *impossible* thing for God to do is remember our sins once He has forgiven them. Those are powerful words, and that is what we must do. I guess," she said slowly, "that rules out the false idea of forgiving but refusing to forget, nullifies such thought. We're now healed."

"Verdad!" Star nodded. "That is why I refused to be blown like a straw in the wind, refusing to allow those who see the power God has put into my hands to be used in a wrong way. I will not be tempted to use that gift of strength as a substitute for what only the Master can do in spirit. *Comprehende usted, dear Madre Mia?"*

Rachel frowned slightly in concentration and admitted that no, she didn't understand—at least not totally. She only felt a whisper that truth was dawning.

"I speak of the valley between us at one time because of misunderstanding. I know you want for me more schooling, and that is what I was fighting. I know, too, that you do not wish for me marriage. But more I am listening to the call to heal through my drawings, letting love lead. Give me time to listen for God's voice to tell me His will. Not mine. Not yours."

"Darling, I understand. And you are right. Take all the time you need—as you and Patrick are doing. Now, let's talk about what you and Patrick have unearthed. Are you free to say?"

"Not to all the world, but to you, *si*, I am most free to share with you my all. With Scot as our guide, we have searched both where *Señor* Bixby, the traitor, first buried the treasure—and yes, oh, *si, si*, the money was real. But naught did we find. This we knew would happen. It was—*como se dice?* To look again?"

"A double check?" Rachel guessed.

Her daughter's quick nod said the guess was right. "We had witnessed the removal by two strangers, recall? 'Twas there we tried the second time. But it was gone, and we know not who took the treasure. Should we not keep this secret? Patrick says so."

"And Patrick is right. Until the right time. Oh Star, you two have been such a help. And it is you who will know how to tell only what you feel necessary to the children. They will hear rumors—"

"It will be my job, but not as a hero. The real hero, as I have explained to the honorable judge, is Scot. And we must honor *el perro* for I have a sad feeling about him, as if—as if—I am being warned—"

"About what, darling?" Rachel asked anxiously.

The great, dark eyes turned to her pleadingly. "This, too—this pre-pre-premonition (*correcto?*)"—at Rachel's nod of affirmation, Star went on to say that people would think her strange, as before.

There was a chilling silence. Then softly Star murmured in a tone usually associated with the velvet tones of eulogies, "He no longer barks at the birds. His tail seldom wags, and sometimes he refuses to dine. And he looks so sad, so apologetic. My hands cannot heal, Mother Mine—else he would continue to bounce. And after the horror we witnessed, I am not sure it is a good thing. Do you understand now?"

Rachel, her heart feeling as it were being shredded, reached out to Star. And Star, her darling Star, walked into her arms. . . .

Buck spent more and more time at home. Rachel had no need for an explanation. He was readying her for the pain of separation. Neither knew when. It would come "like a thief in the night," as Paul had likened Christ's return to earth. And the biblical writer warned that His followers must be prepared.

"All right, I will do the best I can, Lord," Rachel promised.

She and Buck tramped in the woods in search of wild grapes, late-bearing blackberries, and huckleberries. Together they made their family's favorite marmalades, laughing to hide their tears. They took precious time to return to the neglected art of "visiting around," the renewing of old friendships around the countryside. There the men talked political issues while the ladies sat fanning themselves in the porch swings, just enjoying themselves leisurely, talking of domestic affairs, and sometimes listening to the "man-talk." But always, *always* skirting the clouds hanging overhead.

"Someday," Opal Sanders said uncertainly, "us wimmen'll be havin' t' worry our way through such matters—that is, when th' time comes that we're smart 'nuff t'vote. Right, Rachel?"

Opal bit a string from the needle she had used in patching her husband's overalls. "How we gonna prove *that*?"

Rachel felt her own back stiffen. The issue always stuck in her craw, as Aunt Em put it. Then her sense of humor took over. "I doubt if that's holding up the issue, Opal. After all, some of the men I've seen going to the polls are downright dullards! These things happen, but not overnight. Change is slow, as we've learned in dealing with founding a city here. But vote we will. And, should our intelligence *need* testing, we're sure to score high on the issues we ladies are working on." Was she steering the conversation a wrong direction? Better end it. "But to close the matter, let me assure you that men are less critical of us than we think—that is, taken one-by-one. It's just a matter of pride that forces them to stand pat on male supremacy. I personally don't feel chained, unliberated. But I do feel that we ladies are moving closer to being recognized as having equal rights. I can feel it, sort of like the river being sheeted with thin ice, but underneath there's a burble leading to a thaw."

"Oh Rachel, you're so smart." Opal's voice was filled with admiration. "Me—I cain't always understand thangs 'cause I see ever'thang so literal-like. You know, that the sumac's a-turnin' an' what with cannin' all done, well, I guess you're right. Th' river'll be sheetin' over afore we know it. Time changes thangs."

Rachel smiled gently and patted her longtime friend's hand. "There's nothing wrong with that kind of thinking, my dear Opal."

Holding hands that evening as she and Buck walked along the "safe side" of the river, Rachel pointed out the mountain peaks thrusting upward between eiderdown puffs of clouds, but said nothing to spoil the glory. The fat-cheeked moon smiled down as if to bless them, and somehow she knew that the time had come.

"Oh Buck, when all this is over *(Oh voice, don't you dare betray me with a quiver!)* well, can we be 'just plain folks'? I brought sunshine to Opal today. It feels so good to do just small deeds. The rewards are so great. Just a smile, but great."

A bit of a breeze curled down from the needled canopy overhead. Almost fiercely, Buck turned and folded her to himself. Huskily, he whispered, "Yes, my darling, and that time will come. That special feeling you get from serving is like the cup of cold water Jesus spoke of. But I feel that He would want me to serve these people, too—"

The next morning Buck was gone. She had known he would be. Duty had led him into the eye of the storm. But this was his cup of cold water.

12

Battle Hymn

For a brief period after Buck's departure, she felt totally alone. Star had gone to assist at church camp. Rachel approved because, in her own mind, her daughter needed time to be alone to sort things out in her young mind. Too, loving nature as she did, Star would have an opportunity to ponder its beauty, perhaps do some drawings. But that left Rachel completely out of touch with anyone who knew the facts of Buck's mission, or so she thought.

On the other hand, Star would be bringing the children home to Rachel. Mary Cole and the twins could shake the rafters on their own. But, she smiled, with them would be Yo's two, Roland and Baby Emmie, and Brian, Dr. Ames' nephew (she must remember that he went into a tailspin when called "Brian-boy" now!). So she best use her solitude wisely. At least she had Scot, her shadow. Star had declared that the little dog would be disruptive during the dwindling days of instruction, but Rachel knew better. It was Star's premonition concerning the loyal Scottie.

Now might be a good time to preview the classical books purchased from the several endowments set aside for that specified purpose. Miss Annie had promised her help when she found time. When would that be with all the problems continuing to crop up? Slay one dragon and another reared its ugly head. She grabbed a claw hatchet. *Work—she must work.*

Prying open a packing crate, Rachel blew the dust from the clothbound book. Surely she had misread the title. The dust had blinded her. But no, it *was Woman Suffrage, Early History of*

Women's Rights Movement. Credit was given to no author in particular. Easy to understand, she saw as she thumbed through the enormous volume, for it was a collection of notes (some unsigned) and complete manuscripts from such noted personas as Margaret Brent of the American colony of Maryland who had demanded the right to have a "place and voice" in its assembly. After all, she reasoned, back home in England, representation was based on land ownership. Her demand was refused. But her thoughts inspired women in Virginia and Massachusetts who refused to give up, and they won out. How interesting!

Fascinated, Rachel read on, reviewing the "no taxation without representation" fundamental clause during the American Revolution, which roused the women's ire. Weren't they property owners, too? And oh, here was a copy of the letter written by Abigail Adams to her husband, John, while he was sitting in the Continental Congress:

> I long to hear that you have declared an independency, and, by the way, in the new code of laws, which I suppose it will be necessary for you to make, I desire you would remember the ladies and be more generous and favorable to them than were your ancestors.... Remember all men would be tyrants if they could... we (ladies) will not hold ourselves bound to obey any laws in which we have no voice....

Name after name paraded before her eyes, leading down to Susan B. Anthony (arrested, tried, and fined)...Clara Barton... Jane Addams...Harriet Beecher Stowe...and the prediction of final victory. Women *would* win. Someday she must read this book in its entirety.

But for now she skipped to the section concerning women's part in opposition to intoxicating drink. There was an undercurrent of prophecy, all taken from just bits and pieces preserved in history—and all by women. Something told Rachel to record today's date, retain all the scribbled notes she had intended only for her family as reminders for their sharings. Who knew but that one day, foolish as it might seem now, her notes would be helpful in formulating a history of the state of Oregon? Certainly, there was a dearth so far....

(There were those who passed along history by word of mouth in the generations to come who vowed that the battered bits and pieces bearing the initials R.L.J. simply had to be Rachel Lord Jones, who was a kind of lady-prophet. "You know, th' one with th' peculiar-like daughter. Some say she wuz a dark angel—and it did seem odd that the girl left drawings in a kind uv code. Gargoyles, she called 'em. 'N mankind they wuz ugly! Man 'er beast they wuz other-world creatures." The story enlarged as time went on. And finally people used a record which was "downright"proof that "what goes around comes around." When at last women were allowed to vote, the notes seemed even more prophetic. As for something called "woman suffrage," giving women the franchise which allowed them the right to vote, "Well, will you look at this!" they marveled. "It happened before—just take a look at the part women played when it came to Prohibition! History, just plain history. And about the best we've got.")

This was the year of the "first happening." And it was to come soon.

But much was to happen beforehand. Tomorrow would take care of itself. Rachel's thoughts were sufficient for the day. And today was more than enough for Buck did not return when expected. And much was to transpire during his absence....

Rachel closed the book and went on to another.

—♥—♥—♥—

Her children returned from camp, brown as berries and so filled with chatter that, as their mother, Rachel wished for more ears—or fewer! Star, having heard all they had to say, eyed Scot, her eyes lighting when she saw that he wagged his tail with more eagerness. Maybe her loyal mascot would survive—but not by her hands, more through her prayers.

The children suddenly stopped their chatter. "Is he limping, Star?"

"He grows older," Star answered, choosing her words carefully, "just as we are all growing up. Remember the *haiku* I taught you to write?"

They interrupted, all talking at once. "The oriental poems... yeah, with three lines...17 words...about nature...and stuff—"

"But you are missing the point," Star pointed out sadly. "The poems are about life—how everything born grows up, lives— most beautifully, we hope—and finally dies—"

"No, *no!*" they all objected. "Star, you can make him live. You know you can. You *have* to—"

"Wait a minute," Rachel broke in, "you must be fair to your older sister. Star did not say Scot was dying—just growing older so he isn't as active."

But they were not ready to accept the words either of them had said. "We will feed him," Saul promised, looking to his brother for support.

David nodded. "Good things—all our treats—"

"We need not talk about Scot anymore," Star said gently. "I do feed him. Sometimes he sniffs as if to say grace, but not always does he eat it. Dogs are a gift to us and are one of God's mysteries. We know not where they come from, nor do we know where they go. But their job is to love us, and that they do very well."

In Star's face there was pleading. Rachel saw and responded. "Not one of you has told me about camp," she said brightly.

Star appreciated the change of subject. She needed time to formulate answers to their questions. Rachel understood, but within minutes wished she had chosen another topic. They began to talk nonstop. Oh, they'd met the new teachers—yes, two of them—and they were all right (they shrugged) "as teachers go." The Reverend Elmo was super with the Bible class. Mary Cole won the blue ribbon in the spell-down, going past everybody else in spelling names, syllable by syllable, in the Old Testament. Rachel *did* understand, didn't she? "You know, like 'Hab, *Hab*, ak, *Habak*, kuk, *kuk*, Habakkuk!*" (Saul patted a yawn which his twin brother David ignored.) "And that's not all either. She had put all the books of the New Testament in ABC order. I'm proud of my sister!" Obviously, his sister was proud of *herself* as well. "It takes brains, Saul," she said, a quality he himself lacked, her tone of voice inferring. Then she returned David's compliment. "It takes brains, too, to figure out what age Jesus was at the time He was crucified. But we *all* knew *why* He died."

It was at that point that Yolanda's son, Rowie, entered into the conversation. Giggling, he told of the "funny something" they saw when the entire class attended the big, big church in Salem. They all began laughing even before he burst out, "It was a—a—

toilet right in a little closet. And it was inside—and guess what! It had a horse collar on top!" More giggles until Brian, adjusting his thick glasses soberly explained, "He means a top, and there was a lid. We're laughing only because one of the boys from 'way back in the hills called it a horse collar. But Auntie Rachel, did you know that a very smart man came as a guest and spoke about the great classics?"

Rachel, who had been watching Star, studying her face, turned to Brian quickly. "That's interesting. What was the man's purpose?"

"He told us that there were certain classes offered—in Oxford, I think—which assigned only reading of the great classics—"

"*Only?*" Star looked at Dr. Ames' nephew with surprise. "Do you realize how many there are and how difficult to comprehend?"

The other children shrugged the matter away. Brian, however, gave his understanding of what "the very smart" man meant. "I know they are hard. Still, what I thought—well, I supposed it took years and years to be a doctor, so how could he decide which pills by just books?"

"There are different types of people called 'doctors,' Brian. Not all of them are medical men. What the speaker had in mind were those who went to school at home. No, I am unable to say it well. Mother Mine, please help me."

"People who study at home perhaps? By the way, Star, do you know that we have some of those classics, known as 'The Great Books,' right here?"

"In this house?" Star's face lighted up. Rachel wondered why the fact was important only briefly. What mattered was the change in expression. There had been such a faraway look, such a look of something close to sadness and concern. Momentarily the look was erased.

"We all need to talk," Star announced to the group. "I have some games we will play—games which you will need to play by rules. It is most carefully you must listen as we walk partway with Brian and Rowie."

"Tell us ... we want to know *now*. Are they scary?"

As the children clustered around Star, shivering deliciously, Rachel felt her own spine tighten. How in the world would Star prepare them? But prepare them she would. As for herself, Rachel felt the horror of it all sweep over her in a tidal wave of memory.

No, I will NOT think about it. Help me, Lord!

She was almost glad that a minor crisis was in progress as the group prepared to depart. To the surprise of them all, Scot had managed to pull himself erect with a little whine and, with a wag of his tail, follow. What had crippled the family pet so prematurely?

"Look, Star, *look!*" Mary Cole shouted. "See, you *can* help him—"

"But he doesn't want to go to Rowie's or Brian's," Saul said excitedly. "Look! Scot wants to go back to you-know-where—"

"Toward where the evil one was, do you think?" David asked uncertainly. "We ought to go *there?*"

"Certainly not!" Star said. "Come, Scot, come with us. We need you to accompany us. Now come, all, and we will talk about the games. They are about that place. See? Scot is obedient, and you must be, also. Just a moment. I have something for *Madre Mia.*"

Star, opening the door while keeping her head turned backward to keep an eye on her charges, tossed an envelope to Rachel wordlessly. Scot, deprived of going his chosen direction, eased inside the open door unnoticed by the group. *Poor little dog—not old, but weak and sad....*

Once the children were gone, still chattering like magpies, Rachel withdrew the note from the previously opened envelope. Still standing, she scanned the contents. It was brief. Shattering to Star, she was sure. Confusing to herself. And answering fewer questions than it aroused. Her legs felt as unstable as summer-churned butter. Only then did she sit. What could it mean?

At the third reading, the note was no more clear. In fact, Rachel found herself dissecting each sentence, phrase, and word for hidden meanings:

My darling Star: I am leaving this quickly penned message with the Reverend because he will be carrying a heavier load while I am away. Yes, it is necessary that I leave Lordsburg today. Notification is sudden, reaching me by means of a telegram wired to another party. I am unable to tell you where I am going or for how long. However, while I am there I will check carefully on the higher degree attained by the reading followed by the oral and written testing plus the dissertation. It will drain students of all time and energy, leaving room for naught but concentration. Then upon my return, you must be prepared with an answer before we go before our first Board: *your parents*. You will please help Reverend Luke as much as possible with the youth groups; and, Star, I beg of you two things: 1. Let nobody know that I am away (if questioned, say honestly that you have no knowledge of the matter); and, 2. *Stay clear of our watching place*. My love, P.

My darling Star. That term of endearment was entirely too personal—unless, of course, Rachel was right all along. But Star had said something quite different. Why? Why when Patrick stated later that Star was to prepare herself to answer his question? Didn't that sound like a proposal? Realizing that her thoughts were disjointed, she hurried to what surely must be of concern to Star: *Where had he gone—and why?* The degree through digesting such heavy reading was only a detour, revealed by the phrase "while I am there." She must not pry, but *why* had her daughter wished to share the letter? *Why?*

There was no opportunity for a private talk. A sudden visit from Yolanda took care of that. "Yoo-hoo! I'm feeling neglected. May I come in?"

Rachel surprised herself by laughing. "You're already in!"

Yolanda showed no sign of having heard. "Our children were too deep in conversation to recognize me. Rowie grabbed Baby Emmy then went back to Star's instructions, with me left out in the cold. But seeing that they were safe and not bleeding to death made me feel unneeded anymore—"

"You know better than that. It's just that they're growing up and we must prepare ourselves instead of clinging." *Who am I to say that?* Rachel said to herself while quickly turning the conversation other-directional. "What *really* brought you, Yo? My coffee?"

"Well, it would help. But Rachel," Yolanda bit her lip to stop its sudden quivering, "look at this first. Does it mean—?"

Rachel accepted the yellow envelope, knowing in her heart its message. She was right. Dr. Killjoy was summoned to assist with an identification. The doctor was to bring with him the younger minister. "Vague as usual," Rachel whispered. "But we know, don't we?"

Yolanda nodded. "Now, at least, you are no longer alone. The three of us can talk with one another: you, Star, and me."

"But we're made custodians of highly classified information, which means that we must make not the slightest slip. Our people are already living beneath a cloud of fear. Our job is to somehow create rainbows even *before* the storm those clouds portend."

Not an easy task. But to their advantage was the group of loyal women, so busy with keeping the law that they almost welcomed the fact that "business" reduced the population of men as a challenge to prove their equality. No question about it.

Just before the ladies were to assemble again, Miss Annie came to assist Rachel with reviewing the books for the library. She, like Rachel, was fascinated with the collection of notes, letters, and diaries compiled into *Woman Suffrage, Early History of Women's Rights Movement*. This, she said, simply must be shared with the growing number of members. Of course, the burden of proof lay in putting their theories into action, but the opportunity would come. It was to come much sooner than she or Rachel could have guessed—at the next meeting, to be exact.

"Now t'git down t'sharin' whilest we work on my rainbow quilt," Aunt Em announced after greetings and exchanging bits of domestic news were completed. "First, lem'me check makin' sure we got ourselves complete privacy—"

"No cause for worry, our husbands have their heads together in a game of checkers—yours and mine," Miss Annie said. "Let my Elmo have a bit of fun before—" she broke off quickly, causing Rachel to wonder just how much she knew as to *why* the Reverend would be busier. Thank goodness, nobody else noticed. They were too busy adjusting the quilting frames in preparation for their hearing "the latest."

"I volunteer to start, if you will indulge me," Miss Annie volunteered. "Remember what Paul told us in 1 Corinthians 9:25: 'And every man that striveth for the mastery is *temperate* in all things'?"

"As I recall," Miz Lily responded in her gentle, sweet way, "the ladies were always opposed to strong drink and used such passages to strengthen their position—probably behind the movement to outlaw the selling of alcohol completely in some states, and squeaking past the legislature in outlawing it in certain states like ours."

"Yes, indeed!" Miss Annie was quick to agree. "Unfortunately, however, interpretations of the Bible got in the way in some other instances—agreeing, if you will, with the men. The Good Book was accepted so literally and men accused women of going against its teachings. Women backed away—confusing, very confusing, I admit, until the more enlightened ladies thought it through and saw that some men probably had never so much as cracked open the Good Book. They simply used the Bible as a ploy in proving themselves superior. As such, they simply *had* to cling to their authority over women. That is, the mass majority—not all."

"No, not all. I'm glad you included that, Miss Annie," Yolanda interjected. "My mother used to tell me that some of the men regarded women as absolute angels, goddesses, queens, choose whatever word you like that elevates women to sit on a throne, be kept on a pedestal, or ride on a cloud—"

Several of the women groaned. "I can see through that one, too," someone from the far corner of the quilt muttered. "Flatter women to shut 'em up. Poor things probably never heard the word 'protest.'"

"But they suffered uh heap," Elsa pointed out. "We kin tell that by th' name suffer-age which hasta mean what they endured fer us, huh?"

Miss Annie tactfully explained the difference. "No, pain and women's rights are not one and the same. But," she smiled triumphantly, "both boil down to *endurance.*"

"'N we got that, aint' we just?" Emmaline Galloway called out.

A bystander would have found their militant yells comical.

Energized, Miss Annie went on to tell about what had happened in other lands, according to history. The women organized, marched, and drove Parliament to mental distress.

"So will we. So be it," the aroused group yelled louder. "Now back t'th' rum-runnin' over our county line...."

And that's when it happened—the incident leading to a change in history.

Rachel spotted the two men first. They were behaving strangely as they walked down the street. Were they staggering? Just as she pointed toward the two strangers, the two drew attention to themselves by bursting into boisterous singing. A sailing-ship song? She wasn't sure.

"Wish th' sheriff wuz hereabouts. He'd git 'em fer disturbin' th' peace," Aunt Em grumbled. "Is he still on Bixby's trail?"

Nobody answered, aware only of the drunken tumult. Drunken they were, Rachel suddenly knew, even before she saw the enormous bucket they carried between them. The container was strung on a stick. And even from this distance she was able to discern the heavy load of foam atop the contents. That spelled (and smelled of) beer.

"They make me uneasy-like," Opal Sanders whispered. "Anybody know them two?" There was heavy silence.

Aunt Em rose from her chair and called through the screen door, "Lower yore voices, please. We have laws in this town forbiddin' bustin' up meetin's with rowdiness!" When their singing grew louder, she added, "Stop it! What're yuh Bohemians doin' 'round here? Best yuh hightail it 'fore we ladies make uh citizen's arrest. *Git!*"

One of the pair stepped toward her. "Come on, lady, git down off 'n that high-horse. Jest soak yore head in th' brew here 'n git happy," he said coarsely. "We double-dog dare th' whole bunch uv yuh—" and, at that point, he began unbelievable insults.

"He's intoxicated," Miss Annie stated flatly. "Most likely that's home brew or," she paused to think, "it could be from the county across the line. Either way, they do not belong here!"

As the men advanced threateningly, all the other ladies rallied behind the two speakers. "We warned yuh onct. Now hit's twice. Ain't a-gonna be uh third time," Aunt Em said, her voice dangerously low, her eyes ready to burst into flame.

"Ah, come one, hussies. Have uh good time while yore men's gone—"

There was a rush as if the ladies had mapped it out in detail beforehand. Boldly, they advanced. And nobody ever knew for sure who ran at the intruders, grabbed the bucket, and sloshed the contents on the first stranger, then clapped the container over the head of the second.

They went dashing away screaming like animals whose tails had been set afire.

Rachel regretted later that she had paid no attention to the retreating men's direction of escape. But her mind was in turmoil. Two questions burned inside her—questions which *must* be resolved—even as the women around her burst into triumphant singing as they raised the quilting frames to their rightful place: "Glory, glory, hallelujah! Glory, glory, hallelujah! Our God is marching on...."

Rachel shook her head causing the world to spin dizzily before her eyes in an effort to clear her senses. "Battle Hymn of the Republic" was a fitting title. *Battle.* That was one of the things bothering her. The idea somehow must be cleared up. Was she responsible?

But for now, the other matter was more pressing. Swimming before her eyes were the face and the mode of dress of the man bathed in the sour-smelling beverage. It was familiar. She *must* remember. One moment it was there, then it was gone. Who? Where? When? *Please, Lord!*

13

Recognition

Time seemed to crawl on its knees at points, only to leapfrog at others. The difference, Rachel supposed, lay between the heart and the mind. Buck should have been back long ago. His absence sent arrows of pain through her chest until the ache became unbearable. But there was no reasoning with her heart when her mind contradicted every positive thought. "He will be home soon. I am to keep my faith strong and keep things in order here," she would tell herself staunchly, knowing how much she must do. "Oh, *are* you now?" her mind would mock. "And live a lie? You know something is detaining him, probably will for ever so long. Can't you recognize the signs, with more and more people called to join him?" There was no escaping the truth. There would be further delay. She must work as she waited. That was when time whisked past in seven-league steps. . . .

School opened without the usual flurry of activity. Paramount in the minds of the entire adult population were the problems at hand—problems which necessitated that children be accompanied by an adult while walking back and forth. For the most part, the men took charge. Conspicuously missing were Star and Patrick, but nobody asked questions. Construction began on the meetinghouse. The ring of hammers lent an air of normalcy.

"How many would you think know the whole truth?" Yolanda asked when at last the overcrowded schedule allowed a coveted meeting between herself, Rachel, and Star.

"The real truth?" Star asked quietly. "None of us."

"True," Rachel said. "The three of us come closest, as far as we can tell. But," she frowned, "so much puzzles me. I am still concerned over the identity of the two men and their reasons for deliberately goading us women. Our reactions bother me, too. It was unbecoming no matter what their purpose."

Star looked questioningly at her mother but said nothing.

It was Yolanda who told her of the incident. But as for the women's behavior—well, hadn't the men asked for it?

Star seemed not to have heard. Still looking at Rachel, she said instead. "*Two* men, Mother Mine? What, may I ask, did they look like?"

"They were strangers—" Yolanda began and paused. "What is it, Rachel? What's wrong?"

"I—I—remember," she said breathlessly. "I knew I had seen one of the men. It was only a brief encounter, but I know it was the same man! He came into Aunt Em's Eatery, let's see, about the time the Hathaways married." She closed her eyes and behind the lids she saw him plainly, a gaunt middle-aged man, hatless with hair askew, no coat and running as if to win the Olympics.

"Like this, Mother Mine?"

Rachel had been unaware that she was speaking until Star held up a quick sketch. "Yes, that's the man. Oh, darling where did this come from? You know him?"

Star shook her head in perplexity. "I cannot tell you how I know—perhaps by the words you speak, perhaps in a vision. Does God tell me these things, or am I strange? Oh Mother Mine, Auntie Yo—it is frightening, causing me to tremble. Let us not tell, lest I be called a witch. That—that is why I must be most careful with how I use the sometimes-power I feel in my soul as it creeps into my hands—"

Both Rachel and Yolanda knelt beside the girl who was momentarily again the little lost girl she was so long ago. The three of them huddled together. Words were unnecessary. Love speaks a language all its own....

It was a beautiful interlude, one which brought the three of them closer than ever before—and closer to God. "God is love," Star, clear-eyed and unafraid, said on rising. "And 'Love casteth out all fear,'" her misty-eyed mother replied. Yolanda choked out an emotional "Amen." All inhaled deeply with a smile.

Star spoke first. "The man you speak of—he is one of the evil men who found the buried treasure. I cannot say how I know, for when I saw him there was no recognition, no memory, I thought."

"But the other man was a stranger," Rachel said. "I had never seen him before."

"Nor had I. But now I would know."

Yolanda studied them both, while shaking her head as if to clear it. "I needn't pretend to understand. You two are a breed all your own. Why on earth would he stick around? Didn't he take the money? I mean wasn't it moved—gone?"

"Wait! It all comes back," Rachel said, the words tumbling out together, her heart racing wildly. "That jump-jack of a man served to spread the news when Judge Hathaway called the town meeting—"

Yolanda paled. "Then he knows. Oh, how can we tell the sheep from the goats? I'm plain scared for us, our children, and," her voice rose, "most of all, our men. They're gone—and—Rachel—"

"Try to control yourself, Yo, for all our sakes. Bear in mind what God's love does for us. And for our men, we must be brave."

When Yolanda nodded, Rachel turned back to Star. "Why is he so brazen? Bringing alcohol here is sure to cause commotion, draw attention to himself—"

"For a purpose perhaps? Satan wears many faces, *verdad*?"

"*Verdad!* And this man has done so before. But the purpose?"

"Could it not be, *Madre Mia*, that he wishes to draw attention to himself while something more large—*larger*—happens elsewhere. Do I say it well?"

It was Yolanda who spoke, her voice now in control. "Yes, darling, very well. And you mean that we three must watch quietly."

Star's face went through an immediate transformation. Gone was the look of impending storm. Up came the sun in all its vibrant glory, setting the great, dark eyes to glistening, bringing up the corners of her beautifully curved mouth into a brilliant smile. Rachel could almost hear her heart break into song. Surely the angels in heaven would join in....

—♥—♥—♥—

Before parting, Rachel, Yolanda, and Star laid careful plans. They would be cautious with their words while doubling their watch for anything irregular. Meantime, would Yolanda and Star give her a hand, Rachel asked, in attempting to discourage the women's corps against becoming too militant? It was one thing to work together peacefully to achieve a reasonable amount of independence. But these things took time. History was slow in the making and they could be—*would* be was better, implying promise—a vital link in the rise of women to their rightful place in history. But they *must* not attempt to violate the words the Lord Himself spoke to women. *Yes*, they would help!

"Mother Mine, I must have Daddy-Buck mark a notch on the record the way he once did. I feel myself grow taller."

"I guess we can all play that game," Yolanda said humbly.

Rachel nodded, a burden lifted from her heart. How tragic, she was to think later, that we had not time to put our plans into action.

14

Searching for Truth

Aunt Em announced at church on Sunday (after complimenting Reverend Elmo's sermon and ending with "Applied more t'my neighbor than me") that this week's meeting of the women's corps would be postponed a week. "Best we take uh breather 'n show uh pinch uv hospitality t'th new teachers. So, you ladies know what t'bring t'th' nex' meetin'—bits 'n pieces, makin' sure they're colorful!"

She lifted her eyebrows knowingly and for a breathless minute looked on the verge of winking. *Oh no!* Rachel willed and was relieved when her treasured friend settled for a wise look. It was easy to see that the men were puzzled. Easy to see, too, that they were as "curious as all git-out." Rachel suppressed a smile at the pleasure spread over Aunt Em's face derived from male curiosity.

"This is a day for dreaming," Yolanda said wistfully as she and Rachel walked home following the worship service, the sun warm on their backs.

"And worshiping," Rachel whispered reverently. Together they examined the sunny meadows aglow with golden-eyed daisies, the brilliant splashes of sumac, the orchards of overripe apples. The entire world was autumn-lined—soft, sweet, and melancholy for a summer gone. And an unspoken pining for a husband gone, too. Yes, a day for dreaming, but (Rachel squared her shoulders and looked heavenward) a day for praising the Master Painter who had provided such splendor.

They walked silently for a time, each buried in her own thoughts. It was Yolanda who broke that silence surprisingly, with a laugh.

"Be funny, wouldn't it, if we all showed up with our arms full of these bright leaves as the colored scraps Aunt Em asked for?" When Rachel made no answer, she sobered. "Was I right in sensing a double meaning?"

"We know what she wants, Yo: information. Information such as you, Star, and I are not ready to share, although some others may know, too. Frankly, I'm disturbed. I dislike being afraid to trust—"

"And you didn't much like the double meaning, did you? I mean, Aunt Em's misleading the men. She *did* mean colored scraps of discoveries instead of quilt scraps? Why is that so wrong? We were told to be on guard, watch for unusual behavior. Well, *weren't* we?"

Rachel nodded. "*And* reporting it to the authorities. Now we are being secretive, pretending to share with one another and holding back. Something feels wrong. Besides—" she began and then stopped.

Yolanda attempted a laugh and failed. "Now look at who's holding back!"

"I simply feel it's best left unsaid. I may be borrowing trouble."

"So what if you are? You *know* you can trust *me*. You know, too, that I won't give you a minute's peace until you get it off your chest."

Very true.

"I have reservations," Rachel admitted slowly, "about pushing our assignment too far, confusing it with the rights to which we women feel we are entitled. And I *do* agree—always have. You know that. But Yo, equality does not mean superiority. I *like* being a woman! I want to fulfill women's purpose. Would you have it otherwise?"

Under different circumstances, Rachel would have been amused by the sudden enlargement of the pupils of Yolanda's eyes, the way her brows lifted in shock. "You mean have a dumb husband? A dullard for whom I had to mark 'This end up' all over myself? No thanks!"

Rachel felt a little alarm sound within herself. No, that was not what she meant—not at all. How could she make others understand that, unless they combined common sense with their efforts, they could lose something sacred between women and their families, find themselves poles apart from their loved ones? There had to be a healthy balance. *I have always felt that God fashioned women for softness, love, and peacemaking, trusting us with the key,* her heart softly whispered. But how could she put it into a language anyone else would understand, saying that the key they held was love? *Powerful* love—love so strong that it could rewind time and strengthen relationships, instead of weakening their position. But first they must back up and take time to clear their thinking. Only then would women's key work.

"So?" Yolanda interrupted her thinking. *Was she able to answer?*

"I love my husband and children more than life itself—love them in the sort of way that one is unable to measure by scant spoonfuls. I—I meet their needs because I love them, not because I am chained. I discipline our children for the same reason. Just as our heavenly Father disciplines us—"

"Isn't there something about that in the Bible? But I'm not sure what that has to do with—well, I'm confused, too," admitted Yolanda.

"Nothing—and everything. About the reference: Yes, 'whom the Lord loveth, He chasteneth' is put into words or implied throughout the Bible, but not to be cruel or harsh. 'God is love,' remember? I guess I'm an old-fashioned girl," Rachel smiled, "at heart—"

"Me too! I'd rather hug than spank. Just an old softie—that's me."

"That's love." Rachel felt the words come to her lips from the Great Somewhere. "There has to be a balance, and there has to be a balance in how we achieve our purpose in *all* relationships—equal rights, but gently. Yolanda, am I coming through to you?"

"Clear, very clear!" Yolanda's voice was triumphant. "Open, patient—"

They walked on, talking and planning. Their thinking was clear. Unfortunately, their timing was off....

—♥—♥—♥—

No plans were made for the ladies to make themselves acquainted with the new teachers as a group. Rachel suggested that she, Yolanda, and Star visit school alone—that is, just the three of them. It was a demanding day. It was a mistake, they laughed later, to tell the children in advance. Naturally, each of them demanded that all three guests visit their rooms. That took some doing, Yolanda moaned, as she rubbed her feet and stripped off her lace-up shoes. "When will women rebel against these pointed-toe shoes? Since when did somebody shackle us with such a style? If God wanted us to have tiny feet, He'd have had no trouble pinching them in shape or making His shoemaker's last bigger."

Star giggled. "Is this not why we wish women's rights—to dress ourselves as we choose, each in her own way?"

But, they agreed, the visit was worth the discomfort. Mary Cole, obviously the head of her class, wasted no time in keeping it secret. She had to be reminded to raise her hand and wait to be called on instead of blurting out all the answers. Yolanda wondered aloud if everybody noticed the way those eyes flashed at the reprimand. (*Notice?* Rachel had thought her heart would break. Mary Cole's eyes were so like her father's. *Oh Cole, Cole, I wish you could see our daughter!*)

The twins tried to outdo one another, of course. Saul, always the skeptical one, all but contradicted each statement made while David, buried deep in thought concerning the constellation (topic for the day), seemed to forget his mother's presence. The teacher repeated his name three times before he heard the question concerning Orion asked of him. He answered, then added studiously, "Such a beautiful constellation that great conquerors sometimes sent out decrees that it be renamed for them—"

"The names never lasted," Saul interrupted.

And Yolanda's Roland interrupted Saul. "Too bad as Sir Roland was one of them—others being Alexander, Napoleon, and—"

The teacher's face reddened which said they had never acted this way before. Rachel, embarrassed herself, forced an understanding smile, longing to speak the truth: "Really? You should see them at *home!*" And then go one step farther: *"And you know it."*

Brian Ames, shoving the thick-lensed glasses to their rightful place on the ridge of his nose, made a formal try for attention.

"Dear teacher, I wish we could take a nature walk, climbing the hills of the Holy Land where the people of the Bible lived and studied the natural objects. They loved Orion—"

From that point it was a free-for-all. "Yeah, the Bible talks a lot about the stars"... "Sure, that's how sailors navigated"...Just read about Job"... "That's right, teacher. I know some of it by heart. Brother Patrick had us learn about the glories of God"... "Which alone spreadeth out the heavens, and treadeth upon the sea. Which maketh Arcturus, *Orion*, and—" Another student broke in to tell about mythology, how Taurus the Bull halfway up the eastern sky—"

Star had been sketching all the while. And now, as if from another world, oblivious to her surroundings, she spoke: "But Sirius, most brilliant of all stars, beckons. Sirius, beautiful Sirius, the dog star."

Teacher looked at her gratefully and called a recess.

That teacher was Callie.

Poor little Callie. Now they could laugh. But then she needed support which she got after the children made a whooping exit, pushing and shoving to the schoolyard.

Yolanda's sister, beautiful eyes filled with tears, made her way to her guests. "I can only pray that nobody was trampled to death in that stampede. Oh," the tears spilled over then, "will I ever be a teacher—a *real* teacher?"

"You are a wonderful teacher already, my darling," Yolanda assured her as she drew the younger girl close. "They had to show off."

Rachel agreed. But it was Star who spoke as if inspired. "Yes, dear Callie, *you* are one of those shining stars. One does not get the real education from books alone. The wise teacher allows her students to think, search for truth, then think some more. Is this not so? Thinking for one's self is the freedom we seek."

"Oh sweetheart, you said it all, bless you. You are so wise," Yolanda commented now as she bent to lace on her shoes. "Rachel, don't you think Star should attend the women's corps meeting with us?"

Star shook her head. "No, *gracias*. I will be busy otherwise. There are sketches I must make. Too, Scot needs me—"

Yes, Rachel realized, the little dog was growing weaker. That fact and all that had taken place today she must record as history.

"Sweetheart, will you make some sketches? Somehow, it seems fitting that Scot be included in my notes." The little dog only slept now, unable to play hide-and-seek with the children. Heartbreak lay ahead for them. Did it lie ahead for the whole of Lordsburg? A feeling of apprehension crept along Rachel's spine....

15

Bustin' th' Barrels

Rachel slept fitfully the night before the day scheduled for the meeting of the women's corps. Now, as the long gray fingers of dawn clawed at the windows, she rose. Breakfast was out of the question. What she needed was a time alone to meditate, a time to listen for the voice of God. This she needed to get her through the day.

Outside, the breath of the morning was sweet with flowers hiding in the half-light, which the sleepy twitter of night birds said would not last long. Already the satin-smooth horizon was softly rainbow-hued, no longer mackerel-toned. Then, without warning, a rim of an eager sun peeked over the horizon in preparation for its journey across a late-autumn sky. Shadows fled as the bright rim enlarged and became a full circle of fire-opal, leaving behind a trail of flame. The purple mountains sent back a glow of rose.

Rose. Of course, roses were the source of the heady early-morning perfume. Rachel walked to the nearest bush, remembering Yolanda's letters written after her family had arrived in the Oregon Country. How inviting her claims that "here roses are in eternal bloom" were to the ear of a young, adventurous girl on the Eastern Seaboard, where ice-coated shrubs still tapped against the windowpanes.

"And Lord, it is true—and You have made it so," she whispered in reverence, lifting a full-blown red rose between her forefinger and thumb. Who but the Creator could put together anything so perfect? Surely it communicated the deepest, most meaningful message of love.

Leaning forward, Rachel buried her face in the fragrant petals, only to pull backward with a sharp intake of breath. A prickle of pain had stabbed the back of her hand. Surely it was too early in the day for bees, and a bee sting did not draw blood.

Why, a thorn, of course, she realized, pressing the back of her hand automatically to her mouth with the next throb of pain. And, in that position, she stood like a garden statue. The message was so clear it was almost frightening. The answer she had sought was there, implanted on her heart. But, like that garden statue, she would never be able to put it into words. Maybe it was enough just to understand. The confusion was gone. In its place was a deep, beautiful message.

Surely a rose was the queen of all flowers, fashioned as a symbol of love, a love that reaches so deep into human emotion it begs to be touched like the tender sweetness of a baby's skin— velvet-smooth, filling the lungs with a born-again sweetness each morn.

But anything so fragile must be protected. The thorn, then, had not been God's afterthought. Yes, there must be a balance. God had said it through nature. Rachel pondered a moment. Let the rose speak for itself today. Happily, she ran for the shears and carefully clipped the very rose she had held, careful to leave a long, thorn-lined stem.

Suddenly she was ravenously hungry. She and the children would have pancakes. All were up except Star. They whooped when Rachel shared the plan. Mary Cole began setting the table while the twins hastily grabbed for the butter, honey, and maple syrup. Rachel struck a match and set the fire to blazing in the great kitchen range. Kettle on to boil, griddle on to heat, she lifted her skirt a hitch and took the stairs two at a time to call Star. But Star was not there. Strange. And stranger yet, neither was Scot. A bit of the morning's sheen was gone even though the meal was festive—so festive, in fact, that the three children were too busy stuffing themselves, thank goodness, even to question their older sister's absence for once.

Apprehension turned to fear when she heard Britches whistle. "Telegram, Miz Rachel!" he called, his voice echoing against the canyon walls.

She accepted the yellow envelope uncertainly. The message must be urgent, else the telegrapher would have waited for Star's daily trip to the post office. Her appetite fled at the thought.

"Hit's all right, Miz Rachel—honest." He met her eyes squarely, only to have a tide of red rise from his frayed collar and flood his face. "I'm sorry. I—I did'n' mean no harm. I hafta read th' meanin' when I tran-sa-late the Morse code to words."

"Thank you, Britches. Wait, please, until I see if there's an answer—"

"Ain't no ad-dress—" Britches replied, looking at his shoes.

The message was brief. Brief but wonderful! Rachel wanted to reach and hug the young man. Happiness must have shown on her face. His next words were, "I *tole* you hit wuz good! Don' thet mean Mr. Buck'a a-comin' home?"

"Yes—yes, I guess it does. Oh, thank you, thank you—"

Whistling happily, Britches trotted away, leaving Rachel to reread the words: FINISHED STOP HELPING OTHERS RE-SEARCH STOP COURSE LOOKS FAVORABLE STOP LOVE B. Interceptors would find the words meaningless.

Twirling about the room with the precious telegram pressed against her heart, Rachel pleaded aloud that Star would return. It seemed important somehow that they share the news. Then she stopped suddenly. It was equally important that Star and Scot come home unharmed. The sun was rising higher. Where had time gone? But wait she must.

Just as the children had failed to notice Star's not joining them, they paid no attention to Britches' visit or his strange behavior. They were still gulping pancakes and carrying on a heated argument about how a bumblebee could fly when it was impossible "scientifically." They were talking with their mouths full as usual. Rachel should correct them about both, but there simply was no time.

"Hurry up, you three! You're all going to be sick—too sick to go to Rowie's. Enough now."

They loved going to Roland's. And today was even more special. The plan was to sort their rock collection begun at camp with Reverend Elmo. Even so, they dawdled.

When at last she was able to hurry them along, they were still saying a bumblebee's wings were too fragile (Rachel noted their growing vocabulary) to support so big a body. Mary claimed temporary victory by saying smugly: "Anything's possible with God!"

Dressing took longer than it should have even though her garments were simple. Drawers stuck on the swell-front dresser, catching her black stockings. No runs, thank goodness. And the lightweight, nobby-cloth, early-fall suit was a wrong choice. She had donned the winter-white pleated skirt, piped in red, before discovering the semifitted jacket was missing a pearl button. A small matter, but not when she had trembling hands. And where on earth were her tortoiseshell back combs?

Yolanda came before Rachel was dressed. "Aren't we late?"

"Yes, and I'm having trouble here. I'm happy, but scared—"

Yolanda laughed. "You can't be both at the same time. Let's talk about it on the way to the meeting. I already have my stopper planned. I'm going to point out that marriage—a *real* marriage— can't be cut and dried. And that applies to women as well as men. You know, like husbands saying, 'My job ends with putting clothes on their backs and stuffing their mouths full of bread' then forgetting that we need to feel loved and be treated with respect. You know, like men's recognizing we have sense enough to vote. Any more than wives can say . . . Rachel, you're not listening to a word I say!"

Rachel felt herself blush. "Sorry, I was listening for something else. But first, here—read this." Thrusting the envelope into Yolanda's hands, she laced up her shoes.

"This has to be the happy part. Oh whoopee, and praise the Lord! I could use a good husband back home where he belongs. What am I saying?" she giggled. "Isn't that what men say about *us*? Well, I can see you're still not listening. What's wrong with you, Rachel?"

Hurriedly, Rachel explained. "Is *that* all?" Yolanda drew a deep breath and blew it out in a whistle. "Just a daughter walking a dog?"

Was that all? How could women expect men to understand them when they were unable to understand one another? She suggested that Yolanda go ahead without her. Yolanda refused. And that accounted for their being late, which, for better or worse, altered history. . . .

"Here they come!" Yolanda's announcement caused Rachel's heart to flutter in her chest like a caged bird. "She's carrying Scot—"

"Yes, he's unable to walk." Feeling tears sting her eyes, she went on to explain that Star cared for him as if he were a baby, laying his head on a pillow ... feeding him from a spoon. "He's still young—but the injury, remember? And what scares me is that—that she says Scot won't live, that she must let him go—"

Yolanda's eyes met Rachel's squarely. "You mean—Rachel, do you still think that Star has special insight—special power in her hands?"

Rachel was spared answering by her daughter's entry. "Mother Mine, I see that I have given you cause for concern. I am sorry. You must understand that it seemed important to take Scot to a place he knows so well if I am to make the sketches most proper."

"Oh darling, you mean you went *there*?" Why remind her that it was dangerous? She knew. And she was safe at home. So—

"Show her the telegram. Quick! We *must* be on our way." Yolanda's voice was almost a plea.

Star's eyes brightened momentarily. Then, without comment, she returned to the little Scottie. Gently laying his head on a pillow, she swallowed hard and addressed him as if the two of them were alone. "I was so proud of you. You stood up. You sniffed. And you tried to dig. And you made a discovery—I know you did. There is something you know that we do not, something that will be of help one day. I have a feeling deep in here." She patted the little animal's chest.

Scot lay very still, as if exhausted. His eyes remained closed. But seeming to recognize the feel of Star's hand, he moved his tail in a small wag of appreciation and made a comfortable sound that resembled a human sigh.

The meeting was in progress when Rachel and Yolanda entered Aunt Em's Eatery. Fat chance Yolanda would have in making her presentation. Nobody even noticed she and Rachel were there. Everyone talked at once, and no one heard. In such bedlam it was impossible to make sense of the layers of hysterical words piling on top of other loud words. Rachel held her breath and tried to hear the jumbled sentences.

"Bootleggers" ... "won't put up with setch" ... "lawbreakers" ... "unfittin' fer th' human race" ... "over th' county line" ... "iffen men won't protect our young'uns, wimmen's gotta go t'war" ... "bust 'em" ... "said afore us wimmenfolks dared 'em in Lordsburg" ... "yeah, saw 'em big as life, sneerin', a-laffin'" ... "squads, on guard!"

Rachel had seen such fury. Mob control was needed to quell it. And it had been somewhat justified, a battle of "good" against "bad." But among women, the peacemakers, the keepers of the flame of everlasting love? Something was wrong—terribly wrong. What had brought this fury on? What had happened today? She made an unsuccessful attempt to swallow her heart which clamored in her throat. Unable to force a scream for attention from the cotton-dry throat, she took a step forward, raising her hand in an effort to gain attention, then stopped, catching her lips sharply between her teeth.

Two heads emerged from the bushes forming the barrier near the county line. She tiptoed to see above the heads of the milling women in an effort to recognize the bent-over intruders.

Recognizing them, she tried to scream—but too late The two men rose, lifted their buckets and, with a mighty heft, sloshed the sour-smelling contents through the open doors and windows, soaking the women to the skin. There were howls of rage as each grabbed the weapons apparently assembled before Rachel and Yolanda's arrival: axes, shovels, picks—anything they had been able to put hands on.

The men swaggered reproof—a definite dare. Decoys, was Rachel's guess, and when they picked up speed in retreat, she knew she was right. One of them (the one she had not seen until they made their first unwelcome visit) looked over his shoulder, eyes ablaze, hand caressing an unshaven chin. The other, apparently the leader, spat out an oath of command to hurry his partner along. His eyes glowered and his voice, not unlike the rasp of a sawmill's attempt to start, rasped at Rachel's taut nerves. The man was dangerous and should not be antagonized. Star should be with them, after all. She had recognized both men.

All this she had thought in a fleeting second. And in that second lost she had failed to see what the women were doing. A tug at her sleeve and Yolanda's scream alerted her.

Oh, no! The women were in pursuit.

Rachel repressed the startled scream of warning on her lips. She knew it would be useless from the steel in the eyes of those around her. Anger had destroyed their reason, and they were nearing the county line! *We have to stop them*, she mouthed to Yolanda, knowing that the wind would suck all sound from her throat. Yolanda nodded. She appreciated God's making it possible that they understood one another, but wished that He had added more strength to their legs. These women must not cross the county line. They were, as the sheriff would say it, "armed and dangerous." And, oh horrors! There loomed just ahead the dread words: "Saloon! Be Our Guests!"

Was it possible that she and Yolanda could overtake the mob and stop them?

It was. And they did.

Panting, the two young women ran ahead and, at the risk of being trampled to death, stopped with heels planted on the line of the neighboring county. Stretching arms and spreading legs apart, they linked hands together, then extended the opposite arms to form a fragile barrier.

How did cattlemen stop a stampede? *Oh quick, Lord, HOW?*

Sing…yes, sing. What made no difference. Surely the Lord provided the song, for Rachel found herself singing, and Yolanda followed:

> Where He leads me I will follow,
> Where He leads me I will follow,
> Where He leads me I will follow,
> I'll go with Him, with Him
> All the way…

A miracle that the mob stopped some might say. But the real miracle was—well, which was it? The strange silence which fell over the crowd? Or, wonder of wonders, the fact that curious heads began popping through the windows of the saloon followed by awe-stricken gunmen staggering through the swinging doors? The men removed their hats. "Well, whadda ya know?" one said.

The women saw and continued with song. The roles had shifted. Now, without their knowledge, *they* were serving as decoys. Rachel and Yolanda had realized that the two men Star identified as the pair who stole the loot hidden by Bonaparte Bixby had dodged somewhere out of sight. They held a key to the entire plot, and their behavior may have boomeranged.

"They've been had," Rachel whispered.

"Our ladies?" Yolanda managed to find the breath to whisper back. "Yes—misled and misguided. Or do you mean the men? I'm suspicious—"

"Oh Rachel, *look*!" No sheet in the Monday wash could have been whiter than Yolanda's face.

Rachel's gaze followed the direction Yolanda's finger pointed and she felt the blood drain from her own face. There, hidden among the heavy growth of button-willows clumped along the river, were—yes, it *had* to be—buildings. Putting a cautioning finger to her lips, she dropped to all fours and crept along the edge of the screening trees. She could feel Yolanda crawling silently behind. Several times she tugged at Rachel's skirt, a gesture Rachel ignored. Suppose—just suppose—they found a boat. She shut her eyes in a desperate attempt to flag her imagination. There had to be a boat. There *had* to be, she whispered to herself, as if through her impassioned repetition she could will one. A boat would mean rum-running, after all. Why was she so sure? Unless—unless it could be—no, it was impossible Or was it? Maybe the adjacent county was not bootlegging the liquor here.

Shaking her head to clear it, Rachel explored the possibility the stuff was being stilled right here under their very noses. After all, who would have thought there was a regular ghetto as she supposed the shacks were? For the first time, she stopped and squatted to massage her raw knees. Yolanda pulled up beside her and opened her mouth to speak. Rachel shook her head and pointed to a sign: "Teeth Jerked, Two for Price of One" and then another: "Fillings While You Wait!" hanging crookedly on the neighboring shack. *Two* dentists—*here*? False fronts, of course, but how stupid did these people expect anyone who discovered the hideout to be? But what *did* they shield?

This time it was Rachel who pointed. Putting a finger to her ear as a signal to listen, she then pointed it to one of the "barbershops." Cautious sounds came from within, and then there was dead silence. In that silence, Rachel realized that there had been a low hum of machinery of some sort and a sloshing sound which she supposed came from the river. The door swung open and a hooded creature emerged and stopped. The great white beast seemingly held its breath in suspense. And then it stumbled ahead, tripping at one point to reveal its burden: two half-barrels. Alcohol—it had to be. But what could two women do?

Two women? There were women everywhere, arriving at exactly the right time. Or was it the worst? For just at the moment of their arrival, the door of the second building eased open. And there inside, unbelievably, was a makeshift bar behind which were barrels and barrels of what could be nothing other than strong drink.

The rest became a dream. The room was dim and smoky. Men lay on the floor in a drunken stupor. Men, she realized with a faraway sense of horror, that she knew—friends. Her head was too light. And she was walking against her will, her feet touching a floor that wasn't there with the lightness of a toe dancer. No, no! She was being pushed helplessly forward. *Scream. Scream a warning.* But she had no voice....

The women were surging toward the barrels. Rachel remembered later that she tried to restrain them. But how does one restrain a raging storm? There were screams of "Bust 'em!... smash ever' one...knock off th' spigots on ever' cask...show 'em what wimmen can do...."

The world began to right itself as Rachel felt a tide of cold liquid wash over her feet. She made no effort to lift her skirts. Let the stuff rise higher without cresting. Let it drown men who would do such things. An anger such as she had never known flooded her being when she saw Elsa O'Grady's husband staggering in an effort to rise to his feet. Elsa was weeping, trying to help him, and praying that God would forgive him.

Forgive *him?* He needed support and prayer when yielding to temptation. What about the evil in mankind that allowed them to prey on the weakness of others? The Bible overflowed with warnings about giving one's brother strong drink. And, her scalp tingling with righteous indignation, Rachel remembered the command that one was to obey those who had rule. And certainly it was against the law of Lordsburg that liquor be made, transported...oh, this *must* not be allowed...better that a millstone be placed around the offenders' necks and they be thrown into the river. And, above all, rose the question: *How did we let this happen?*

The back door swung open and men, wild with anger, pushed forward. "We will kill ye, ye she—" Oh, she must blot out the words. She must—

Suddenly something cold and steely was pressed into her hand. Somebody behind her, a man whose voice was familiar, commanded: "Take these—both of you. You *do* know how to shoot?"

The sheriff! Sheriff Brimmerton was home!

And Yolanda was answering. "Better believe we do! How can anybody make it over the Oregon Trail without knowing how to use firearms?

"Then get at it. *Now!* Shoot them barrels chockful of holes. *Emmaline!* Get here this minute! *Here*, put this to good use while me and my men round up the transgressors. And you, Miz Lily— let 'er go, Galliger!" The sheriff and his "merry men" were off.

Who among the ladies fired first? What difference did it make? There was a volley of thunder and Rachel, who deplored violence, felt no remorse. In a sense of near-hysteria, she looked at Miz Lily and wanted to laugh. Who would have thought it? Immediately, she sobered. *Oh, dear God, forgive us if we are wrong.*

But the few ladies the sheriff had chosen to deputize went on pumping lead into the barrels. Beer shot all directions, like geysers spewing from a thousand overheated mouths of the earth. Foam rose to the ceiling, blinding the infuriated gang. They sputtered, coughed, and stumbled while filthy blasphemy was washed down their throats. Helpless, they were easy prey for lawmen surrounding the buildings.

Sheriff Brimmerton basked in the limelight. "Get the outlaws shackled!" Brazenly going over the heads of government agents in full dress, he ordered, "String 'em together like a chain gang. If one so much as mumbles, gag 'im!" Then, turning proudly to his all-women posse, "Heard all the commotion and congratulate you, one and all. You did the job your men failed to see . . . clung like a leech to your convictions. Now," his voice rose, "you curiosity seekers make haste back across that gerrymander!" They made haste. . . .

But where were the two leaders? The question stopped Rachel's heart. *Could they have followed Star?*

16

Reconciliation

Is there any word sweeter than "reconciliation"?

Lordsburg folk would say, "No!" And with just cause. Each family had to face up to mistakes made and forgiven, walls built up and walls torn down, each without pattern or design. Throughout the years to come, Rachel was to remember the rose which circumstances never allowed her to use in illustrating her idea of how human relations worked: the protective thorns which kept some from ever catching a glimpse of its beauty, its need for pruning lest the vine grow out of control. And yet, it was that very pruning which allowed for new growth. But in the healing that was to follow, her sharing the unexpressed message at the women's corps meeting played a part in the reconciliation which took place—all because she shared with the aged but wise Reverend Elmo and the youthful but rapidly growing in stature and in wisdom Patrick O'Grady. "Patience and understanding," they preached, each in his own words. Its softness, its protectiveness...did God Himself not demonstrate both in the beautiful gift of His only Son? The blood...the suffering...the rejection...and the acceptance which led Jesus to the cross but led the redeemed to life everlasting. Yes, reconciliation—no matter what the price—is beautiful.

"There has to be a first start. Make it!" was the ministers' message. "Repent. Seek forgiveness. And move on in your new life...." What took place in private homes was just that: *private*.

But in the hymnals one page in particular was worn thin: "O! Be Ye Reconciled...."

There was the Lord to thank for His inspired writers of the Bible. But the ancient prophets were gone, and yet time marched on. The world had no need for another Bible. But there should be a history.

Remembering, Rachel continued with her notes as if the Creator Himself had appointed her to do so. And Star continued with her drawings.

"Downright uncanny, so 'tis," old-timers were one day to pass down the word. "These scraps uv goings-on is like somebody knowed 'twould happen—er could hit be thet hit *did?* Yuh know like somebody—don' rightly rek'lect 'is name—said, history hasta be relived iffen folks don't larn from hit...." Eyes would widen and the older generation would huddle around winter fires and tell their children's children the story of Oregon... always reminding them to read both the Old and New Testaments in like manner.

And generations later, a few collectors clung to a few yellowed and tattered notes when the Women's Christian Temperance Union became an ever-enlarging organization. It is a matter of history that women declared war on the consumption of alcoholic beverages and brazenly took up their inflammatory banners and marched with a purpose. Oh yes, they were armed. And with axes and hatchets, they hacked every barrel in those "dens of iniquity" to pieces. The new law of prohibition was added to the Constitution. As a result? The women liked to think so. Cause and effect, you know. Bible was on their side.

Women who delved into history proclaimed that women of the New World suffered from the rigor of the law...refused any rights to an education...punished for speaking in public...and some (hard to believe but true!) were hanged for being "witches." And even after a measure of enlightenment, "Give 'em uh inch and sure as shootin' they'll take uh mile!" men protested. "Humph!" women scoffed, "Yuh menfolks never *give* uh inch in yore stubborn lives—we *earned* it!"

Earned? Even the men conceded that at least women *worked* for it. Over a century later, the women of Lordsburg pulled away from "thet silliness 'bout women bein' subject t'their husbands," long after overcoming their exclusion from the right to an education.

"Someday th' world'll see th' light," they declared, "'n we'll vote right along with th' best of 'em ('Best—ha, let 'em think it!')."

The battle was long. There were hardships and disappointments. Women's struggle in the state's history is one which has rarely been equaled, *never* surpassed. But it is a matter of record that Oregon adopted the woman suffrage amendment well in advance of many older states. Strange, many said even then. "But then," people say today with a shake of the head, "it's just another part of the Oregon mystique, as was *she....*"

—♥—♥—♥—

Notes and pencil firmly in her grip, Rachel raced home, leaving Yolanda behind talking with two other women, strangers to Rachel. They were the two new teachers, she was to learn later. Yolanda's report came as a shock. Rachel had been so immersed in the mystery and danger which plagued the city that she and Yolanda had failed to meet the ladies, detained as they were in Callie's room.

And now, drawing close to home, reality of the day's events struck her full-force. *Was* she responsible? True, she was a woman ahead of her time. *Why* so? was not the question. The question was *Am I responsible either directly or indirectly? I knew that the other women thought of me as a leader. Oh, what is Buck going to say? And how can I explain?*

There was no time to formulate an answer. Preoccupied, Rachel—pledged to be on guard every minute—failed to see the oncoming figure. Amused, he allowed the two of them to collide before bursting into laughter.

Buck! Oh, how she had dreamed of this moment... its tenderness... its sacred beauty... its intimacy. It was none of these. Anger, born of tension and fatigue, exploded within her. "How dare you—" she sputtered, "you *let* this—*let this* happen—*made it happen*—while I—oh Buck—"

And helplessly she fell into his arms, sobs shaking her body.

Now came the tenderness, the beauty, the intimacy. Buck's arms enfolded her, tenderly at first, his heart thudding against her own. And then she felt the muscles ripple along his forearms as he drew her closer, ever closer, until she was unable to breathe. But she made no protest. *What a wonderful way to die!* She relaxed and stopped breathing. Until—

Oh mercy! Why did she have to hiccup at a moment like this?

Rachel felt the heat of her blush of embarrassment. And then they were *both* laughing.

"Wh-what are we—we laugh-ing at?" she hiccuped, feeling wonderful.

Relaxing his hold only enough to allow her to inhale, Buck said, "Oh, my darling, I wish you could see yourself. Your hair looks like an inverted mop—and what on earth have you been wading in? Your skirt has shrunk to a new style. What is it you ladies call those tight-around-the-hem skirts—oh, hobble-something. You *look* hobbled—hobble-top?

"*Peg*-top."

"Whatever, it's up to your knees." He was still laughing. "You, my dear, look like a lady of the night. Now," he sobered and made a poor attempt at scolding, "can't I leave you alone *ever* without your getting into trouble? Oh Rachel, don't start crying again. You know it breaks my heart. It's serious, isn't it?"

"Very serious," she choked. And then, words tripping over one another, she told him the whole story. "So," she ended, "it was beer I was wading in."

His reaction was what she should have expected from this wonderful man she was proud to call "husband": concern for her, shock at the discoveries, and amusement—pleasure actually— at what the ladies of Lordsburg had done. Reconciliation? Between them none was necessary.

"But Star? Yes darling, there's cause for alarm—" he said. "Let's go."

17

Crossroads

What was this? Rachel's mind had had more than it could take. Why were all these people swarming about their house? Slapping fingers gone numb against her mouth to hold back a terrified cry, she froze in her tracks, colorful imaginings taking control. *Star*... Star had disappeared... the rum-runners would retaliate... oh, why had she acted so irresponsibly? *Oh Star, Star, Star!* And her dull mind suddenly took a turn for the worse. Who knew but that the other children were with Star? More and more lurid became her thoughts as the once-blurred faces swarming in the coming twilight took on shape and, she supposed, developed a pulse. At least they had voices. But who could fault her for the bizarre memories which rendered her speechless?

"How long have they been missing?" someone asked.

Missing? Then they *were* missing—or were they? She knew, but knowing was no comfort.

"How long? Where were they last seen? Th' new Miz Hathaway—Cappy, th' Judge calls 'er—declares she seen 'em playin' sumpin' like cops 'n robbers (So 'Mrs. Maxton,' now Cappy Hathaway/Agent Hathaway, Rachel's mind wandered, is back too) sez a passle uv 'em wandered off—could be hidin' out fer fun, dun'cha know—kep' a-callin' thet animal critter. Course he never had sense 'nuff t'come—"

"Idiots, yes, I'm a-meanin' th' whole caboodle uv yuh!" Brother Davey, oh bless his heart, here he came breaking all speed limits for a wheelchair. "I jest pray," he panted, "thet uh rare rush uv common sense comes t'them hat racks y'all keep claimin' t'be heads! Me 'n my Emmy-Gal take offense when folks accuse our gran'childrun. Hidin', my foot! Th' whole pack uv yuh blunderheads heerd His Honor's wife talkin' 'bout games. Ten t'one them's *war* games—"

"Course, Davey-Love," Aunt Em had joined her husband. "Thet bein' how our brilliant Star larns 'em 'bout out-foxin' th' enemy—"

"There's a search party combing the woods," Dr. Killjoy, white-faced, said. "My advice is—"

"—to call it off at once!" Buck commanded.

Rowie's father nodded. He had made a quick-fire conclusion and somehow Buck had read his words before they were spoken.

"We love you all, and God bless you, but please return to your homes," Buck went on to say. "We will need the doctor here, and Miz Lily, the nurse—just in case."

"Plus all of you who have been away on your missions," the Reverend Luke Elmo said quietly. "Assemble here quickly. We know where the children are, do we not?" His eyes searched for Buck. But Buck was gone.

Rachel's mind righted itself. Why had she been standing like a dummy when the children were lost? she asked herself. "Yes, yes, we will find them with God as our helper. And yes, there *is* something the rest of you can do, the most important part of all. Pray—pray with all your hearts. Reverend Elmo, would you lead them, perhaps to the church? I know you had planned to participate in our trip—"

"I serve where I am needed," the dedicated man said calmly. "'Come ye that love the Lord'—come with me."

Tears stung Rachel's eyes. "Thank you," she said meekly, then, lifting her voice, she told the crowd already assembling as Buck had requested, "I want to thank you again, and your prayers will have us back within the hour. Meet us *then*, Reverend?"

The man of God nodded. "Both myself and my beloved wife. Will you join me, Miss Annie?"

All eyes were on Rachel for a split second. "What a woman!" they would say. "Mighta knowed she'd be able t'take charge—inspired, she wuz, jest plain inspired. Flesh 'n blood though. On hearin' news what would do other folks in—well, Rachel Lord Jones would meet square-on. She'd whiten—thet wuz natch'ral—

then she'd be cool as a cucumber. Right now, jest lookin et 'er puts strength in th' legs, grit in th' craw." Wordlessly they hurried to catch up to the Reverend and his wife.

Rachel had *not* met the situation "head-on." Her mind had exploded in a thousand fiery slivers of fear. But they were right in saying that she rallied from shock. The sinister suggestions her mind had made were the works of the dark hands of evil. But knowing that such thoughts were unendurable, unconsciously she had reached for the bright hand of good. Afraid? No. Alone? No. God would walk with her.

Now fearlessly she spun on her heel and rushed down the shadowy path to the river.

Half an hour later those appointed were back in the Jones' living room. It was quiet—too quiet. Fatigue was written over their faces, but all eyes were unnaturally bright. All were eager to speak. And yet, where to begin? It was Star who made the first move. She simply dropped to her knees and gathered the shivering little dog into her drenched skirts. The twins knelt beside her, each laying his tousled head against a shoulder. At Mary Cole's motion, all the other children huddled with them—waiting for a signal from their undisputed leader, their Star.

If only grown-ups could learn this lesson, tears in the eyes of the adults said. But it was Star who said softly: "There is much to tell, so much, but first we must thank our Lord for all He has revealed. May I ask that you all hold hands? Joining hearts as well. Touching gives strength, yes? This day we have reached crossroads—and we need You, Lord."

18

A Miracle—in Color

"...and a little child shall lead them," the Reverend said after the prayer.

Star lifted her head, ripe-olive eyes abnormally large and even blacker than usual. "I am neither Jesus to whom Isaiah referred, *verdad*? I only walk in His footsteps," she said humbly. "Nor am I a child!" The smile she gave him was dazzling. Did she imagine it, Rachel wondered, or did her daughter exude an otherworldly glow?

It was as if a spotlight from an unknown source flooded down upon the group, sending showers of glorious colors like a rainbow—and lifting Rachel's spirits the way rainbows were prone to do. She must clutch at the colors, hold them close to her heart, letting them shine on and on, no matter what was to follow in the maze of reports. Oh let them shine...shine...in the perhaps tragic possibilities....

Surely the others felt it. They might have been carved of stone.

"I beg, oh, *por favor*, I beg on bended knee that you do not think me strange. You see, I saw a vision again, a colored vision, and I have brought it home—"

Patrick rose, walked to where Star still knelt. Gently, he lifted her to her feet. "They will believe you, dear Star. If this dedicated young woman is to be called strange, then count me strange also—"

"And us!" all the children chimed. "Star made us see, and it means something."

Patrick smiled and put a finger to his lips. The children obeyed.

Yolanda met her husband's eyes and those of Brian's uncle. Dr. Killjoy smiled crookedly, and Dr. Ames turned palms up. But their perplexity, Rachel knew, concerned not Star but their own charges. Yolanda's eyes then locked with Rachel's. "If they minded that well at home," she mouthed silently, "we'd all drop dead!"

"Go ahead, darling," Buck said gently. "We need to hear."

All eyes were on Star now. And all were approving, supporting, and loving. Yes, it was intended that she should tell her story....

She had gone to the place Scot loved most beside the river, the place where he was himself—the self he used to be. There she was able to make the sketches for generations to come. "The sketches and the notes recorded by Mother Mine will show, pray we, the Oregon Country as God created it. Perchance it will be as if this were the garden in which He walked in the cool of the evening."

She handed the drawings to Rachel.

The hooded creatures did not come, Star explained. These were the best sketches of all. She was inspired, in another world. And so engrossed was she that the rustling in the bushes went unnoticed, just as her presence and Scot's went unnoticed by those who spied. Why, she had wondered, did the little dog not growl when the sound grew loud? He was so different there—so young, so strong. No evil had stolen his healthy body. It was Eden before Satan entered. Just as their ferny dell had been before the "evil one" came. And Scot knew that one day life would be like that again. God would restore it, and all would be peaceful and calm. Though wars might rage about them, they would be on an island of love. But still wondering at his not barking all intruders away, she laid her paintbrushes down and looked for her model. That's when she knew Scot was gone. But he had never left her before.

"Scot," she called. *"Scot!"*

Something warned of danger. She could feel it, touch it. And something whispered, "Rush—it is urgent—*rush!*"

Again she called. But there were no shining shoe-button eyes, no wag of the fluffy tail. Forgetting that she might be in danger, Star searched the ferns, then, shading her eyes, ran to the river's edge—*forbidden territory*. Star strained her eyes. But it was growing more difficult to see. A mist had risen, thick like molten silver—thick and strangely illuminated.

The sinister silence was alive, rising and falling, its throbbing patterns in cadence with her pounding heart. Fear had risen like the eerie fog. She didn't imagine it; she knew she didn't. There was something out there—something breathing in and out with the current of the moving water. An island? No, islands were stable where God planted them, yes?

A boat? *Sure?* Yes, she was sure. And moving toward it was— oh no, it couldn't be, but it was! Scot was swimming toward it, ears back, little nose sniffing the water to follow a scent he had picked up. Again, Star called, "Scot, oh Scot, you are not strong enough—*come*! Oh Scot, you will never make it back!"

And that was when, without caution, she waded in....

Star would have been swept into the fast-moving current of the river had it not been for the unbelievable strength of her pet. "My heart was pounding—pounding so hard I am sure that it was responsible for the sudden churning of the water. I tried again to call to Scot; but the water drowned my gasping and panting as I was sucked to the very bottom of the river in that grave I had occupied so long ago. And then, surfacing for the last time, I felt a tug like unto that of a strong hand, then a pair of steady eyes met mine. There was something in those eyes—so ageless, so supreme. Oh, try to understand! But how can I ask you to comprehend something I am not able to comprehend myself? I only know that what he did was impossible without help from the Great Hand which created him. The same Hand which lifted the fog and calmed the waters. The ship was gone. But Scot's collar of rainbow hues remained."

There were questions. Mary Cole, David, and Saul, who had sat in silent fascination, now began their own questions among themselves. After all, their beloved mascot was gone. Wasn't *his* safety worth more than any silly old ship's? Could God let this happen—and with Scot such a good dog?

Yes, there *had* been a ship. And yes, Star believed Scot drew her attention to it. Its cargo? Star could not say. Perhaps the buried treasure which had been found and moved several times... perhaps intoxicating drink...but yes, Scot knew what his purpose in life was and he had led her to it. One is not to know all, only to see "through a glass darkly."

"But Star," Sheriff Brimmerton pressed, his voice almost beyond recognition in its newfound softness, "you *do* feel that all these things are tied together: the noises, the ship, the behavior of your pooch—uh, brave dog. Is this what you're telling us?"

Star nodded. *"Si, señor.* Do not all things work together for good—how does it go, Patrick? I am tired—so tired—"

"All things work together for good for them that love God," the young minister finished for her. Then, looking at the others assembled, he said, "Star is exhausted. I think you understand—and will excuse us."

He moved to lend Star a helping hand. But suddenly, the fog was gone. And so was the memory of it. Star, like the fragile little dog whose life was ebbing away, was filled with renewed energy. Her eyes were filled with vibrance, ageless and supreme.

"Yes, do excuse us, *por favor.* We need nourishment for the body now. You children may play the riddle games while Patrick and I serve. We have no loaves and fishes, but the two of us cast not our nets, but our votes for pancakes!" Patrick laughed, his eyes adoring her.

At the door they paused. A radiant Star glanced over her shoulder. "Reverend Elmo, is it not proper to break *pancakes*?" she asked roguishly. Smiling, Patrick turned to lay a blanket over the sleeping dog.

There was a ripple of laughter which cleared the air. Rachel exhaled and realized that she was now prepared for the reports. Her head was clearer than it had been in months.

Aunt Em leaned back, reached into her paisley bag, and withdrew her quilting scraps. "Might as well keep these hands occupied along with my tongue. Why do I git th' feelin' thet one uv these bright days we a-gonna need a-nother quilt?"

Rachel sought Buck's eyes. In them was understanding, and with sudden tranquility she realized that they were agreeing and that when the proper time came...well, there would be no objection at all....

It was time to get down to the problems hanging over their beloved city. But, of all people, who should delay the matter but the shy, pink-cheeked Miz Lily. "But before we start a nex' quilt—well, shouldn't we—uh—complete the one in the making?"

The other women turned curious eyes her direction, causing a deep flush to stain her fair skin. "Not t'worry," Aunt Em said, comfortably rocking to and fro. "We got plenty time—lotsa meetin's ahead fer th' double-weddin'-ring 'un. But this rainbow hues design'll take careful plannin'. Onct, uh long, long time ago, along th' trail leadin' over th' mountains, her gran'ma—thet's whut I'm known as—made a little girl uh coat-uv-many-colors dress—'n now—well, carry on!"

" 'Bout time yuh be givin' consent, Emmy-Gal. Wimmen—funny breed, talkin' quilts when we're a-sittin' on uh powder keg. Take over, judge!"

"Thank you, Brother Davey," Judge Hathaway almost smiled. How he had changed since renewing his vows to Cappy. How we have *all* changed, Rachel added to her thinking. No, *grown*. "Grown" was a better word.

"The house will come to order!" Judge Hathaway said, once again a "judge."

19

The People's Right to Know

"Hear ye! Hear ye! Let us consider that court is now in session," Judge Hathaway said. "Our city manager here was within his rights, both as our host and because of his position, when he turned away the newspaper reporters. Agreed?"

All agreed. Buckley Jones was heir to the throne, so to speak.

"Then with your permission, let us consider this a grand jury of sorts. It is a most extraordinary situation. Borrowing from what I consider the masterpiece of logic, Lincoln's Gettysburg Address, I suggest that we remember that neither this city nor the world will note what we say here tonight. But they may never forget what we *do* here. Let our prayers be that those following will continue our unfinished work. Affirmative?"

"Affirmative!"

"Are there comments or questions?"

"Well now," Brother Davey said, obviously proud of his sometimes failing memory serving him so well, "ain't he th' president what said a house divided cain't stand?"

"Right you are, Davey-Love," Aunt Em smiled as she bit off a thread, "but I'm believin' th' Good Book said hit first."

"Yep! Thet was my nex' point. Anyways, we gotta git our own houses in shape. Yuh men be knowin' whut I mean?"

Yes, they knew. One glance said that. But a second glance said that they did not care to comment at this time. That report best wait for that "unfinished business" the judge had made mention of.

Rachel studied Judge Hathaway's face. He looked tired and the dark smudges beneath his eyes were slightly swollen, which suggested lack of sleep. Small wonder. The dear man was carrying as heavy a burden as had the noted president he quoted—for his time. And it was a burden in which they all shared.

His eyes caught hers. "It would be my thought that we start with your daughter's report, Mrs. Jones," he said formally. "Would you be willing to review the background leading up to this?"

Caught off guard, Rachel wondered just how far back she should go. "I—I'll be as cooperative as possible, Your Honor," she said with equal formality. "I will need help, of course."

"Of course," he nodded.

"There are no strangers among us," she began, "so I am assuming that we all recall what Star referred to as the 'watery grave.' You remember who tried to drown her and how we disposed of him. And you will remember who, to our surprise, rescued our Star—"

"But he had to stand trial, and met a tragic end himself. Let's not canonize *him!*" Dr. Killjoy's voice was laced with anger.

"I believe," the judge intervened, "that Mrs. Jones is only suggesting that we must proceed with caution. According to the law, it would be better to let five guilty parties go free than to punish one accused who is innocent. Proceed, Rachel."

The name slipped out. But it amazed Rachel how much use of her Christian name relaxed her. She was able to summarize quickly and accurately from that moment. Star's sketches had served as the one piece of final evidence needed for identification of her would-be assassin—those and her visions, her dreams. "I cannot explain what my daughter herself does not understand, but I am willing to accept it."

"And if you will allow me, let me add that the child—young lady—has the keenest mind and the most skillful hands I have yet to find in my practice." Howard Ames spoke with conviction.

"Best in seven counties, yep!" David Saul Galloway said proudly, a statement which added little, but touched the hearts of all.

"Thank you, Howard," Buck interjected. "Dr. Ames is responsible for the little Scottie being alive. He brought the dog back from, one might say, the dead after the attempt on his life."

"So you, Star's parents, put complete trust in her report—including that which concerns her pet?"

"We do," Rachel and Buck said in unison. Oh, the beauty of those words! It was probably due to the long day of crises—how many could one day hold?—which whisked Rachel's mind back, back, *back*. Back to the sad-sweet day when she and Buck took their sacred vows before the Reverend Luke Elmo. Praise the Lord for memories. . . .

The judge cleared his throat. "That being the case, all reports to follow very well may lead us back to Star's account and its verification with Patrick's support of the part his eye could see. Star sees differently, a matter which is not to influence facts such as the rest of you are able to supply. Would you agree, Mr. and Mrs. Jones?"

Buck nodded. Rachel was a bit hesitant.

"Rachel?"

"Yes, Your Honor, other than—well, we cannot dismiss the reality of Star's sketches, in my mind. I should like to offer them as evidence."

Judge Hathaway asked that they be brought forward and marked "exhibits, numbers to be decided, and viewed by others after all reports."

Rachel saw his eyes open with shock when she delivered the sketches—but only for a moment. And then J. Quentin Hathaway was judge again, laying aside the sketches. The burden of proof lay ahead. . . .

"Sheriff, sir, have you a report regarding your search for the missing man—either his whereabouts or activities?"

"You speak, of course, of one Bonaparte Bixby," Sheriff Brimmerton said as he scratched his head. "Seldom have I had such foul luck. I combed every hamlet between our state and the Canadian line, picking up many a false lead. Followed 'em all, but you good folks know the old saying 'All roads lead to Rome'? Well, now I'm about convinced of this truth. For certainly none I followed," he grinned almost impishly, "me—the Sheriff of Nottingham, as young Ames has chosen to rename me, and me merry men, well, we found neither hair nor hide hereabouts." He turned palms up. "How can a man just plain drop out of sight? Easy matter for him to change his name—he's been known to do just that—but the pictures? The likeness is convincing. Nobody, excepting a mule, has ears like that!"

The judge cleared his throat. Point of order. His Honor took over.

"Well, the court has shown that one Bonaparte Bixby was connected with Julius Doogan, otherwise known as Jules Dunigan, now deceased. Begging your pardon, Miz Lily. This must be embarrassing for you, his aunt."

"Embarrassing, but true," the sweet-voiced spinster replied.

"Thank you, Miz Lily," Judge Hathaway resumed. "It is also established that the missing man located the money taken from the train robbery, hereinafter known as the 'buried treasure,' and that, according to Star Jones's testimony, it was buried then relocated by two other persons whose identity is yet to be established."

Rachel bit her lip. It was hard to withhold evidence. Correction: It was in the judge's possession, marked "exhibit number—"

But an excited murmur went around the room, gathering volume with every tick of the grandfather clock. Judge Hathaway rapped on the claw-footed library table serving as a desk with his bare knuckles. There was silence.

"We must, of course, continue the search. Have you people representing our United States government any comment at this point?"

One man, standing tall in his uniform, answered for the several other agents scattered throughout the room. "Not at this time, Your Honor. Perhaps I should assure you that we will continue here as long as deemed necessary—a matter to be decided in Washington, D.C."

All nodded approval. And Buck was called next.

Rachel felt herself tense. She had known his mission. She did not know the outcome. Buck had been sworn to secrecy. Her husband inhaled deeply, paled slightly, and revealed that he and "helpers" had, upon finding human bones among the ashes where animal sacrifices were made by the satanic worshipers, then sought help in identifying the skeletal remains. Yes, they were human. That had been verified. But no, identification was as yet unknown. Two of the group assisting would be recognized, Buck said in completing. They were doctors who had served Lordsburg: Dr. Frederick Greer, the more experienced doctor, and Dr. Norman Ambrose, the younger who had studied under the older man. *And* both planned to come back to Lordsburg. "Norman has wanted to return all along," Buck finished, "and, since Dr. Greer plans a semiretirement, he is considering coming along to work on a part-time basis and also to continue research on this project."

"For those of you who may be new, I'll add that both are excellent," Yolanda's husband said. "Dr. Ames here summoned them to assist when I was the target of a flying bullet." He paused, then resumed: "They're good, very good, I might say—both of them." Dr. Killjoy then added, "Very well may have saved my life or," he grinned, "at least, postponed my death—"

"Oh Maynard," Yolanda whispered with a sort of desperation, "don't say such things!"

Rachel sucked in her breath, a feeling of apprehension prickling her scalp. No other person's ears seemed to intercept the wife-to-husband words as the meeting went on without delay. Maybe, she thought, I am conditioned to listen for danger signals, preparing myself to protect Yolanda. Her dear friend had been strengthened, but could she withstand another loss? The question hung unanswered, and Rachel forced her mind back to the meeting. Mrs. Hathaway was speaking.

"—and I would have preferred to hold back the name. But, as I understand, we are to reveal all findings—except any which would seal our lips because of national security?"

The spokesman for the government agents nodded soberly.

"Then, may I ask that the name not go beyond this room? We do not wish to cast a blight on the otherwise untarnished name of—you will take this objectively, Yolanda? It is your sister I am assigned to interrogate—"

"*Callie?*" Yolanda sprang to her feet as she echoed the name. Two crimson spots burned on her cheeks and her eyes were black with unspeakable emotion. Her voice shook when she protested. "Callie—my baby sister—you *can't* suspect her of deceit—"

Agent Hathaway's face whitened, but her voice was steady—steady and sympathetic. "I suspect *nothing*. And I would be the last to accuse. My job is only to follow orders. Persons in my position do not so much as *think*. We only compile information and report to our superiors. Until then secrets remain secret—"

"*What* secret?" Yolanda's voice rose to an unnatural pitch.

Maynard stood and, placing a supporting arm about her shoulders, eased her back down beside him. "Let her finish, Yo." His voice was gruff.

"There's nothing more to tell. So far, dear Yolanda, I have unearthed nothing. There is no confirming evidence, not a trace of suspicion—and there need not be. Her name would not have been included except for her—uh—association with Bixby—the engagement—"

There was a ripple of shock waves which traveled full circle. Yolanda burst into tears. "I can't bear any more! Take away your pitying eyes—"

Rachel rose quickly from her wing chair and, picking her way through a maze of feet, hurried to kneel beside Yolanda. "Our eyes are not pitying, darling—they are understanding. We all love you." Then she, too, gave way to tears.

"Alas and alack," Cappy moaned. "I feel wicked—no, guilty, as if I were caught stealing sheep—stealing her reputation instead."

"Spare your remorse," Maynard said with a hint of steel in his voice. "My wife will be all right. She is hurt—maybe more surprised—but that will pass. Buck up, my dear. We will talk. The woman is only doing her job, as are we all."

There was an awkward pause. There was more to be said, but nobody seemed to know how to say it. Rachel let her mind drift to the kitchen where, from time to time, she had heard Star and Patrick conversing while rattling pots and pans. Sometimes the conversations were low and serious, at others, playful—almost to the point of being giggly. It was good to hear Star border on silliness. Patrick was good for her. How could she have thought otherwise? She didn't—not actually. Rachel realized then that it would be hard to let go no matter the age. But she was stronger now, strong enough to realize that Star was capable of mature thinking and in no rush to be married.

More talk, and with it the mouth-watering smell of sourdough pancakes. Was everybody as hungry as she? The judge must be—

"Thank you, doctor," His Honor said. "There is more to clear up, admittedly. But, for now, the hour is late and I do believe the time has come to adjourn. We have established the main facts and—"

There was a wave of protests: no adjournment until the main episode of the day came to the forefront. The ladies must be heard!

"There have been no arrests, as I understand. Right, sheriff?"

"Correct, Your Honor—nor will there be!"

Rachel hid a smile. Not likely since Mr. Brimmerton had joined in the free-for-all. Something in her mind clicked then—a memory of the sheriff's carrying the matter even farther as she herself hurried away. There had never been good blood between the two counties: one clean (Lordsburg folk), the other "dirty." Troubles stemmed from the free-flowing alcohol "over thar" and "them bloomin' brothels." Certainly Brimmerton had done nothing to mend the differences when, frustrated because of the getaway the two men made right beneath his nose, he turned on the curiosity-seekers "over yonder" and yelled: "Away with you—*all* of you. If ever another steps across this line—"

What would he do? Rachel failed to hear the rest of his warning. Looking over her shoulder, she doubted if the others heard either. "Get," he had said. They got!

"Furthermore," the judge added, "it is not our purpose to contest the will of our ladies. Any differences are to be settled in the home, bearing in mind that we men encouraged the organization, setting no limits as to how far they should go. Should the church think differently—"

The church did not. The Reverend, bald head shining like a full moon rising above the dark horizon of his near-threadbare black robe (a relic from his circuit-riding days with which he refused to part in spite of Miss Annie's gentle coaxing), made that clear. "Let him who is without sin cast the first stone."

"Then—" the judge tried for adjournment again.

But the government agent who had served as spokesman all evening again stepped forward, saluted smartly, and said, "Begging your indulgence, Your Honor, but may I speak?"

"Proceed. You have the floor."

"It is my understanding that plans are to call those turned away from this meeting together to inform them as to circumstances. I agree wholeheartedly with 'the people's right to know'— with one reservation, as referred to by Captain Hathaway. But we are compelled to act in secret at certain points. Had we followed that point to the letter of the law, no mention would have been made concerning Miss Lee. I must order that this matter be kept within this group. Reasoning will tell you that any party under investigation—and we must keep personal feelings from such investigation—be regarded as a matter of national security. Any leak will alert such person, altering behavior. Do I make myself clear?"

"Very," the judge responded. He glanced Yolanda's direction and seemed satisfied with the look of relief on her pale face. In Rachel's mind this was debatable. She would ask Buck about the phrase "intent of the law." This would crush Callie, and later Yolanda.

Suddenly the room filled up with the pungent odor of golden-brown pancakes and amber coffee as Star and Patrick entered, each carrying great platters. Star did not set hers down. Instead, without awaiting permission, she walked directly to the judge and, holding the platter above her head, reached for her sketches.

There was a faraway look which, like shutters, had closed over the lovely face. She appeared unaware that Patrick took her platter.

"These are the men—the ones who replanted the treasure!" She held up the sketches.

There was a loud chorus of women's voices: "Them 'causin' trouble today."

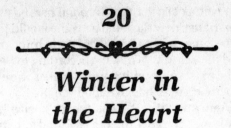

20

Winter in the Heart

For the next two weeks Rachel was so absorbed with her thoughts she scarcely noticed that autumn, beautiful autumn, tiptoed out. Here it was December—mild, but December all the same. The reds and greens of Christmas were there by nature's hand. Fir trees, faithfully green throughout the calendar months, held their arms high to catch a first snowflake. Maples and oaks, more easily intimidated by winter, shed their summer garments in anticipation of an ermine coat. Now, through the thinned-out leaves, the dogwood's red berries were more visible. Bright-cheeked apples strung every branch as if reluctant to leave the parent trees. A few Canadian honkers, late in their flight, warned of coming frost even though the sun continued to brighten their feathers.

How like Lordsburg, Rachel admitted to herself. Her eyes were grasping all the signals and tucking them in some far corner of her heart. She was holding onto summer's reassuring warmth and autumn's brightness, while there was the chill of winter in her heart.

Idle wishing would not take it away—not when she knew that the fires of love were burning dangerously low around her. Secrecy prevailed of necessity, and secrecy bred suspicion. She must go on, clinging to a faith which—given time and, yes, action—would clear away the ugly part of mankind and let the beauty shine through again.

Meantime, neither she nor those around her must ignore their blessings. No matter how dark the way, she would let herself be borne upon the wings of that faith, bearing in mind that God *was* in control and the world was moving according to *His* plan. That meant that she must serve with a smile. Smiles were contagious. And, she remembered, although nobody enjoyed adversity, from it came a certain strength. Patrick, whom Rachel had come to love, had made mention of something she had jotted down when he was in conversation regarding his findings about the Great Book degree he and Star would seek. How did it go? Oh yes, research during his time away led him to quote about thankfulness. "The English word, 'thank,'" he told Star, "derives from 'think.' If man would but think he would be thankful." To which Star had said thoughtfully, "So we are approaching *Think*sgiving." That had been November and summarized it well.

Well, there was plenty to be *thinkful* for. The library was overflowing now with great books, just as the larders overflowed with food preserved for less-plentiful months ahead. The barns' ribs were swollen outward with grain. The church was growing by the proverbial leaps and bounds. The women, ever-watchful and a wee bit more conservative now, worked with renewed zeal. There was a certain restraint, regrettable but necessary. "We can be relieved that whatever wounds there were between husbands and wives have healed," Rachel confided to her own husband (thinking how sad it was that not every woman had a Buck). He had smiled, a hint of amusement near the surface, and said that the pastors had taken care of that well.

How appropriate that they had chosen "peace" for the sermon just after the ladies had descended upon the bootleggers, doing their duty as they saw it. "Be grateful for peace, my beloved brethren," Reverend Elmo pleaded. "Our Bible says it clearly: 'The Lord will bless his people with peace' and, quoting again, 'Great peace have they which love thy law; and nothing shall offend them.' And how glorious that peace begins in the home— no greater gift can man and wife give their children than the perfect example of harmony. Home, home, sweet, sweet home, the cradle of love. Husbands, greet your wives each morning as if it were your first day of marriage. And wives, end each evening down on your knees together as if it were your last—"

The O'Gradys had held hands and wept.

Remembering, Rachel thought back to the promised meeting of the general public which the judge had promised when they were barred from the fact-finding session. Rachel had opted to remain home with Mary Cole who was running a slight fever. Rachel also agreed to watch Yolanda's children and Dr. Ames' son, Brian. And yes, Star was to go. She and Buck could report to her. And yes, of course she would watch out for the wafer-thin Scot. He would present no problem. Secretly, she wished the little dog would complain, demand attention the way Mary Cole was doing. "I wish Star would think of a replacement for the doggie. She'll be so broken up when he goes." Rachel wanted to say the words aloud, but it would be bad for Mary Cole. And the way her daughter was behaving, she decided, maybe she should threaten to replace *her*. One minute she was moaning, groaning, saying she was dying and getting no attention immediately, until Mother had to assure her that most people did not succumb with one eye open! The next minute Mary Cole was whimpering to get up. Why must she stay in bed when there was absolutely nothing wrong with her? Mother then had to remind her that it was inadvisable for "dying people" to be trotting around in public. The laugh they shared was probably better for her daughter than the chicken soup.

Howard Ames dropped in unexpectedly. His face was a welcome sight, and Rachel would have found that hard to explain. Anxiety perhaps . . . unexplained fevers . . . sympathy for the little dog . . . the apprehension which Lordsburg shared . . . everything lumped together.

Rachel greeted him with a smile and offered coffee which he refused. It was then that she noticed a look of concern on *his* face.

"Meeting over?" she had asked lightly, pointing to a chair.

Dr. Ames nodded, running nervous fingers through his hair. "I came for Brian. Might as well take Rowie along—save Killjoys a trip—"

"Is something wrong?"

He looked at her questioningly. "Yes and no. I mean, I would have come for them anyway. But yes, I guess I'm concentrating needlessly on the chilling mystery that goes on and on. We'll have to double our guard on the whereabouts of the children. I don't want to frighten you—"

"Well, you're doing a good job." Rachel's attempted laugh came out flat. "Come out with it—please do. I'm not good at games."

"It's nothing new, Rachel, just the way it was said. The audience took all the reports in stride, offered to help. Everything's out in the open except for withholding the items we mentioned. But I guess I did not expect the government agents to be so adamant about everybody's staying away from the river—especially the site of, well, the horror. They've staked it out and said parents would be fined if their children were found near the place. Not that the fine matters—"

"I know. It's the implication of danger." Rachel's heart was thudding, but she promised to assist even more than previously, watching 24 hours a day if necessary. He looked relieved.

They chatted briefly until Howard relaxed visibly. Rachel asked him to check on Mary Cole. He obliged and, to her relief, Mary Cole giggled and teased as he thumped on her chest and pressed her ribs. "Fit as a fiddle, except for the elevation in temperature. Always wise to keep children in bed in case of fever. I'd advise that you keep her away from the other children. Someday maybe the powers in our profession will believe us when we say some ailments not considered contagious can be infectious. Now, young sprout, you mind your mother!" Mary Cole giggled again. Howard turned away and winked at Rachel. She would be all right.

"I think I'll accept that coffee now. Oh, let me take a peek at poor Scot. I've cared for him before, you know. It angers me that he'll meet a premature death," he clenched his fists, "because of these ruthless men—devil's helpers, every last one of the—forgive me for the word I was about to say. Names wouldn't help, anyway."

They lingered over the coffee even though it was past the children's bedtime. Did Rachel know about the arrival of the two other doctors recently? Yes, they were at the meeting. Yes, Greer and Ambrose—both staying with him. House seemed too big now with Mrs. Maxton—that was, Mrs. Hathaway—gone and—and—well—well, *her* having left such a nightmarish memory—

Her meant Barbette, of course—the evil woman who pretended to be the wife of Howard Ames and mother of the doctor's adopted son (and nephew), when she was neither. To the horror of Lordsburg, she proved to be the missing link, "Queen of the Rum-Runners." Of *course*, the child needed stability.

"I do understand," Rachel said quickly.

Howard called the reluctant boys, paying no attention to their objections. His mind obviously was elsewhere. At the door he paused.

"Rachel," he said hesitantly, "has Yolanda said anything about Maynard—I mean, any change in his behavior, or complaints?"

The question startled her. "No, but regarding what?"

"Nothing really. All right," he grinned, "no games, I know. As a doctor I have to bear in mind that he was the target of gunfire, too."

Rachel felt her legs wobble beneath her. "You didn't get it all?"

"I thought you knew." With that he was gone, leaving her in shock. Yolanda could not stand another loss, and she could bear no more burdens.

Buck's arms moments later were a blanket around her heart. But that was then, and this was now....

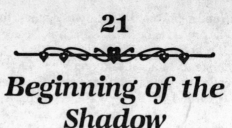

21

Beginning of the Shadow

Christmas came and went. Lacking was the spirit of the season. Oh, true, there was a candlelight communion service at the church—beautiful, as usual, but robbed of its full measure of beauty by knowledge that the partakers were surrounded by lawmen for protection. It was as if the shadow of the cross fell over the manger.

The school board decided that the annual pageant, providing equal pleasure for bright-eyed child-performers and parents beaming with pride, be held in the afternoon. The children protested loudly, some tearfully. It *had* to be evening. Jesus was born at night while shepherds tended their sheep. And how could there be a Christmas star? Stars did not shine in daylight. The arrangement would take away all the shine, all the purpose. Wasn't He the light of the world?

Adults, having promised to make as little as possible of the threatening situation, agreed that the children had a right to know—*must* be told, in fact. Rachel and Buck agreed that it was handled well. "Actually, it is best to let children know the truth," Buck said. "They're little rocks, always bearing up better than grown-ups expect. Still, it's too bad about the ugliness that necessitates it." Rachel nodded, her heart too full to answer. It was obvious that they were scared. A certain anger was growing within her. It wasn't fair!

There was one uplifting scene when in the semidarkness created by dark-green window shades drawn against the lights,

Mrs. Shepherd, the widowed teacher who was an accomplished musician, accompanied the all-school chorus. The woman played the piano without reserve, inspiring the children to forget the situation and sing their hearts out. Surely nobody had ever heard the carols ring out with such triumph, such beauty—possibly rivaling the heavenly choir.

"Mankind," one man leaned over to whisper to Rachel, "that woman sure can tickle them ivories!"

Rachel nodded with a smile. But her eyes were picking up surprises throughout the room—all happy. She shook her head in dismay, causing Buck to put his arm around the back of her chair and draw her as close as was proper. "What's going on, sweetheart?" he whispered, his eyes saying more.

Taught never to whisper in a public gathering, Rachel drew back demurely and pointed discreetly at points of interest. First, there stood Sheriff Brimmerton beside the still-slender Mrs. Shepherd at the piano, leaning over gallantly to turn her music. Wasn't he supposed to be on guard? What possessed the man to abandon his post to do a job any one of the pupils would have delighted in doing? Mrs. Shepherd, sitting soldierly tall while her patent leather button-down booted feet danced all over the foot pedals, glanced up appreciatively with each turning. Her cheeks were bright with color the exact shade of the red-ribbon bows holding her braided crown of silver-threaded brown hair in place. A faint smile carved itself on Rachel's face. The way in which God went about His surprises would never cease to amaze her. For one precious moment, her own heart felt light. And, proper or not, she leaned back into the warm curve of her husband's arm. When she looked up again, the sheriff was gone, undoubtedly torn between duty and love. It did not take Aunt Em's news that it *was* love—"beholdin'" in her language. "No, nobody outright tole me, Rachel-hon, but iffen it looks like uh duck 'n walks like uh duck—" Yes, of course. Rachel tucked in the corners of her mouth to suppress a smile. *Then it WAS a duck....*

Having forgotten that she was snuggled too close to Buck, next she pointed to Callie. Rachel had never seen her so happy. The great eyes had captured a million stars. Why, she was practically lighting the room. Obviously, she knew nothing of the cloud of suspicion surrounding her Why then—? There was no answer. Rachel spent no time seeking one. It was enough to see Callie so happy that she was clumsily, self-consciously dropping her program, stumbling—so downright clumsy when she was normally so graceful. Where was her stage presence?

It was by coincidence that, in seeking for the object of Callie's attention, her eyes met Dr. Greer's and then those of young Dr. Ambrose. Would they remember her? They did. Dr. Greer nodded without expression. But Dr. Ambrose curled his fingers in a small wave. She was reminded again of the young man's handsomeness, remembering then his deep faith and commitment to it. Oh, if the men would only settle here. Something clicked, but the thought was cut short by the memory of their mission. And the awful truth came back, remaining even after she spotted Star and Patrick seated together. Star, she noted, was in deep thought.

Later Rachel was to learn that Star was listening intently to Mrs. Shepherd's music, enjoying it and more. "Mother Mine," she was to confide, "I have spoken with the *señora*, played for her—*como se dice?* Ah yes, what she refers my playing to as 'by ear'—I do not understand."

Rachel's spine had tingled. How many more gifts did this child of mystery possess? "It means that you have potential, my darling—that you have an ear for understanding music even without the notes."

"This I did not know," Star said humbly. "The lovely *señora* wishes me to learn to *read*—read the notes, she says. Perhaps this is the way our Creator would have me use my hands. I *feel* the music in my soul, feel it travel from my heart to my fingers. And there is life. Will others find that strange also?"

It had been a tender moment. Buck had held their daughter close and said through clenched teeth, "Oh little sweetheart, you are to follow your calling, tuning out what others think! I am tired of such petty thinking and would welcome their silence. Let your heart decide. Some believe that the *stars* 'know'—and you're our Christmas Star."

Her heart decided to take the lessons, of course.

After that, Rachel and Buck saw little of Star. Rachel wondered if she ever slept. The crack of lamplight shining underneath her bedroom door when they retired was still shining when they arose. The music, spoon-feeding of the little dog, carrying him gently in and out periodically (allowing no one to help), the difficult studying—yet somehow she found time to continue with her sketching. Sometimes Rachel would awaken in the deep night hours and hear Star and Patrick pondering over what Poe would have referred to as "many quaint and curious volume of forgotten lore." Once, thinking she heard a noise outside (as she often did but kept to herself), Rachel had tiptoed past the library where Star and the young minister were studying. Not that caution was necessary. Nothing would have disturbed the two. And small wonder!

"Oh my word!" Patrick moaned. "I was hoping *this* would not be among those we are to digest." He read a line to Star and laughed. "You should see your face—"

"I do not understand—*no comprendo*—"

"Small wonder, it's French. No *comprendo mucho* myself! Well, do not worry your pretty head. Fortunately, the book is translated into several languages I *do* understand." He paused. "You know what? We are in luck. Your Mrs. Shepherd speaks French fluently. And come to think of it, all our doctors—as well as Miz Lily, being a nurse—know Latin."

"What, may I ask, is the title of this difficult book?"

Patrick laughed again. "Bear in mind that you asked! It's *Propheties*, written by Michel de Nostredame, commonly called simply Nostradamus, about 1544. The title translates into *Prophecies* logically—"

Logically? Rachel felt as if she were going to have a nosebleed.

"Like Revelations?" Star wondered.

"Well, yes and no. The book makes no claims to being divinely inspired. In fact, it was frowned upon at one time to the point that, well, even in the court of Catherine de' Medici—she kept the writer around to cast the horoscope of her sons, you know—some readers were relieved of their heads."

Rachel gasped. A thought too horrible to verbalize came to mind. With people wondering about Star, oh, what would they think or do if they knew about such reading? She must hear more, even though her feet were freezing on the cold, bare floor. Noiselessly, she pulled a braided rug toward herself with one toe. There, that helped. And now to listen—

"Well," Star sighed. "I shudder to recall that our Holy Bible was cast into the fire at one time. Always there is evil in the minds of those claiming piety—"

"That is the idea: conflict in the thinking of mankind. Only God knows the truth. Our purpose in wading through this heavy book of rhymed quatrains is to compare it with Revelations, test it, see how much has come to pass. We will make it together—"

"Together," Star repeated. "I very much like the word. And with God's help, of course."

—♥—♥—♥—

In late January Callie declared herself "settled," having hung the last ruffled Priscilla curtain in her bedroom. The Hathaways had chosen to build only a small house—cabin, actually, by choice—about a quarter-mile from Lordsburg. Away, they proclaimed with twinkling eyes, to be spared the noise. What kind of a judge did that city have anyway? newcomers asked. Probably crooked as a barrel of snakes. Why, even a peace-loving citizen who required an ear trumpet to hear it thunder could pick up the pandemonium, particularly on Saturday nights when all you-know-what broke loose.

Rachel and Buck shared a good laugh. Marriage had brought out the best in the judge. Their real reason for choosing a site on the outskirts, of course, was in order to keep a watchful eye on the comings and goings outside the heart of the city. Any stranger was subtly investigated. And there were certain persons everybody knew would be nabbed on sight. Those law-dodgers must have known. They kept out of sight.

And all had been quiet—too quiet. Rumor had it that no less than a dozen shoot-outs had taken place in the adjoining town last week. But then what could you expect when demon rum flowed down every street, road, and gulch? Lordsburg was different, living up to its name.

Had people become a little *too* complacent? "No," Buck reassured her. "All the light-touch—'ballyhoo' as Aunt Em calls it—is just the little boy whistling in the dark. Deep down, I think we're all as afraid as children ourselves because—well, Rachel, we have to face it, the darkness will close down over us, too, one day. It has to."

Lordsburg woke up one Saturday morning to find itself wrapped in the first snow of winter. Oh, how pure, how magnificent! Children whooped, engaged in snowball fights (without interference from parents), and made angels in the snow. Aunt Em declared open house and dished up snow ice cream throughout the day. "It is Eden before sin entered," Reverend Elmo declared and rang the church bell to summon all to a prayer meeting, which was well-attended. Farmers heard the recently acquired clarion bells and flocked in to praise God for the cold which locked in their wheat seeding at exactly the right moment. How, Rachel asked herself, could there be such a thing as evil lurking in such a pristine setting? She was soon to know....

Callie was there, glowing still. She hugged Yolanda almost fiercely, and then turned to Rachel. "You two are invited to come along home with me. Don't you dare say 'no'—either of you. I want to show you what a homemaker I am!"

Homemaker? In Rachel's mind that accounted for the new shine. But who, when, how? Wouldn't Yo have told her? But Yo didn't know.

Callie, almost as if avoiding questions, teased through their invigorating walk. "Just wait. Are you *ever* in for a surprise!" And then, growing more and more exuberant, she told one amusing story after another. The cabin was built and abandoned by prospectors...no, a count from abroad...or was it Captain John Smith from the colonies? Cozy though—windproof and rainproof, you know, caulked with saplings and mud. Thatch roof, nice fir door. Too bad the Hathaways forgot windows. Had to keep coal-oil lamps burning all day.

"Callie, Callie," Yolanda interrupted, wiping her eyes from laughter, "what on earth's gotten into you? I've never seen you so profuse and downright funny. Right, Rachel?"

"Well yes, I was wondering why the Priscilla curtains—"

"Oh, they corrected that—cut out squares *for windows*," she laughed gaily.

"My sakes! Get on with you—enough of this banter. Get going before I turn you over my knee the way I used to do," Yolanda commanded.

Still clowning, Callie did a little pirouette in the snow, jangled her keys, and ran ahead. Rachel did not see Callie stop and gasp raggedly at the door of the beautifully constructed, peeled-log cabin. She was looking at Yolanda instead. This was the first opportunity to follow through on Dr. Ames' question regarding Maynard's health.

"Our men have been entirely too busy, huh, Yo? Does your doctor seem to be holding up all right? Buck seems tired."

Yolanda looked surprised. Then, after thinking a minute, she said slowly, "Yes, now that I think about it, Maynard *does* act tired—but men! Just *try* and slow them down. Of course, they say the same about us. What's wrong with Callie? You *did* hear her scream?"

They ran the few steps separating them from Callie. No need to ask questions. There they were: men's footprints soiling the snow—big as life and of different sizes. All were beneath Callie's window.

Inside the inviting room, Callie held out her arms to restrain her guests. All stood still. "Do you detect a strange odor?" she asked, white-faced.

Detect? How could anybody miss tobacco? And there was a peculiar too-sweet scent about it that Rachel had smelled before. But where? So few she knew smoked. Memory was near the surface but elusive, unpleasant.

"Callie," Rachel whispered, "shouldn't we go—wait for some of the men? How," her whisper became almost inaudible, "do we know if he—or they—are lurking—"

"No place to lurk," Callie said shakily then. Lowering her arms, she hurried into the bedroom. "But somebody's been here—I just sense it."

"Nothing's upset—" Yolanda began.

Callie appeared not to hear. She was busy checking drawers in her highboy. "Nothing *looks* disturbed. Gloves on top," she inventoried, "stockings underneath. But wait, I always keep them in order by color . . . and my extra corset's on the wrong side. It's all been searched, every inch, and put back neatly to hide it. Oh my goodness, look at my clothes!" Callie had opened the doors to her wardrobe. "See? My coat's sagging on one shoulder, and one pocket's turned wrong-side-out."

She was searching feverishly now in spite of Yolanda's objections.

"Nothing's been taken, honey, so why stew around? You come home with me—"

"Look! Even my rosewater and glycerine bottle has been moved. Whatever they were looking for had to be small—minute—"

"A map maybe?" Rachel asked, and then wondered why.

Callie stopped her searching, her face gray. "Could somebody be suspecting me of something? Ridiculous! What could it possibly *be*?"

Rachel and Yolanda were spared what would have had to be an inadequate answer by the arrival of the Hathaways.

Cappy Hathaway became *Agent* Hathaway immediately upon hearing about the odd invasion of Callie's room. She agreed that Callie should stay here rather than go with her sister. "After all, in my position, I'm prepared for a return visit. She's safer here—"

"And I'll be on my way, ladies," the judge said from the doorway. "I'll gather the appointed men so we can hurry to Callie's classroom. Rachel and Yolanda, if you will be so kind as to get your men to meet me at the church. And I'd suggest you gather the children inside. Too much exposure to cold is bad—"

Aunt Em's Eatery. That was a good compromise. They would all be sick tonight from too much snow-cream. But Rachel was sick already. . . .

Callie's classroom was searched with less discretion—ransacked from top to bottom. Everything was in shambles. Clues? None were left. All they could do was double their guard again . . . and again . . . and *again*.

All this Buck told Rachel when he came home safely, for which Rachel breathed a prayer. They held hands outside briefly, watching the full moon riding high and serene in its circled orb while cutting paths of light on the untracked snow. "So inviolate up there. Hold me close, darling." He did . . . warming her winter heart.

22

All Tracks Lead Somewhere

The snow lingered. Not a good sign a-tall, the older generation said gloomily. "Jest a-layin' 'round waitin' fer a-nother," Grandma Evans grumbled at a meeting of the women's corps. She was right. But how could one feel as glum as her voice sounded, what with a blinding February sun be-diamonding the white-mantled earth below, the brilliance of multicolored scraps the women cross-stitched together for the two quilt tops Aunt Em (with a Chesire-cat grin) insisted be completed as they shared informational scraps to be pieced together like the quilt . . . not to mention the remembered reflection of the February-shine in the eyes of Mrs. Shepherd and Callie? Several wondered aloud how the two teachers carried on so calmly under all the bedevilment. Why, they'd be confused—*utterly* confused and frantic to the point of wishing the mountain would fall upon themselves for cover. Oh, not that! Why, that's what they feared: evil to fall on them.

Brother Davey had wheeled in at one point to comment. "My good women—uh, ladies—ain't nothin' t'fear from up yonder. Hit's th' rats what tunnel undergroun' gnawin' away et th' foundation."

"Now, now, Dave-Love, don' go scarin' our company. I think they both're in good hands."

"Meanin' th' Lord? Yep, sure thang. Still," Brother Davey scratched his remaining hair, "we gotta be on th' lookout. Oh, I see! Yuh be speakin' uv them watchdogs—er, bodyguards—what appointed theirselves, eh Emmy-Gal?"

That question brought about a flurry of questions from the ladies as they lent a hand of assistance to Aunt Em who was letting down the quilting frames. Rachel was curious herself. Catching Yolanda's eye, she lifted her eyebrows in question. Yo responded with an I-don't-know shake of her head. She must be worried about her sister, considering the tracks—

And tracks were the topic of conversation now. "Do any of you patronize Mr. Franchot's 'Dream House,' adjoining the dress-maker's?" The question came from a Nella Taylor-Smith, new in town and wife of the architect who was building a larger hotel in Lordsburg.

"I don't move in such exalted circles," someone replied, an answer which Mrs. Taylor-Smith ignored.

"I had my hair restyled," she said, patting a heaped-up do which rivaled Martha Washington's, "and may I recommend him highly? He is French and knows how to blend face powder so expertly that it scarcely shows."

"So?" Brother Davey interrupted, refusing to see his wife's signal.

"One does hear such interesting news there. It is my under-standing that our sheriff is keeping *special* watch—if you know what I mean—over Eula Shepherd. Yes, that's her name. Mr. Taylor-Smith and I made her acquaintance before coming here. Mr. Brimmerton's never been married, you know, and her being widowed—"

"So?" Brother Davey repeated, more loudly this time.

"Thet makes sense," Aunt Em interrupted, her voice carrying the edge of a newly-honed butcher knife. "After all, this snow's good fer somethin'—easy t'track down tracks. Lots uv 'em 'roun' th' school."

"And some continue to appear around our door as well," Cappy Hathaway said as she entered the room and closed the door behind her. "I wanted you to know. *However*, I would caution all of you," Agent Hathaway paused to glance significantly at the patron of Mr. Franchot, "that rumors and gossip do more harm than good."

"What does it all mean?" Yolanda spoke for the first time, and Rachel felt a pang of concern at the chalkiness of her friend's lips.

"It could mean that we are on the right trail, dear, or that the tracks are some vague sort of warning—just a watch-your-step kind of warning," Cappy said kindly.

"Warning!" Yolanda leaped to hear feet, her scraps of fabric scattering over the floor like autumn leaves in a windstorm. "Who's protecting *Callie*? You *know* she needs special protection—"

Too late she clapped a hand over her mouth. The gesture aroused more speculation than if she had violated the gag rule. Mrs. Taylor-Smith was watching.

"Oh, I wouldn't worry," Mrs. Taylor-Smith soothed as she patted her hair again. "The young lady has triple protection: a government *supposedly* secret agent, the judge himself, then that handsome new doctor—what's his name—*Ambrose*. He hurried right over—"

The aged Grandma Evans saved the moment. "Well, they's gonna be mo' snow jest lack my faithful *Pore Richard's Almanac* don' sed. See how th' sky's a-cloudin' over? Shore is 'n thet's uh he'p from above. Don' go 'way a-thankin' thangs is safe with all th' roads them tracks be makin'. All roads lead somewhere!"

Rachel left with her head whirling. She wished with all her heart she could concentrate on the possibles—the lovely ones. Oh, why must the ugly ones head her concentration list? She must hurry. There was an urgent need to tell Buck all these things, to be held safely in his arms—and, she realized suddenly, to outrun the approaching storm!

But Buck was not to be found. Instead, a note was propped against the pewter vase filled by the hands of the children with snowdrops and wild holly: "Darling, the tracks led to the river. Must check. Love, B. P.S. Same design on sole. Lock up!"

23

But Why, Why—WHY?

The new hotel was taking shape, according to Buck. Yes, the city council had known about it, approved its construction. And the place called Dream House? Yes, on that one, too, but he knew very little about a Mr. Franchot and had never seen Mrs. Taylor-Smith, just was aware that the architect was married.

"I want to find out more about her," Rachel told Buck over their morning coffee, almost screaming to be heard. This was the thirtieth day of being snowed in. The sun came out long enough to tease, only to hide its face behind another coverlet of snow-filled clouds, so filled that they no longer could bear their load and chose Lordsburg as a dumping place. School had closed. Snow was no longer a novelty. Children found safety valves in teasing their pets, engaging in pillow fights, and in general driving their mothers crazy.

"And I want you to, sweetheart," Buck replied above the bedlam. "I want you to know how much I appreciate your self-control through all this. It's different with us men: wearing snowshoes, getting together. And please don't suggest that you ladies could wear them, too. No equal rights in this area—it's for your own protection. By the way, the extra bones we found in following those tracks to the river *were* human and the doctors say they'll be helpful in establishing identity. The coroner agrees. Greer and Ambrose are staying, as you know. And come to think of it, they plan to move into the new hotel. Maybe they have an eye on the lady, too."

"Aren't all newcomers screened?"

"Good question, Rachel. Men are, particularly those who want to establish businesses. But," he grinned, "here we go again with preferential treatment. In this case, I'm not so sure which way it works. Maybe we *men* are suspected of being the more evil."

There was a whoop as a feather pillow sailed through the door. Rachel picked it up, gave a whoop herself, and walloped her husband. *Her* whoop alerted the children, and there they all stood at the door, pushing, shoving, and shaking the rafters with laughter. Behind them were Star and Patrick.

"What kind of family will I be getting into?" Patrick asked, adding his laughter to theirs.

"A wonderful one," Star answered soberly.

Rachel scarcely noticed that the two young people were speaking openly of their relationship now. She was concentrating on the fact that Star was holding Scot in her arms. How the weakened little animal clung to life was a mystery. It was as if—yes, as if he, like those who had dominion over him by God's decree, had a mission to fulfill. And, as yet, it remained unfinished....

The snow thawed enough for Rachel to venture out on the first Saturday in March. Good timing, as Buck would be home to keep an eye on the children while Rachel paid a short visit to Aunt Em. From there, she decided, she would stop by Yolanda's and together they could call on Callie again. She felt a need to resolve something in her mind. It was as if Callie were calling out for help.

Bundled as she was, Rachel felt the brisk breeze penetrate to her skin and noted that clothes, laundered by the more courageous, were swinging stiffly on the lines—frozen. The idea made her feel the cold all the more, so she paused beneath the overhang of the next building. It surprised her to find that it was the Dream House. And what she saw through the polished window surprised her even more.

My goodness! How did such a place become a part of Lordsburg? It belonged in Seattle, Portland—or were those cities prepared for such? Back East—maybe even France! One glance revealed silver-gray carpet, rose velvet chairs, an Empire sofa which surely must have come from Paris, as did the Florentine dressing table which was laden with priceless crystal bottles containing cosmetics as foreign to Rachel's mind as the decor.

But the furnishings and priceless collection of impressionistic paintings lining the wall were less shocking than the patron wrapped in a velvet robe trimmed in touches of color to match the glamorous surroundings. The lady went unrecognized, but what was this? A ridiculously elaborate pale-gold wig stood high on a hatbox on a shelf beside the patron. Rachel shivered. The wig created an illusion of Marie Antionette's head after her decapitation.

Recovery was quick. A glimpse of the owner of the hairpiece was all it took. Rachel wanted to giggle when she caught a glimpse of her in the long mirror. Hairnet drawn tightly over the skimpy mouse-colored hair . . . face slathered with a mask of cold cream . . . chin strap beneath her chin and tied over her head. . . .

Something warned that she should not be caught peering in the window. Turning quickly and almost slipping made the quick getaway she planned impossible. She had been spotted—that she knew from the drawing of the drapes. Thank goodness her back was to any spectators and, with the fleecy collar of her coat turned high, recognition was impossible. Now why had she thought that? Nobody there knew her—well, did they? Why was she uneasy?

In that split second there came to her nostrils the peculiar, too-sweet smell of tobacco—some foreign brand, certainly not akin to that which her father had used in his pipe. The startling thing was that the odor was familiar.

Pulling her head scarf up to her nose, Arabian fashion, Rachel dared look back. And then she had the shock of her life—no, not one, *two*. The door swung open and a man emerged. The shock was almost too much. It was—it *had* to be—one of the two men who incited the riot at the illegal bar, the talkative one. Or did she imagine it? How could he be there one moment and gone the next unless—Yes, that's what happened—he went back inside. Frozen, both from shock and cold, she stood a moment trying to recall something else she had seen. A sign—that was it—a gold-lettered sign: Turkish Tobacco. And beyond it sat the same patron, recognizable now that the undersized, quick-moving Mr. Franchot—with many a twitch of his pencil-thin moustache—was adjusting the now-familiar wig in place. Mrs. Taylor-Smith!

Then she did *not* imagine the man smoking the Turkish tobacco. And he was leaning over the woman, placing something minutely small in her well-manicured hand. Rachel fled, stumbling as she ran.

Words tumbled out senselessly as Aunt Em massaged her cold-whitened fingers and, in spite of all protests, unlaced her boots and plunged the unfeeling feet into a basin of mustard water.

"Ain't surprisin', Rachel-hon. They's uh connection somewheres, but I'll be switched iffen I can figger hit out. Sure yuh're up t'th' trip to Callie's? But they's no changin' thet mind. Time's learnt me—so, *Davey-Love!*" Aunt Em raised her voice and Brother Davey appeared as if by sleight of hand. "Keep yore eye pasted on th' hominy—ain't ready t'slip yet. Jest make sure hit don' go scorchin'. So good with spareribs," she said, turning to Rachel who was lacing her boots back on. "Butchered last night. Let's take uh mess t' both Yolanda 'n Callie. An' Davey-Love, iffen yuh'll git some ready fer Rachel. Oh, 'n keep th' doors locked—"

There was a what-you-wimmen-up-to look on his face, but Brother Davey must have been struck dumb and said not a word as they took leave for Yolanda's.

Yolanda hesitated. "Much as I want—*need* really—to see my baby sister, I'm not sure what to do. Maynard's not himself, and I'm wondering why."

"I regret having mentioned the subject," Rachel said sincerely.

"Oh, I'm glad you did," Yolanda said quickly. "Otherwise—well, never mind. Give me a second to put this meat away. And I *do* thank you, Aunt Em. I'll be ready., The children are—"

Rachel nodded. "All with Buck. What would I do without him?"

Yolanda sucked in her breath, started to speak, and changed her mind. Rachel was sure it had to do with Maynard and wished with all her heart one could be more sure about life.

Callie met them at her door, anxiety in her face. "What's wrong?"

"Now, what makes you think something's wrong? Can't people who love you drop in without bad news? And do ask us in. We're freezing." Yolanda faked a moan. "Brr-r—"

Callie murmured an apology. "You know you're welcome, but—" she began, hesitating.

"But what?" Aunt Em's words were more of a command than question.

"I guess I was going to say that it's lonely being a solitary woman, but I don't like to cling."

"Aha! Then it's true what we hear, that you have a someone who's going all out to watch over you, be depended on, loyal, reliable, and very handsome? Well, he has good taste—and I'm happy for you, sweetie." Yolanda was almost bubbling over.

Callie gave her sister a reluctant half-smile. "Take a chair, all of you. I should offer coffee—"

"That would be nice," Rachel answered, thinking it would be better for the girl to have something to do.

Callie appeared not to hear and neither did she explain why she did not prepare the coffee she had offered. The three guests watched her in silence, their thoughts obviously following different paths, none of them pleasant. And where was Callie's glow? Always so self-disciplined, so in control that she appeared in complete repose, she was pacing the floor restlessly now. Strange.

"You know about the tracks," the girl burst out suddenly, "and the searching of my room and classroom. What are they looking for, and *why*? They keep coming back, in spite of Norman—uh—" Callie's face flamed, "I mean Dr. Ambrose. And yes, you're right, big sister. I am in his debt. He is a friend, someone I can depend on, but nothing more. I—I don't even know why he took me into his care."

Yolanda smiled happily. "*I* know." She glanced at Callie's face. "I appreciate your talking so openly with me, sort of. But what are you holding back? Maybe I can help. Has something gone wrong?"

Callie stopped pacing and concentrated on the melting snow where patches of emerald grass showed like vivid scatter rugs. "No," she addressed her sister, "there's no way to help. You wouldn't understand."

"Want to try me?"

"Why not?" Callie laughed bitterly. "It goes 'way back. Norman (this time she did not change it to Dr. Ambrose) acted interested in me when he and Dr. Greer came the first time, and there was promise in his voice when he said he'd be returning. Of course, I was younger and entertained romantic ideas." For a fraction of a second the glow was back. Then the desolation returned, an unhappy droop to her lips. "I don't *know* what happened. He was genuinely glad to see me again. We talked for hours that first night. He gave me reason to hope, helped me forget the ugly past, made me feel it was so trivial that there was no need to make mention, so I foolishly let my heart start dreaming again. Business occupied his time, but I understood."

So that accounted for the glow: hoping, waiting. "Nothing wrong with that," Yolanda said. "Give him time, darling. It's unfair, you know, men's having all the advantage. A man can ask to see a woman again or walk away, but the lady has to wait. Same with a proposal. The choice is his."

"Oh, we weren't to that point! It's just—just that suddenly he was back, watching out for me, then just going away. Never a word about our so much as walking to prayer meeting, not even a good-bye. Now," she said fiercely, "you tell *me* what's gone wrong. It's Bixby, isn't it? Back to ruin my life, get even. Well, *isn't* it?"

"No, baby, it's not. He's gone—and for good, we hope. It's—"

Rachel cleared her throat warningly. Yo had come dangerously close to disclosing that Callie was (foolishly in Rachel's mind) under investigation because of the man. "It will turn out all right, dear Callie. Nothing is normal right now. We have to control our emotions and, oh, Yolanda, will you *look* at the time? Our men will have searching parties out! No time for more talk. Come on, Yo. *Now!*"

"I know why you rushed me," Yolanda said, looking a little embarrassed, once they were out of hearing distance. "I nearly spilled the beans."

"I wanted to say 'Shut up, Yo!'" Rachel admitted, with the bluntness of a seasoned friendship. "You think all this hush-hush is unnecessary and so do I—you know that. But we have no choice."

"Men do, of course!"

"You know better than that. Women are involved in this as much as the fellows. We have to leave it to those better prepared than we are. Try to understand that."

"I don't understand any of it!" Yolanda burst out furiously. "I don't understand why all this had to happen in a God-fearing city. I don't understand why my husband, an innocent party, had to be shot, and why he just may continue to suffer the results. Or why that little dog must linger to suffer. I don't understand what became of that outlaw, Bixby—how he disappeared when our officers claim to be on 24-hour guard. Why that glamour-tramp showed up—strike that, but I don't trust that woman calling herself Taylor-Smith. Mark my word, she's up to something—manages to blind our men. Or why those medical men came back anyway, just to torment my sister! So what," she shuddered, "if they put those bones together to make a skeleton? That's something we have no need for. The past holds enough of those—"

"Oh, snap out of it, darling. Please do." This time Rachel's voice was pleading. "There are things we may never know. Cling to faith."

They embraced and ran opposite directions as the long rosy fingers of sunset shot up in the west as if in warning. Rachel stiffened. *What, I wonder, is the reason why Aunt Em didn't say one word?* Obviously, she knew something she did not share. Another *why....*

And then all the other *whys* took a backseat. Why were all the people gathered in the yard of her home? Something had happened! *Oh Lord, I need You....*

24

A Heaven Full of Stars

Everybody was talking at once. "Scot's gone—disappeared.... Somebody musta stole 'im.... Now who on this green earth would take a three-quarters dead critter like that?... Well, he's gone, ain't he?... Sompin' queer—downright queer.... With a city's life at hazard, anything is possible.... Could be he's lived his nine lives.... Dummy, it's cats havin' that many.... Hush up, cain't ye see how disturbed these chil'drun be?... This is significant, otherwise the government wouldn't be organizing a searching party...."

Searching party? Rachel looked wildly about her. Where was her family? Nothing she'd heard made sense. Any outsider would have found amusement in the situation, she thought fleetingly. And that included the two farmers who at that very moment rattled up with their wagonloads of onions. Was there a warehouse hereabouts?—had to find a shipping harbor. They spoke of the eye-watering vegetable in terms of tonnage, explained that they were European immigrants, said onions were a staple in the diet "over th' waters," told that their crossbreeding was "bound on bein' world's finest" and she was to watch for the name "Oregon Sweets."

She should worry about *onions* at a time like this? Their unfamiliar accent was hard to understand... she knew nothing of shipping onions... and her eyes were filled with onion-induced tears.

"Try Portland," Rachel said, hoping the information was helpful while praying that the men would hurry on. But they lingered.

"Treble heah—a piece o'service we can do, kind lady?"

Wait a minute. The drivers had brought their crop upriver through forbidden territory. But there was no time for explaining—just for asking. "Did you gentlemen see anything of a small dog, a Scottie?"

Yah, yah. A weakened ani-mule overloadin' tha brain wid wonder how he cud carry on—poor love. Went that away, he did.

Rachel was not surprised that he pointed to the site of horror which continued to turn her dreams to nightmares. Why, oh *why* had she allowed Star to return, risking her very life for *sketches*?

Turning on her heel, she sprang forward, her body so filled with adrenaline that a panther might have found it difficult to overtake her. Unaware of Buck's screaming, "Rachel, Rachel darling—wait!" and ignoring the thorny blackberry vines which tried equally to hold her back, she raced ahead. Through the dark of the forest, somehow she saw with nocturnal vision. And there she was: Star, her darling Star.

Murmuring words of endearment, Star lay over the lifeless body of her beloved pet. Clenching her fists and forcing her now-weary legs forward, Rachel felt that her pent-up anger and grief would explode inside her. Her face was sticky with tears. Her body ached, as did her heart. But once she felt the warmth of her daughter's body lying prone as if to acknowledge a farewell and deep gratitude, she felt the lump in her own throat grow smaller. In the distance there were voices. But here all was silent, calm, and still—a certain peace.

"Don't cry, Mother Mine. Scot's mission is fulfilled. It is our responsibility to follow a now-secret message he left hidden. And do you not know that our Scot's spirit left us long ago? The vision—it pointed out the way for us. That you must believe."

The voices were closer now. Why? What were these people looking for?

The children heaped themselves over Star, weeping hysterically, until Star spoke soothingly, but with a conviction which quieted them. "Do not weep, dear ones. God would not be pleased. It is not Scot you weep for. You weep for yourselves." There was instant silence.

"Good grief!" Mary Cole, always able to do a mood swing, was gazing over her shoulder, wide-eyed.

Rachel wondered what the perceptive child had seen, but put a finger to her lips to signal a "quiet please." The solemnity of the moment must not be violated. And none of them should be here. They must get away. They *must*! But her head began spinning as she stood on spongy legs. Did nobody else notice the white apparition which the moon, rising above the serrated blackness of the treetops, revealed? A small breeze stirred the silhouette of the firs, wiping out the view. But Rachel was sure that a figure stood on either side of the tall white creature, certain, too, that this was what Mary Cole had seen.

"Oh Star," Brian was sobbing in anguish, "tell us. Dogs *do* go to heaven, don't they? Scot was so good, so kind, kept all the commandments he could. And he loved God—I *know* he did!"

Crying is contagious. All the other children were weeping again.

"Wipe your eyes, *por favor*. You are right, dear Brian. Oh, I wish all human beings would be as kind. But I am not wise enough to answer your question. The Bible does not speak of the matter—"

"So God doesn't say they don't, huh, Star?"

"No, David. But look at the stars in the heavens, all of you. Remember our findings among the constellations? We need have no fear for Orion's safety this winter night. The beloved star is no longer in danger from Taurus the Bull. Can you see him halfway up in the eastern sky? There is peace in the heavens as there must be peace in our hearts. See? Sirius, the dog star, has never flamed so brightly."

Rachel's heart was so touched that for a fractional second she forgot all fears and misgivings, concentrating only on the breathtaking beauty of God's handiwork. He had hung the shimmering stars overhead with his own fingers. How they twinkled, and her own Star had understood. Sirius seemed to stand alone in its bluish-white magnificence. The stars' only job was to bless mankind with their gleaming, darting points of spiny lights—eagerly, it seemed, as if they did their work with a sort of joy in shining. . . .

She jumped when Buck touched her arm. "We must get her away, and the others will follow. It is not safe. Help me all you can."

There was no chance to answer. Buck had pushed through the throng (larger than Rachel had realized) to the children. Gently, he covered the little dog's remains and picked the dog up as carefully as if it were still breathing. He whispered something (a promise of a memorial tomorrow, Rachel learned later). Star nodded, whispered it to the remaining children, and led the procession home.

Patrick caught up with them, removed his own coat and put it around Star's slender shoulders, comforting, understanding. Aunt Em was waiting at the gate when they arrived home. Without words she placed a small, tufted silk comforter in Star's hands. Star embraced her "Gram'ma Emmy" wordlessly. "An' his own ruffled pillow—I'm uv th' notion Scot'll be put away real nice. My Davey-Love," she wiped her eyes, "good man that he is, right now's whittlin' uh headpiece. Don' go doin' a heap tho', 'specially over yonder." She inclined her head to the site where Star had found Scot. Rachel's eyes followed. That's when she saw that the crowd had gone their separate directions.

Inside the house, Rachel suggested hot chocolate and cookies. Mary Cole followed her to the kitchen. "Mother, I've *got* to tell you now. It's important. White boots the woman wore, white dress, white face, white hair all piled up. She looked *dead!*" Nella Taylor-Smith? Rachel shuddered....

25

Discovery of Scot's Mission

Star agreed that it was risky to return. The burial must be brief, simple, and very quiet. But no, Scot could not be laid to rest in the Jones' garden. Yes, it would be nice to put fresh flowers on the small mound daily. But he had to be returned to his preferred grave site, there with his own kind, those innocent ones who had met an untimely death before him. Why? The faithful little animal alone knew, and his secret would be buried with him.

"We will bow our heads in silence, nothing more unless Dr. Ames chooses to say a word. It was he who kept him with us."

The sunrise service was small, as Star had promised—just the immediate family and close friends. The younger children had found shooting stars, the harbingers of spring; and Dr. Ames allowed Brian to sacrifice their one indoor hyacinth, its purple fragrance filling the purity of the early-morning air with sweetness. Holding hands, they bowed their heads while the doctor repeated a brief Greek myth. A beloved youth was accidently killed by Apollo, Dr. Ames said. Overcome with grief, Apollo caused a beautiful hyacinth to spring from every drop of the slain youth's blood. "Let us thank our Creator for giving us animals to love, knowing that He does nothing without a purpose. Good-bye, little Scot. You did not die in vain."

Patrick, aware of an audience of government agents standing guard, picked up the shovel. "Star, if you would like the honor of lifting the first shovelful, we men will do the rest."

Star with her usual composure, accepted the shovel. Effort-lessly, she plunged the sharp edge into the damp earth. And immediately she stopped, color draining from her face. "Some-thing is there—"

"Yes, I heard the grind—metal against metal." He reached for the shove, attempted to push it deeper, then lifted it and tried another spot. All watched breathlessly as he continued the shovel-ing, then gasped when he whispered, "A box! it is—it *has* to be—"

"The buried treasure! Here, let us give you a hand—"

Rachel inhaled deeply, then did not exhale, Her nostrils had picked up the familiar and frightening odor of Turkish tobacco!

"Quick, we *must* go. Please, *please* don't delay, even to open the box. Just dig the small grave in another spot and let's go! Take my word for it, we're being watched!"

Without question, Patrick quickly prepared a grave, gently laid Scot's remains inside, and allowed Star to rearrange the silken coverlet before the other children sifted a bit of sod over the coverlet, then quickly began covering the hole and smoothing it flat. Brother Davey's shingle-marker, lettered "Scot" was put in place and flowers scattered over the burial site, and all was complete.

It took no urging. The small group hurriedly picked their way home—the adults to escape the danger lurking nearby, the chil-dren to see what the box contained. Although purposes for the quick exit differed, their thoughts did not. Star was right. *Scot's mission was finished....*

Sheriff Brimmerton was waiting for them. Eula—that is, er, Mrs. Shepherd—had alerted him, having gotten a whiff at the beauty shop and sniffing out the rest herself, he said. He had suspected (so he claimed). So the two of them *were* friends! But why should she think of so light a matter when the long-sought treasure was in the process of being pried open? Rachel won-dered. And then she was glad she did. The mind must travel at a great speed, Rachel supposed.

"Just a minute, sheriff. Two quick questions. One concerns Bixby—" she asked shakily.

Mr. Brimmerton's eyes were on the box. Well so were hers, but this was important, too. "The government agents came too, huh?" asked the sheriff. "Oh, to answer your question: nope. It's like he dropped into a fracture in the earth just as it was closing. If you'll excuse me—"

More than that. She'd accompany him. But not before her second question. "I understand Eula Shepherd is a friend of Mrs. Taylor-Smith?"

His eyebrows arched up almost to his hairline. "That woman sporting the peroxide-blonde wig? Not that I've heard. Funny, because Mrs. Shepherd said she hadn't met a soul when she came here to teach. 'Course it's different now, what with you marching ladies," he indulged in a grin, "and Star's taking music from her—really talented she is—glad Eula's getting acquainted."

"Then there's you," Rachel teased back. *Marching ladies*, indeed!

"But not that Taylor-Smith vamp. I don't rightly trust her."

Somehow Rachel wasn't surprised. What did surprise her was her ability to jest when moments ago she had been hypnotized with fear—still was for that matter. But she suspected that some pieces were coming together, strategic pieces that nobody had realized were missing. She was *sure* when Mr. Brimmerton turned to say: "Found this scrap of paper at the edge of the woods when I came looking for you. Think it means anything? Oh, they've got the lid open!"

His eyes focused on the unearthed box, the sheriff tossed the folded paper to Rachel. *Mean* anything? It was a map leading to the burial site of the children's dog—the same site as the remains of sacrificed animals and (she shuddered) at least one human being. But neither was what the mapmaker had in mind. It was where the box was buried. Yes, the box. She hurried to the table to see the contents which held all those huddled around it so spellbound.

Money! How many stacks of greenbacks? And gold and more gold.

"Wait a minute here," Cappy Hathaway was saying with a command in her voice. "Rip the top of the suitcase. It's far too heavy. See? What did I tell you? I've never seen so much jewelry in all my born days put together: solid gold, diamonds, sapphires, rubies . . . and take a gander at all the men's stickpins and pocket watches—a *fortune*."

"To be confiscated by the government, of course." One of the men in uniform stepped out of the shadows. "The robbers took everything of value the travelers had—not to mention killing the engineer for the government payroll. The riders of the train were hysterical—those who survived—so information was pretty skimpy. Robbers made 'em turn pockets inside out into a flour sack—laughing, taunting, insulting, pointing muzzles of shotguns and handguns at their very temples, shootin' 'em dead if they didn't cough up valuables. Never could get the details straight, but some victims managed descriptions which identified Doogan and some accomplices. Peculiar, there was a woman involved—innocent party but had heaps of jewels. Got herself caught in cross fire. When her companion saw the little red-bluish hole and her eyes staring blankly, well she up and outright pulled a revolver from her pouch bag, aimed accurately, and mowed one robber down. But some stranger, another female wearing a black veil, grabbed the jewels and made a clean getaway. We're led to suspect some descendant's got the jewels—I mean, some more are missing, best we can tell."

"If Scot were here, he'd know," Star said, then looked away, her thoughts reaching into something half-remembered, Rachel thought.

"Or maybe he *did*. I have one sketch more—"

26

Dearly Beloved

Rachel and Buck talked throughout the night. So did the Hathaways, apparently, because the judge pulled the latchstring, sending a tinkle of bells throughout the house as they finished breakfast.

"We've put it all together—that is, except for the parts which very well may be lost," he announced before hanging his beaver hat on the hall tree. "Star's last sketch was an answer to prayer—her last one, wouldn't you say?"

"Identity of the two men? Yes, and the figure in white as well." Buck pulled out a chair for their guests and poured coffee without asking. "I'm supposing you've decided that the two strangers are in on some scam with the Taylor-Smith woman?"

"One calls himself Taylor, and the other is Smith. Not very smart."

"Where did you get your information, Your Honor?" Rachel asked.

"Brimmerton. He outright cornered the woman—even has her in his custody, as well as the other two scared rabbits. Your questions alerted the sheriff. Not that he'd admit it. Says he smelled a mouse—"

"I thought he might," Rachel said, "that's why I mentioned her claim at being acquainted with Mrs. Shepherd. I'm not sure why."

"Why the woman calling herself Taylor-Smith made mention? Oh, to establish herself as one of you. It took Mrs. Shepherd a long time to remember her—saw her without that straw stack on her head at the French shop. Something unhealthy about a man's engaging in that trade. Anyway, memory of having seen her under a different name came. Would you believe her husband had no idea—"

"Mr. Taylor-Smith?" Rachel gasped. "He never suspected?"

That was correct. Checked out his claim, found him innocent. And yes, the Jones' were right. Taylor and Smith were hired hoodlums, same pair who insulted the ladies, bootlegged—all those things and more. And yes, the map the sheriff picked up was the folded piece of paper Rachel had seen change hands. Rachel was right again. There was a connection also in suspecting that Taylor and Smith were followers of Bixby, who was a part of the Dunigan—or Doogan, whichever—gang. How did Rachel come to suspect there *was* a connection between the woman and the teacher keeping company with the sheriff?

"I heard her comment on the beauty of a bracelet Mrs. Shepherd wore—even tried to buy it, claiming it was identical to one her grandmother owned. I put it together when the government agent went into details about the train robbery. Then all those jewels—"

"I'll warm our coffee," Buck said absently, and then asked very suddenly what brought the judge to call so early. "More information that I believe you both suspect—all of which we have to discuss with our group—plus some announcements. I'll need both of you, of course. Know why the young doctor demands to be released from his watch on Callie?"

"Yes—yes, I think I understand," Rachel said hesitantly. "But she must have a guard until we find out about Bixby. We'll talk about it. Might as well bring it out in the open—her relationship with the no-good. Or does everybody know? Can't she be told why she's being watched? On the other hand, can't this be kept still?"

"No reason for spreading the news. She's had enough to contend with, and very well may be facing more. Can I depend on your being there?"

Buck assured Judge Hathaway that they would be there. But Rachel found herself puzzling over something he had said even as she handed him his hat. What had he meant when he said Callie might be facing more upsets?

Rachel was unable to keep the promise her husband made for her. Something so unexpected came up that it changed their plans. And, although Buck insisted that it took priority, neither he nor she realized that the frightening summons was to change not only the evening's commitment but the entire future of Lordsburg as well.

"Go on ahead, darling," Rachel told Buck. "I want to gather up my notes and make sure that I have all Star's sketches. She and Patrick are in the midst of an assignment, and the sketches will tell the story. She's late, having taken another music lesson."

"Then that will leave Mrs. Shepherd free to give her testimony. That's good. I've a hunch that the lady caught in the crossfire during the train robbery will prove to be her own grandmother. That would leave the Taylor-Smith woman's ancestor to be the one in the black veil who grabbed the jewelry and disappeared," Buck speculated. "Well, tonight will tell. And," he smiled, "you're right again, my little investigator. There *is* a romantic attachment between her and Brimmerton. Are you the matchmaker?"

Rachel laughed. "Nope, just a lucky guess. Now, run along—"

"No way. It's nearing sunset and if you think for one minute your spouse dares leave you alone—"

"Don't trust her, huh?" she teased.

"It's the men I don't trust. Hurry up!" Buck playfully pinched her upper thigh and she let out an indignant yelp—one which was never finished because of the terrified scream of a child. Her first thought was to wonder as to the whereabouts of Mary Cole, David, and Saul.

"Brian!" she gasped when she saw his face and noted his lack of color and his inability to say more. Obviously, the child had been running. "What is it, darling? Tell Auntie Rachel, what is wrong? Is it one of the children? And where's Rowie?"

"Rowie's with them. We—we found flowers, and—and—he's supposed to stay h-here with—with us," he panted.

"Calm down, Brian. Is there an emergency? Think! Why are you here? One thing at a time. We'll need to know where all the children are and what you're so excited about. That comes first!" Buck's voice was shaking in spite of his obvious determination to stay calm.

"Oh, Uncle Buckley, I don't know, but my father, I mean my uncle, you understand—anyway, Dr. Ames sent me. There's something wrong and they won't tell me—don't want Roland to know either. I—I just know Auntie Rachel has to go—"

"Go where, honey?" Rachel's mind went a dozen directions at once. "Am I to help find the children? You never told us where."

"We found the flowers and all went to put them on—on that lonely little grave. But they'll be all right. It's Auntie Yo that needs you *now*. My Uncle Howard—my Daddy—is there. There's something awful wrong, and the lawyer's there—oh, here they come!"

Buck hurried to the window, not sure who was coming. "Thank goodness, the children—and with sheepish faces. I'll take care that they dare not do this kind of thing again. But what's Mary Cole holding?"

The room was whirling madly around. Rachel hardly heard when their daughter said, "Oh Daddy, look! Look what we found when Rowie moved more dirt on the mound: a half-melted watch. I've seen it before, have you?"

Rachel failed to hear his response. She was gathering the sketches and her notes, hardly aware of what she was doing. Yes, Star would mind the children. And yes, Rachel would accompany Brian. But nothing made sense....

James Haute met Rachel at the door. What was the lawyer doing at the Killjoy house? For that matter, why was *she* here?

The lawyer, his little moustache twitching nervously as always, answered her unasked question. Jerking his head toward the darkened room, he said quickly, "You're here as a witness—legal matters, you know."

No, she didn't know. But there was no time to ask. Mr. Haute murmured something unintelligible, his head buried in a briefcase, a pencil clenched between his teeth. "I guess it's best that you awaken Mrs. Killjoy," a voice behind her spoke in guarded tones.

Dr. Ambrose was here? And wasn't that Dr. Greer? Where were the other doctors: Yo's husband and Dr. Ames who had sent Brian for her? It wasn't real. She was dreaming. In a moment she would awaken and all would be in order. The Killjoys would be preparing to attend the meeting and...

It was young Dr. Ambrose who spoke. "Mrs. Jones, may I present Dr. Johnson?" Rachel automatically extended her hand. "Dr. Johnson is the state medical examiner who will work with us in determining the identity, but for now he confirmed our findings about Dr. Killjoy. I am sure you are somewhat acquainted with the case, being such close a friend to Yo—that is, Mrs. Killjoy. She is suffering from shock and complete exhaustion, but she asked that we awaken her when you came—"

"Yes," was all Rachel could manage, although she longed to scream out a million questions. She drew a deep breath and walked quickly to Yolanda's bedroom, trying the knob gingerly.

"Rachel? Come on in. I'm awake." Rachel walked into the room, not knowing what to expect. What she saw were her dearest friend's dark-fringed eyes wide open, appearing in the fading light to be the unique color remembered of the Atlantic, their childhood home, when there was a storm at sea. Her hair, unpinned and covering the pillow, fanned out beautifully, more red than black. She turned her head slightly, and Rachel had a momentary illusion of a shower of gold. But there was something sad in the stoic smile. It was as if life were suddenly a flickering flame, first with a glow, then dimming.

Rachel dropped on her knees beside her, a strange determination to keep that flame aglow, restoring life, no matter what the price. "What is it, darling? They told me nothing—"

A strange look crossed the other woman's face. "I thought you knew," she answered softly, reaching for her robe. "My Maynard is leaving and I need you here both as a witness—his idea—and to hold me up until I can get used to life without him—"

"Oh, Yo, you're not making sense. Where's he going, and why do you need a witness for his departure?" Rachel asked a bit impatiently as she handed Yolanda her slippers. Yolanda's eyes opened even wider.

"Rachel, he isn't coming back. I—I thought you knew. Maynard will not be returning. The—the piece of shrapnel the doctors were unable to remove—you know when he was paralyzed—has moved to—to the brain. And oh, my darling, don't make me spell it. Just love me. It's inoperable, and I can't get through this without you—"

"Oh Yo! Oh darling," Rachel sobbed. "You know I will—"

Yolanda comforting *her*? She was seeing her friend in a new light. She was facing up, bearing the unbearable. *Oh dear God, how?* Star, in comforting the children, had said, "It is not for Scot you weep. It is for yourselves." But this was different. Her tears were for Yolanda. . . .

White-faced and horrified, Rachel—wishing with all her heart that Buck were by her side—followed Yolanda to where Maynard lay. Doctors hovered over him and the lawyer stood close by. The man lying on the bed bore no resemblance to the stranger who had saved the life of Yolanda when she was bordering on insanity because of the untimely death of the man she was going to marry. Rachel's initial opinion of Dr. Killjoy had lingered. He had never liked her, or so she had thought. How strange that he should reach out to her now, on his deathbed.

Maynard's face was gray, but he managed a wan smile as he took her hand. "If you doctors will give me a moment alone with my wife and Rachel—no, Haute, you remain. And Norman, if you'll send Dr. Ames in, please. Life is to go on. You stay with Callie, enjoy every moment."

Rachel supposed his requests were honored judging by the soft footsteps behind her. "Do you want the Reverend?" she managed to ask.

No, he preferred Patrick. Somehow he'd known that Reverend Elmo was at the important meeting and that Patrick was near. One of the doctors would go for him, Rachel heard from a fog. She and Yolanda knelt on either side of the bed. To Rachel's surprise, Maynard managed to kiss each of their hands.

"The Lord kept me alive until you joined Yolanda, Rachel. But life is ebbing away fast. Thank you, my dear, for all you've done for my wife and now I have an assignment for you. You are to witness my last wish—see that it is carried out. Are you here, Patrick?"

Patrick was there. What's more, so was Star. The children? She was caring for them, including Emmy, in the den. No, none of them were to come in. Neither were they to be at the simple service. "Keep my memory before them alive and vital." He inhaled with difficulty.

"But do not let them grieve. And bear in mind that children need both father and mother. Rachel, do not look so stricken. Yolanda knows, as does Howard. Do not entertain the mistaken notion that a trap is closing in on them. They are to be married immediately—living, I hope, in the Ames' house, as they need no ghosts. Haute has drawn up the agreement. There will be plenty of money—an endowment—also money for the church." He paused to cough, and Howard hurried to his side. "Please make this brief, Maynard. You must rest—"

Maynard smiled then said weakly, "I'll get plenty of rest up there. Rachel, don't press the doctors. They've done all that's humanly possible. Just sign as a witness and see that the memorial is kept simple. Also see that Yolanda does not wear black. It is not my favorite—c-color on her. Good-bye, Yolanda, my darling. I love you, but for now, I-I want to be alone—" Maynard's eyes closed and he slipped into a coma. Yolanda leaned down and brushed the colorless cheek with a kiss.

Star had alerted the judge, and somehow the newspaper had heard. All assembled at the door, a situation which Buck, who had slipped in, took care of immediately. The reporters were to leave at once. Had they no respect for the family? Star gently closed the door to Maynard's room and calmly told the members of the city council about Dr. Killjoy's passing. It was not as if it were totally unexpected. And it was his wish that life go on. "I have prepared coffee. Please join us in the library where Grandma Em is serving chocolate cake, Uncle Maynard's favorite. Remember that he asked that there be no mourning or farewell when his soul puts out to sea. The Savior waits for him in that most glorious of all harbors. Join us, I beg." They followed.

Rachel turned to where Yolanda had stood to put comforting arms about her. But, dry-eyed, Yolanda—having kissed the cheek of her husband—now stood in the embrace of Dr. Howard Ames, who was joining her in silent mourning. Confused, Rachel found herself in the arms of her own husband.

"Oh, my darling, my darling—" she cried out. "Hold me, hold me! Never let me go."

"So long as we both shall live," Buck whispered gently. Then pushing a rebellious curl from her forehead, he planted a sacred kiss in its place. "We were not to grieve. Remember, precious?"

"But—but it's all so strange. Even Yolanda's acceptance—"

Buck held her closer. "It will all work out, sweetheart. Yolanda has matured, and who knows but that she will be content as Mrs. Ames? Beautiful friendships often bloom into deep love, remember?"

"Oh, my darling, yes, I remember—you and me. Hold me."

"I never let go," he said with a playful chuck beneath her chin, but there was deep caring in his voice. Oh, praise the Lord who worked in mysterious ways....

—♥—♥—♥—

The church, decked with golden-throated daffodils, heady double hyacinths, and dainty lavender wood-violets the children had gathered, was filled to capacity. Yolanda, pale of face yet looking ethereally lovely in a pale-lavender dress which matched the wild violets, attended the simple service. She was supported by Howard, Rachel, and Buck. The other doctors stood to one side, hands at their hearts, in respect of their lost colleague—and Rachel was ready to attend to the bereaved widow should she be unable to go on with her plan. Mrs. Killjoy, eloquent in her grief, delivered a touching eulogy, in spite of the protests of all who loved her. Star played soft background music.

"The Lord has called our dearly beloved home." Yolanda's voice was strong and sure. "The greatest tribute you can pay my late husband is to follow him to glory. It was his request that the children have both parents, and so it is that Dr. Howard Ames, his cherished colleague, and I will be married at once. We shall honor that request soon after a private internment, after which we will go into seclusion. God bless you all. He loved you. . . ."

27

No Time for Understanding

Maynard was dead. Yolanda and Howard were settled into their home. And where was Callie? All the recent happenings were jumbled in Rachel's mind. All she could recall clearly was Maynard's last request: She was to stand by Yolanda, comfort her, do whatever it took to help her in these hours of need. Other matters niggled at her brain, half-remembered, but not the priority. Buck's report must wait. Didn't he understand?

"Rachel, I understand, but we *must* talk—the watch—young Dr. Ambrose's decision—the orphaned children—Are you listening? You *must* understand—"

"I must care for Yolanda. There is no time for listening. Look! Here is Aunt Em with a quilt—food—"

Buck murmured something she failed to hear. The medical examiner? Oh, yes, Dr. Johnson—but he had only assisted Dr. Ames, Dr. Ambrose, and Dr. Greer. She'd forgotten his purpose....

"Rachel! Rachel, *please* listen. You'll have to testify. We have Mrs. Taylor-Smith taken care of and found where the Turkish tobacco came from," he said with a hint of satisfaction, then frowning, "but the shooting—you *are* listening—I must help—"

She heard no more. Aunt Em was entering, her face sad, neither looking nor sounding like herself. "I cain't invade their privacy, an' not sure th' quilt's proper—but we got a-nother, well, two 'n when this sadness is wiped away—well, yuh be goin'

Rachel-hon'—here Buck, give uh hand with the problem uv settling th' children—"

Rachel accepted the quilt and food, murmured something
about seeing them both later, and hurried to her friend's house—
only to find the Killjoy home vacant and lonely. She paused,
sensing that something was wrong. Oh yes, memory came back.
Yolanda was now Mrs. Ames and was to live in his home. But
what was the other feeling—that of not being alone? And, she
wondered with sudden fear, what accounted for the vague scent
of Turkish tobacco? Buck had said something about it, and what
had he meant about the children? Oh, she should have listened,
should have put him first. Wearily, she realized now that her
husband had needed her too and—*oh dear Lord!* Now her mind
was clear! Buck had said, "But I must *go!*" Go? Go *where*—
without her? Rachel stumbled forward, then suddenly ran.

Yolanda met her at the door, arms wide open to welcome her.
"How thoughtful, my darling, but I am holding up. I will always
hold the children's father in my heart, but the Lord has opened
my eyes—"

Howard Ames joined his wife. "Welcome, welcome into my
new life. Maynard told me about your loss and about Yolanda's.
You are wonderful women. How many others could have endured
the tragedy of the explosion of the mine? And—and on such a
special day?"

The doctor must have seen the pain reflected in their white
faces, revealing that even now the memory was almost beyond
endurance. Yolanda's loss of her betrothed on her wedding day . . .
Rachel's loss of her *husband* . . .

Face twisted in pain for having fanned alive the burning coals
of memory, he reached out to place a supporting arm about
Yolanda's shoulders. "Forgive me—but He—*God* knew about my
great love for this woman—"

"Love?" Rachel hadn't meant to speak aloud.

"Yes, his words and yours, I believe. There are so many kinds
of love. I never gave a thought to marriage, you must believe
that—entertained no such thought—"

"It would have been unlike you. You are an honorable man,"
Rachel said, remembering her wonderful Buck's deep caring
after her loss of Cole.

"*You* of all people understand, my darling," Yolanda whispered. "I'm all right, but I have something more important for

you, dear Rachel. Go back and tell the others that they must cling to every moment, cherish it as the gift from God that it is. That includes you—you and your faithful companion. He needs you."

Yes, he needed her. Now! "I will. Oh, I will—"

Aunt Em was gone, of course. But so was Buck! Calling did no good. And then she saw the note. "I will see you as quickly as possible. I regret that we must be apart, but this must be settled once and for all. Take care of the home front, and then if you still need me, we can put it all together. B."

If she still needed him! Rachel dropped her head against the dining room table and cried until there were no tears remaining.

—♥—♥—♥—

Summer passed, autumn came—and then spring. The wind was almost warm. Clouds played tag in a sometimes-cloudless sky. The holly and snowdrops were gone, but the lady's slippers ventured from beneath the pine needles and the three-petaled trilliums like white stars, thrusting their fragile heads through the moist earth of Oregon while birds sang as in celebration of the resurrection.

Oh, how beautiful—more beautiful than Rachel expected another spring would be—because Buck was home. He was never again to take second place, never again to wonder if she needed him. There was a thin sickle of a moon smiling down on them this last night that Rachel Lord Jones recorded a final note. History for her had stopped. Her work was finished—

But not before the entire world had turned upside down....

—♥—♥—♥—

Rachel was still weeping over Buck's sudden departure when Agent Hathaway came. Cappy asked no questions, suspecting that her tears were for the orphan children about whom Buck had referred.

"It was cruel—inhuman—wasn't it, Rachel? To think that Dr. Johnson would have brought his wife and family along.... None of us had a chance to thank him for assisting with identifying the bones—but he did start. As you know, Buck carried on in Salem—"

Buck carried on? That helped to know. "And Mrs. Johnson?" she asked cautiously, wondering what on earth had happened.

"Yes, she died instantly as did her husband—caught, as far as any can tell, in cross fire. We've questioned the children and followed their leads. They're right—absolutely no remaining relatives."

"So—" Rachel's head was whirling. What was it all about?

"I'm puzzled—completely puzzled. I thought you might be able to tell, Rachel. Why did your dear friend and her former husband choose to leave that beautiful home to *us*?" There were only the Judge and Cappy.

"I don't know," Rachel said honestly, "but they must have had a reason—"

"Somehow the Lord must have known the children would be left and that the house would afford us room for what we have always wanted: a family! But first, there must be a memorial— and the formality."

Patrick would conduct the simple service and James Haute would prepare the adoption papers. He had brought the title to the late doctor's home, as well as his will. But Callie, whom Norman then Rachel had guarded, must have protection from harm. Why was Norman leaving and why was the girl weeping? Rachel promised to look after Callie. "They still have a chance," she said vaguely, leaving Cappy Hathaway looking puzzled.

Two days later Callie ran up the walk. "Rachel! Rachel, help me—" Rachel ushered her in. "A good time to come, darling. The service for the Johnsons is over, but you're still wondering why Norman is avoiding you? Let me quote your sister in saying 'never waste a minute.' You are in love with him, aren't you?"

"Yes," Callie said without hesitation, "but he wants nothing to do with me."

"Who said *that*?" Norman demanded, having run up the walk without being detected.

"You ignored me—would have nothing to do with me—*lied* to me—" Callie gasped. "Oh, go away—go away! You deceived me. How could I love a man like you?" The girl's voice broke.

"But you just said so. You admitted it!"

"Oh bah!"

Norman sprang forward, took the weeping Callie by the shoulders, and shook her. "Oh Callie, forgive me! I love you better than life itself. Why do you think I have lost so much sleep?"

Callie tried to pull away, her lips quivering pitifully. "Don't touch me—you—you spy! Accusing me of being a part of the gang. Let go! I am humiliated having even known that crook called Bixby—"

"I never believed that for a minute, my darling. Neither did anyone else. But *he* wasn't innocent. He was trailing you, and yet I was unable to let it be known. I couldn't keep it secret any longer, asked to be replaced. Oh Callie," he groaned, "I love you! Rachel, help me make her see."

"Callie darling—"

"Speak for yourself, John!" Callie quoted John Aldridge's words to the historical Priscilla. Then suddenly she was in his arms. "Thank you, Rachel," she choked. "Tell Aunt Em we— Norman and I—need that quilt!"

"The quilt," Rachel laughed suddenly. "Of course! And better get your application in to Judge Hathaway for his darling cabin."

But neither of them heard. Norman was holding her breathlessly close. And once again Callie's eyes were aglow.

Youth, with all its glory, had returned to her own heart. *Oh Buck, my precious darling, come home. I understand....*

28

Mysteries Still Unsolved

Rachel's heart must be checked. Which of the doctors should she depend on? The silly thing was tumbling, racing, and skipping. And the tumult inside her head was ridiculous. But reasoning did no good. She had received a letter from Buck! No three ... *three!*

It might as well be spring. It was springtime in her heart. No matter that there were still dirty mounds of snow, in spite of a pale sun. The wind was bitter and penetrating, but oh, the birds were singing. And surely those were apple blossoms losing their winter pout and joining the birds in a pink hallelujah chorus.

Britches stood on one foot and then the other, his face red to his strawish hairline. "I dunno how it happened, Miz Jones. I'm allus extra-careful 'bout yore mail, I plum am. Somehows I got it bunched with th' mail t' be delivered in town, laid hit down, and some well-meanin' soul uppen took it—"

"It's all right, Britches," Rachel burst out happily in her eagerness to read her husband's messages, wishing the boy would go. But he seemed disturbed. Poor Britches, so afraid of making a mistake.

She took a moment to exchange pleasantries. The boy was lonely, she supposed. He inquired about the Johnson children, and then expressed regrets about their parents. Felt particularly bad, almost involved, seeing that he'd witnessed the turble accident—

"You witnessed it, Britches? Then you'll need to testify with me."

"Yessum, I been thankin' as much. 'Course now, I ain't down-right sure who 'twas—uh bunch uv men, none uv 'em goin' t'th Merriweather's barbershop."

Rachel, still turning the letters around in her hand, looked at him questioning.

"Meanin' they go t'th' beauty salon—th' French 'un run by that funny little Fredric-Paul Franchot, I'm thinkin' his name is. Leastwise, I supposed they wuz visitin' Mrs. Taylor-Smith and them other two callin' 'emselves Taylor 'n Smith. But wonder why they keep on goin'. Ain't nothin' goin' on 'roun' here like wimmen fixin' men's hair, is there now?"

"Did you see who shot?"

"Oh, 'twas uh bunch. Never aimed at them pore Johnsons. More like they wuz after Miss Callie—"

"Callie?" Rachel gasped, dropping one of Buck's letters. Britches, to whom the years had brought little change either in looks or behavior, reached down awkwardly and retrieved the mail.

"Thank it could be that Bixby still hangin' 'round? I know he's got more money stashed here 'n yonder, an' he had uh heap followin' 'im when they slaughtered all them animals."

Rachel shuddered, remembering. "Well, Britches, he was never found, neither was the identity of the human skeleton—if there was only one."

"Oh, I 'member now. Mr. Buck's goin' on with th' work Dr. Johnson begun. Ain't he? Not that I'd tamper, jest that some uv yore mail was tore when hit come back. Mail ain't as certain as 'twas. And sometimes I git t'wonderin' if more ain't delayed—yuh know, t'be peeked into. I been wantin' t'make a-quaintance with them Johnsons. I heered them three girls is purty as peaches. An' I'm guessin' I could put th' boy t'work. Wouldn't he be likin' thet? When could I see 'em?"

"Why not Sunday? There's an older girl, another about her age, a wee one—and then there's the boy. Hope to see you Sunday."

Britches dropped his head again. "I been havin' t'work Sundays. Thet's why I need help. Where kin I git uh decent haircut?"

Britches had gone into the woods whistling happily. But before Rachel could rip the first letter in her no-date stack, there were Yolanda and Callie! Together! It was like a dose of spring tonic.

Oh, the untarnished joy of newlywed bliss in true love! True love? Why, the three of them were bubbling over, even though it had been Callie she had in mind. Yet, suddenly she herself had realized how much, how *very* much Buckley Jones had come to mean in her life, how—oh, how could she have forgotten?—he had been the red-velvet jacket upon whom she had walked, the stage property supporting the background for her and Cole to play house, idol that he would always be for them both. Had she ever told him—*made him believe?* She was no longer fearful of losing him either. Men like Buck—or were there others?—would stick by. *If she needed him, indeed!* What was it John said about perfect love? "Perfect love casteth out fear"?

Yolanda, watching Rachel's face, let out a musical peal of laughter. "I guess that is too much, too soon. But your face—oh my darling, who struck gold?" Her tone was not one of mourning.

"I guess we all did when it comes to men. And Yo, I am always glad to see you smile. Maynard always liked you smiling—"

"Yes, that is why I came—that and another matter we'll talk about. But the letter—it seemed almost planted when I was sorting through the doctor's papers. He—he'd seen me grieve before. You'll have to read it. But before you do, I—I'm not sure how to say this—"

"Since when did you start mincing words with me? Just say it!"

"My sister's in love with her husband!" Callie laughed. "Now she understands how *you* feel about Buck. Now, for goodness' sake, stop acting like schoolgirls and read your notes slipped under a slate and let's go!"

Rachel accepted the letter from Yolanda's outstretched hand.

My Darling Yolanda: You are to read this when I am no longer able to speak for myself (it was penned in a medical man's peculiar scrawl). You must have wondered sometimes why you married me—or wondered why I allowed you to do so when you were still in such mental anguish. I was unique, being a doctor, you know. It was impossible for me to think of you other than as my patient—oh, beautiful, to be sure—but less important than men and men's professions. And yet I was unable to free you after your illness, kept you a bird in a gilded cage. It was not totally selfish, my darling. I held myself under a spell, so sure was I that nobody looked after you—and that, nobody, absolutely nobody, must allow another loss. And then I did a foolish thing. I fell in love with my gallant, sunny wife. You have taught me more than I would have dreamed possible, obliterating my arrogance, because it was through Howard that I came to realize that you outweighed my profession. I thank you for those gifts, instilled in my children. But Yolanda, you are destined to be radiant with another mate. You and Howard, my dearest friend, owe me only one debt. That debt, Yolanda, is happiness. Together you have everything. And yes, our darling—Howard's and mine—we will all meet in heaven. There will be no marriage there. I go happily to seek it for us. No more tears—ever. M.

Yolanda was weeping through her smiling, but she *was* radiant. Callie interrupted. "I have the corner on happiness. I'm the bride, remember?" But her smile was gentle. "Put on your boots. I must go to the school, and my Norman will not let me go. We'll slip—come!"

"She'll go alone unless you agree. It's spring vacation and Callie has some paintings she needs a woman's touch in hanging. They're all playing musical chairs, you know—"

"Start on, Yo. I just must scan Buck's letters."

Yolanda understood.

She would want to read them over and over when there was more time, Rachel knew. But the notes had been no more and no less than she expected concerning Buck's activities, *except* that the most recent letter promised to see her in the spring. That could be anytime! "See?" she would tease. "See how I've grown? Just try and lift me!" There was a bad moment when she sensed the same old terror. Be careful, he had warned, things were not settled yet. "I believe that the lady tiger may have some puppets." He could say no more. All his work was necessarily secret. But in the light of his closing sentence, she was happy again. "Oh, if I could hear from you, but I am unable to receive mail." Suddenly her heart turned over. He'd never complained. That couldn't possibly mean a bad omen. Such were old wives' tales. So she would concentrate on anticipating apple-blossom time!

Nevertheless, once Rachel caught up with the other two, she found herself expressing her concerns. "Oh, he sounds like Norman. Whatever happened to women's independence? You can figure out where Buck is by the postmark," Callie said airily.

"It's big business, honey," her sister said quietly. "The government disallows identification when they're involved. And Rachel, I shouldn't allow myself so light a manner after reading Maynard's letter. Please understand that I was grateful—or became so. I—I couldn't have survived without him. Toward the end I believe I fell in love. Certainly, I was a devoted wife and mother. I mourned him deeply, but never alone. Howard helped fill the empty space in my heart, and then something miraculous happened. It was as if a veil lifted and I realized—well, as if it were first sight!"

"Time for fair play. You laughed at me. So let me remind you of what we used to say: 'Who ever loved that loved not at first sight?'"

In so light an atmosphere, the next episode was so badly out of context that a chapter had surely fallen from another book than what one held in hand. Callie simply popped into her room and, with a near-inaudible gasp, disappeared. Rachel and Yolanda screamed her name to no avail. It was then that Rachel realized the room was in shambles. What? Why? Oh, they must get help. No, the kidnapping was too soon. Somebody or some group was holding Callie within the building. Not a shred of doubt that it *was* a kidnapping.

"Grab something, Yo. Grab anything. She's here!"

Armed with a small shovel and a broom that needed replacing, Yolanda and Rachel ran wildly from room to room, clawing forgotten wraps children had left in the cloakroom and stumbling over woodpiles which someone had just upended from the school's neatly stacked rows. Time had no meaning. Callie must be found. She was here. Both sensed it. Either hiding in some simple place or soundlessly being moved from one hiding place to another.

That was when Rachel came too close. Something blunt struck across the back of her skull—twice. The blows came consecutively. But in the split second between, Rachel caught a glimpse of a figure whose head was capped with a flour sack. And then she must have passed out stone-cold. Away in the distance there were voices....

"Rachel—Rachel! We got 'em hobbled, and our Callie's all right. She's right here with my—uh—friend. I planned on coming anyway, helping get ready for when school's back in session, don't you know?"

The first thing coming clearly for Rachel was the sheriff and Eula Shepherd by his side. Foggily, to Rachel's eyes, it appeared strange that a lady's hair need be so tightly crimped to spring houseclean, and then she heard the Secret Service talking to Yolanda...the judge...all of Brimmerton's "merry men"... even Britches. *Why?* She tried to get up, only to have a pain shoot through her head.

"The doctor's coming. Norman went for him for both you and Callie. Have to have you ready to testify with all the others," the judge smiled, "and have Callie ready to trip down the aisle as soon as the rest of the mysteries are solved...." Rachel drifted off again.

29

Identities

Aunt Em was leaning over Rachel that evening before her vision cleared up completely. "Got uh lump on back uv yore head bigger'n th' twins' baseball. Dr. Ames musta broke all records gittin' t'th' school. My Davey-Love's dyin' uv curiosity—"

"So am I," Rachel said, lifting her head and then laying back on her own pillow with a slight moan.

"Yuh gonna feel thet pumpknot uh day or so, Rachel-hon." Aunt Em pulled a small table alongside the bed. "Here. Tuck this soup in—"

Rachel pushed the work-worn hand away. "Thank you, you're wonderful. But first tell me—"

"You gotta keer fer th' inner woman first. Thet's whut Buck'll be comin' home to. Git swallerin'!"

Obediently, Rachel gulped down the soup.

"I *do* feel stronger, bless you."

"'Course yuh do. Now iffen yuh can piece it together, you may jest find you'sef 'memberin' more'n I do. We'll see."

The best Emmaline Galloway could determine, she said, the root of all the evil was still money—which was to be expected. That's right, that half-beast and half-demon known as Bixby had more than their government mint, all taken from his part in the Dunigan robberies. Seemed there was a raft of robberies beginning with early stagecoach days. Even held up the last stage which had gold—some said gold pieces as big as sunflowers—

then chose the trains as a target from the very first one. But then Rachel knew that, just a review. So best get up to date, Aunt Em went on to say.

Now, what happened was this: Nobody could find Bonaparte Bixby. Must have left like his pants were on fire, leaving all that loot buried. But he did have followers, and they heard he'd left some jewels and maybe cash stuck around in Little Callie's classroom.

"That's ridiculous," Rachel said angrily, rising from bed now and forgetting to check on her headache. "Anyway, the Taylor-Smith woman and her two goons are in custody—"

"Sure are!" Aunt Em said with satisfaction. "But," she continued as she stacked the soup utensils in her basket and removed a batch of molasses cookies, "would you believe one Fredric-Paul Franchot was in with thet madam? Thet's whut she proved out t'be, you know. Funny how thangs work out, ain't it now? Britches' comin' here jest in time. . . .

Britches! Yes, she did remember. Not only was he here, but at the school as well. But—

"I don't understand what one has to do with the other."

"Here they come—your brood!" The older woman laughed. "Good-bye, cookies. But I'm guessin' he asked where to git uh haircuttin' 'n went t'th' Frenchman—well, sort of. That 'n other matters took 'im there. Curious 'bout them lady barbers fer one thing—"

Rachel had thought Britches was only making conversation. Now Aunt Em was telling her it was not idle talk. The sheriff had his suspicions the painted women were unwholesome. (*While I slept through it all*, Rachel accused herself. But how much could a person handle?)

"Guess yuh wonder iffen them hussies got picked up. Sure was! Along with thet sneaky Frenchman. Did you git uh notion thet polecat's whiskers wuz false? Bad as uh woman wearin' sachet in her corset t'keep from uh Saturday-night bath! Well, thet little varmit'll git plenty uv exercise without whacking ladies' skulls. We'll all hafta testify come tomorrow night. Oh hello, chil'durn belongin' to'th Joneses. Nope, I kin see yuh 'n Buck's got th' whole generation uv tomorrow—"

And tomorrow's generation was all talking at once, all so filled with news Rachel wondered how Star and Patrick could concentrate. She should set out the cookie tray to muffle the noise and, she grinned, she would except that she wanted to hear the news.

"I can't believe it. It's right, though. Britches is starting to school Monday. He won't begin in chart class though, except for reading and you know why—because he wants to learn to talk properly, you know, not 'swallowing his g's' as Mrs. Shepherd calls it. Miss Lee knows there's something else too. How come *she* knows so much, because she's your *teacher*?"

"Mother, the boys are being disrespectful. When will I meet the Johnson girls?"

"And boy, Mother? She thinks she's ready for *beaus* and for courting just because this is her graduation year," Saul taunted.

David, serious as always, lifted his eyebrows. "Why are you rude to our sister? Isn't it better that the two of us be thinking about our own future? I was considering being an instructor in a Christian school. Strange how few men enter to be teachers."

Mary Cole with suitors. The twins thinking in terms of further schooling. It had all gone so fast. And then Rachel recalled her daughter's question. "The Johnson children, who are to become Hathaways by request, I understand will be at church Sunday."

Sunday reminded her that Britches would be in the congregation. A hero! And still in need of a haircut, she supposed.

"Want some cookies, my dear news reporters?"

There was a round of applause as she set the giant-size molasses cookies before them, followed by a scramble to see which could garner the largest share. Oh dear, such manners! She and Buck had tried so hard to civilize them, and they had been model children. This was a phase, Buck said, something they would outgrow. Rachel hoped so. Even Star insisted that they chew with mouths closed. And once Patrick had suggested subtly that it was best to avoid speech when one's mouth was full. Aunt Em said, "Well now, it all rolled off 'em like rain on uh duck's back. My boy-angels!"

The boy-angels hadn't let molasses cookies slow their conversation one bit. "Oh well, I guess Miss Lee (used to be Miss Callie)—she's got high-hat since she's marrying a doctor—is of a mind that everybody's been bitten by the love-bug now," Saul blurted.

David looked at his brother quizzically. "Are you still talking about Britches? Isn't it schooling he's there for?"

Mary Cole, Rowie, and Brian went on chewing. David alone heard. "It *was*, but I think he's got his eye on the young teacher. Grandpa Davey says it's not unusual for a pupil to go goo-goo-eyed over his first teacher."

Mary Cole shouted above the boys. "May I have your attention, gentlemen! Think you know so much? Listen to this! Grandma Emmy told *me* something, too. Me and Emmy Lee—and she said it was so—she's not in school yet, but she understands. Did you know that Dr. Greer's beholding to Miz Lily? Has been for a long time secretly. Right, Grandma Emmy? Isn't that romantic? They've been writing letters since the doctor was here the first time—"

Rowie shrugged. "Don't—doesn't the man know about marriage licenses? They're no spring chickens, Sheriff Brimmerton says."

The door to Star's bedroom burst open, letting in a blast of cold air. Why, the children must be freezing. It wasn't spring yet.

"Patrick, why not build yourselves a fire in the bedroom fireplace?" Rachel suggested. "Dinner will be in half an hour."

"I'll help, Mother Mine," Star said, "as soon as I explain a matter or so to the children." She lifted exquisite, dark eyes to meet Patrick's. His adored her. But there was another message which flashed between them, something Rachel was unable to read. "A fire would be nice, Patrick."

While Star spoke, Rachel studied Patrick. His was a good face: intelligent, full of character, integrity galore—and admittedly, right for her oldest daughter. How could she ever have doubted? Patrick had not changed. *She* had. With the children, it would have to be the other way around. Oh well, that was like comparing oranges and apples And how on earth had her mind drifted so far? She turned to listen to Star and realized that Patrick was listening raptly. He must have sensed Rachel's look. He turned, sustaining her gaze coolly, even though the color blazing in his cheeks made a loud statement: "I'm in love."

"So you see," Star was saying, "it is always prudent to bridle the tongue. Rest assured that Miz Lily will not consent until the honorable doctor decides whether he wishes to serve the Lord. God would not have her push him. Dr. Greer must accept the Lord for one reason only. It is not enough to believe, at least not just with the mind. One must accept with the heart—to know there is no other way."

"How'll she know?" Mary Cole demanded.

"*She?* Don't you think it nicer to say Miz Lily? Others are helping, and one does not lie about anything so all-important. One does not lie to God. Just remember them in your prayers, the doctor and his nurse. Dr. Greer *wants* to believe."

"He will surrender," Patrick said with conviction. "Did I hear a knock?"

Rachel opened the door. There stood a stranger, a portly middle-aged man, twisting his hat in circles, his glasses looking out of place pushed back on a balding head.

"Mrs. Jones?"

"Yessir, I am Mrs. Jones, and this is my family."

"Except your husband. May I have a moment of your time?"

Rachel invited him in. Star and Grandma Em tactfully took the children out into the kitchen to help. Curious as Rachel was about the unexpected guest, she thrilled to hear Star's tinkling laughter. Yes, they could have pancakes, she promised. Then she and Patrick must take Roland and Brian home.

The man had not moved once he was inside. "I'm sorry. Please sit down, Mr.—?"

"Steward Stonebreaker of the United States Postal Service, ma'm," he said, absent-mindedly handing his hat her direction.

"I'm afraid there's been some mistake," Rachel murmured, hanging Mr. Stonebreaker's hat and removing a light stole for herself from the hall tree.

Mr. Stonebreaker gave her an irascible look. It was then Rachel realized that men in his position seldom made mistakes. She was glad she had said no more.

"There's been no mistake," he said, leaning back and placing the ends of his pink fingers together. "I wonder if you realize how much in danger your life is? Don't answer that! Obviously not, as you seem to be approaching life normally—and it's far from it. What the deuce took your eyes off reality?"

The man was right in a way. Rachel was aware that many matters were unresolved. But she had let down her guard, so excited was she over the talk of marriages—and yes, excitement over her husband's expected return. On the other hand, if this gentleman had something to say, why didn't he come right out and say it?

"What do you mean, I am in danger?" Rachel strove to hide the coldness she felt toward this man, and the squeezing she felt in her heart. "I mean, has something new happened?"

"I shouldn't have spoken so bluntly. Our other government agents weren't sent here for their health. They were to keep a watchful eye on you, particularly while your husband's away on a life-and-death mission."

Rachel let out a little cry.

At the sound, Patrick burst into the parlor. "Will you state your business, sir? Rest assured that Mrs. Jones is cared for."

"I'm sure you *think* she is, young man! But these criminals who're tampering with the mails have their victims under 24-hour surveillance. Don't entertain the notion that they're squeamish. They have tried unsuccessfully to eliminate Mr. Jones. It's to the point that he has decided he'd best make out a will—share and share alike for his children, the bulk going to his widow—"

"Don't *say* that—I can't bear it!" At Rachel's cry, Patrick walked the width of the room and placed a strong arm about her shoulders. "Mrs. Jones is unaware, but Mr. Haute has shared this matter with me—also has Britches on guard, as well as myself. We are all ready to testify. Perhaps you'd best tell us what's expected in the mails now, also a hint of what her husband's mission is. In that order."

"Gold. Looking for the owner of that watch. Guarding your lives. Satisfied?" *Satisfied? Oh Lord, have mercy....*

30

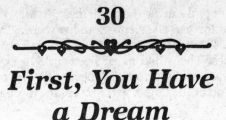

First, You Have a Dream

Rachel awoke the next morning depressed—depressed and frightened. Had she imagined the strange sound around the premises last night when at last the household had settled for the night? Well, certainly she had not imagined the dire, but vague warnings of Steward Stonebreaker. Exactly what was she to look for? And with Star and Patrick away today, she would be alone, except for the children.

She busied herself with the numerous tasks neglected during the past two weeks. Work it off, Aunt Em always said. And certainly she had plenty to occupy her time But a middle-aged woman would sound childish to ask that they remain with her, not that she could now. They left before dawn for a preliminary interview and to apply for a new set of books. They were to meet the three dignitaries from back East in Wilbur and be home before dark. They had received the writ of subpoena for tonight's hearing, guaranteeing an early return—almost a comfort. Then Rachel realized that thought as unworthy. Today was important to their future. What was it Patrick had said that she recorded? Oh yes: "First, you have a dream; otherwise, how is a dream to come true?" She must write that in her notes. It was beautiful.

There was a sudden commotion outside the door. "Mrs. Jones, tell them to come on. Have they forgotten about Illa Johnson-Hathaway's birthday?" *Rachel* had. All too soon her children had joined the boisterous group, leaving her only echoes for company.

Work did *not* take away the uneasiness. In fact, the apprehension gathered force as she went about her work. First, in sorting out the notes she would need for the evening, Rachel ran across Star's sketches. There had never been time to examine them. Now would be just right. Her skill never failed to communicate spirit, as if God in all His glory were speaking through the artistic hands.

The sketches told the story almost by themselves, her mother thought with pride. Each one was recognizable until she found among them the sketch of a man's watch. Hadn't Star said when she saw the gold case that she had seen it before? Rachel tried to recall whether she said she recognized it. Apparently not. The postal examiner had revealed that Buck had the remains of the watch. Remains?

Yes, she found on a second examination that Star had drawn two pictures. The watch in its original state, and the same item after it had been damaged by fire. Rachel wondered if Star consciously remembered the watch or if total recall lay stored somewhere in that otherworldly memory of hers. Something about the sketch turned her blood cold. The feeling traveled beyond apprehension now. There was a hint of something unholy about it. Maybe Britches would know.

Almost as if she had rubbed the magic ring of *Tales of the Arabian Nights*, Britches came trotting through the woods. She welcomed him in, a little selfishly. Besides, she truly admired and respected him.

"Well, here comes the student!" Rachel greeted. "I'm so proud of you. But who's tending the post office? I hear that you are on special lookout."

"Yes, but Burr Johnson is handling the mail. He came askin' fer work. I'll larn—teach, th' teacher tells me—teach 'im the Morse code by 'n by. But Rach—uh, Mrs. Jones, I'm bustin' t'tell yuh. I—uh—this is confidential 'ceptin' fer Patrick, but I know who owned th' watch. They's uh couple uv suspicious-lookin' fellers on th' lookout fer it. Won't yuh tell th' sheriff I'm needin' hep? I git uh gut feelin' somthin's gonna happen. Mr. Buck ain't safe with it in his possession—an' yuh had oughta have company here. They're desperate. I gotta run now. Don' let my teacher hear I'm uh coward—"

Rachel's heart was pounding. "Wh-who owned the watch?" she urged. "It's important, Britches."

"Bonaparte Bixby."

Bixby! Then Buck *was* in danger! The visiting man was right. Both Buck and she were in danger. "Your teacher would never think you cowardly, my dear. I'll take care that Mr. Brimmerton knows."

But Britches was gone.

She would go to the sheriff now. Why wait? Grabbing her apple-green coat and a matching head scarf from the hall tree, Rachel shrugged into them, only to be interrupted by an impatient knock at the door.

Well, the day had turned out to be anything but lonely. She would dismiss this caller hurriedly and be on her way, even though Buck had been adamant about her traveling alone. In this case—

Another impatient knock, more of a bang.

"I'm on my way," she called. "Who is it, please?"

"Open up! It's Steward Stonebreaker, U.S. Postal Examiner!"

His tone of voice said he was accustomed to immediate obedience. It was hard to be polite to such a domineering person, particularly when she was in a hurry. Something inside Rachel stiffened. Squaring her shoulders, she met his eyes with less than friendliness. "Would you mind stating your business? I am in a hurry."

Somehow the man was inside. "I thought you'd been ordered to travel only in the company of another—"

"I am *ordered* to do nothing! Please understand that."

He did not smile. "I made a special trip to tell you that I will walk with you to the meeting tonight. I do not wish you to be alone."

"Thank you. That was very thoughtful. However, Patrick and Star plan to be back. But for now, if you will excuse me, I need to make a business trip. It is important."

"Very well, I will come along. As I told you, Mrs. Jones, you are in danger—"

"Must you keep reminding me, Mr. Stonebreaker?" What did it take to be rid of this man? He really was a stranger; and, while she did not necessarily distrust him, she did not feel like confiding. And for some reason she was unable to put a finger upon, he did not appeal to her.

Before she could convince him, someone called her name.

Norman? What brought him here? Relieved, she called out formally, "Come in, Doctor Ambrose!"

Mr. Stonebreaker looked annoyed. Then, looking at Rachel shrewdly, he talked rapidly. "You do understand that Mrs. Taylor-Smith and her accomplices are all out on bail and can't have a final trial until all facts are in. Hold the young man at bay a minute, there is one thing I must make clear."

"I have invited him in, and there is nothing you and I have to talk about."

Steward grabbed her by the shoulder. He looked desperate. Here was a man who had aged without growing up. Urgently, he spoke, "Oh yes, we have! You are to understand that if anything happens—you know, if your husband does not return—I will be beside you, and my intentions are perfectly honorable."

Rachel stared at him in disbelief. "Let go of me at once!"

A fist shot out from nowhere, grazing the hateful chin which had been dangerously near her own. "Why, you contemptuous beast! How dare you touch Buck Jones' wife! She needs protection all right—from bums like *you*!" Norman's voice was so hot with anger, it caused Rachel's nerves to tingle through her entire body. Or was it delayed shock? What would have happened if the young doctor who had come to check on the bump she sustained hadn't been worried at her delay in opening the door? Rachel shuddered with revulsion.

"The man must be insane!" Norman was saying now.

Rubbing his chin, the intruder muttered, "I'm *very* sane."

Norman laughed contemptuously. "Yes—yes, I guess you are at that. Rachel is a very rich woman. Once you saw the will, you figured to live out the rest of your life a rich man. Well, let me tell you something, you scheming wolf: We don't allow our ladies to be approached in any such insulting manner. You'd be the last man on earth this honorable woman would turn to. And besides, nothing's going to happen to her husband. Now, as to *your* safety—"

Mr. Stonebreaker, hat still in hand, made a hasty departure.

"Don't be too upset, Norman." Rachel had gained her composure. "Sadly, the world is filled with people who are weak, self-seeking—"

Norman was less understanding than Rachel. His face was still drained of color and his hands trembled as he felt the lump on her head. "You know," he said, "that man could be an imposter. Unfortunately, you can't legislate, elect, or appoint a gentleman."

"You go back to your Callie, dear friend. This is not a time for you to be upset with the world. Quoting Patrick, 'First, you have a dream.'"

He nodded absently. Obviously, something remained unresolved.

After young Dr. Ambrose left, something too lurid and frightening to entertain clamped over her head like a hood. What if Norman had the right thought? That this man was an imposter? Could he possibly, Rachel thought with alarm, be masterminding something revolving around Buck—his *death*?

Oh, thank goodness! There, a short distance away, Star and Patrick were approaching on their twin roan-coated riding horses. Star accompanied him to the stable to unsaddle. And Rachel noted that they were deep in conversation. Moments later, they were inside the house.

"Mother Mine, are you all right?" Star asked with concern.

Rachel forced a smile. It must have been unsuccessful.

"What has happened? We were concerned. Something did happen?"

Rachel quickly gave account of the day, ending with Mr. Stonebreaker's visit and too-familiar behavior.

Patrick's face bleached of color. "Why, the very nerve! His reputation preceded him, but it did not occur to me that you were the target until we were well on our way home. It has happened with other widows."

"Oh Patrick, I am not a widow!"

"A slip of the tongue, my dear, but I am concerned—"

"About my safety, Buck's—everybody's? Mrs. Taylor-Smith is out on bail, he told me."

"Not anymore, Mother Mine! The lady was discovered to have insurance policies on three of the men who were killed. It is all a great mystery to me. I did not know that ladies could have insurance. Does it not seem strange when they are neither allowed to vote nor hold property without another party? The gentlemen who talked with us today were from New York and informed us that they are acquainted with the representatives. Patrick sent Britches a message by code, and the sheriff took the transgressors back to jail. And next comes the horrible part— Patrick, you will assist me—I—I no longer have the stomach for such matters."

Star was about to be sick. Rachel should be with her but found herself rendered helpless, unable to move or speak.

"The men who have been spying on both you and Britches, opening mail, on the lookout for something," Patrick frowned, "for more than the treasure, I believe—they are dead. They were coming too close to the secret. The sheriff found their bodies."

I never helped. Maybe I could have prevented it. Her heart was throbbing and it was difficult to breathe. "What—who—?"

"There was no way to have stopped it," Patrick said. "Britches was glad you were not there to be killed. He saw the entire thing. The murderess, Mrs. Taylor-Smith, dropped her pearl-handled pistol as she attempted to get away."

It was all too much to absorb. *Oh Buck, Buck, my darling,* her heart cried out. But Rachel took comfort in the tender warmth of two pairs of arms holding her close in love and protection. Oh, praise the Lord for family! But for now, they must go to the hearing.

There followed not one night, but three unhappy days when Rachel had to testify and listen to the remainder of the evidence. It all had happened before, somewhere back in her past—just a matter of déjà vu. Rachel found it hard to concentrate. They were all convicted. What's more, Mrs. Taylor-Smith had been robbed of her glamor. It occurred to Rachel that the woman objected less to spending the rest of her life behind bars than to being stripped of her vanity. The same might be said for Fredric-Paul Franchot. He no longer hopped about like a mouse sniffing for a nibble of cheese. His drooping shoulders showed that he had lost faith in himself, in his fatal charm over women. Nothing remained, nothing. . . .

Or did it? Buck was not home. Nothing was finished until then. Well, she must dream. Dream—and pray.

31

Searching Blindly

A few days later, Patrick startled Rachel by asking permission to allow Dr. Greer to visit him in the Joneses' home. She agreed immediately, reassuring him that any of his friends were welcome here. Although curious, she asked no questions.

Relief showed in the serious face. "The doctor asked, Rach—uh, Mrs. Jones—"

"Rachel, please," she smiled. "Consider yourself a part of the family."

Patrick's young face scalded with color. "I—I," he gulped.

"Go ahead and say it."

It was hard not to laugh. Patrick, so at home in the pulpit, so congenial at their dinner table, so totally at ease with Star, stumbling as Aunt Em described Brother Davey's proposal, "like a blind dog in a meat house."

"Oh, how did we get into this?" The young lover was miserable. "I had planned this for light-years away—asking your daughter's hand when Buck—uh, Mr. Jones, returns."

Rachel felt her heart turn over. *When Buck came home.*

"Now look what I've done—reinforced the fears brought on by that tasteless government inspector. We were talking about Dr. Greer's coming here. Afterwards I—"

"But Patrick, I must admit I'm concerned—scared to death, in fact. I've cried. I've prayed—selfishly at first, then I asked God to bring good from this. But, oh Patrick, I'm human. I love my husband deeply, more deeply than he knows, and I've had some

179

heart-to-heart talks with God and explained that I have been remiss in never letting Buck know how *deeply* he is loved."

"Don't you think God understands your need, Rachel?"

"Yes, it's just that my world is so empty, meaningless. No, that's not true. I have all of you. It's just colorless—"

"Don't apologize. God understands that, too. He created woman to need a husband." Patrick paused to grin teasingly, an unusual expression for him, and then said, "And that statement has nothing to do with equal rights."

Rachel was beautiful at that moment. Her eyes were luminous with borrowed lights from her pale-green dress which was the color of the young weeping willow leaves along the riverbank. She failed to see Patrick's smile of appreciation. He knew "love light" when he saw it. It was a holy thing.

"Never mind equal rights," the green goddess said. "I will be his willing slave."

Moments later the doctor was there. What was it Patrick was about to say at one point? Something concerning his plans after his talk with Dr. Greer? Oh well, it probably was of no consequence, Rachel supposed, as she went about setting out the silver service. As she worked, bits of the conversation drifted through the open door. At first she paid no attention. In fact, she rattled the flowered china cups more than was necessary to keep from overhearing. Until—

"I find myself wanting to stand before the congregation making a proclamation—just wanting to be a part of the church. But it's as if the devil is battling for my soul. I cannot believe totally on Christ. I'm miserable."

Dr. Greer?

"You are laboring over it too much, doctor. Just relax. God won't let you fall. I would like to have you perform a simple experiment. Repeat after me: 'I believe in the Lord Jesus Christ.'"

Dr. Greer cleared his throat self-consciously before speaking. Then uncertainly he said, "I—believe in the *Lord Jesus Christ*. Oh, I do, something *did* happen! It was as if He stood beside me. I can't wait to tell Miz Lily there *is* a God. I *saw* Him!"

"Mother Mine!" Rachel almost dropped the tea tray. She had never heard Star's voice so loud, so triumphant.

"I know. I heard." Tears were streaming down Rachel's face. But, Patrick told her later, she still looked lovely. Dr. Greer spoke in a stream: "Patrick here and Star have been working with me, patiently praying. And oh, Mrs. Jones, your daughter's hands were always on my head. There's a strange power there that even I, as a doctor, cannot explain. Only a fool would try, but then 'Fools rush in where angels fear to tread.' Not that I'm an angel or aspire to be."

Rachel smiled. "No, but that does not bar you from heaven, either in the here-and-now or the hereafter. Something tells me that I just witnessed a soul's entry beyond, and that same voice tells me that now we should prepare for the state of heavenly bliss below."

A short time later the doctor was "on his way rejoicing." Rachel had never felt so humble, so blessed. If only—

"You're wishing for your heaven-on-earth, too. Right, Rachel?"

"It may be a sacrilege at a moment like this, but yes," she said, near tears again. "Do you—" she swallowed hard, "think—"

"—Something has happened to your husband? I didn't wish to upset you further. But now I feel that I can wait no longer. I'm going to look for him. It will be a somewhat blind search, but I do have a few leads. And without further ado, this is good-bye. Rachel, you and Star must pray for me, and for Buck's safety. I know what torture you have been through. And I heard Dr. Killjoy's wife eulogize him. Both say in essence, 'Don't waste a day.' You understand?"

Rachel understood. A word of understanding and appreciation began deep inside her heart and came out a near sob. "Oh, God go with you. You are right—"

She walked outside to look for signs of a permanent spring. The young lovers must have a moment's privacy. And she must have a moment alone with the Lord, asking Him to assist her in building a new dream...a simple dream...just a man and a woman together again.

That night Rachel dreamed of a black stallion. The great, shining creature was leading a procession, an unoccupied saddle on his sleek back. And across the saddle horn was a pair of boots....

The nightmare grew more and more real each night until at last she spoke with Norman about it. He was very understanding. "I know what you mean, my dear. I had a recurring dream that almost drove me insane while I was guarding Callie, a feeling I needed to unburden to her. It comes from unresolved problems. I do not intend to pry—"

"You're not prying, dear Norman. And you are right. You have helped. Is everything all right with you two? I want to help."

"More than all right. Get ready for the wedding of the season!"

He saluted smartly and rode away. As if, she smiled, theirs were the *only* wedding which lay ahead in what she hoped would be a lovely season. . . .

And then Patrick was home. Rachel knew before he told her. There had been no sign of her husband. It was then that she was unable to hold up any longer. It was a November world . . . gray . . . chilling . . . no longer springtime . . . but on its way to winter, the month of the mournful dead. . . .

32

Just Waiting

Life went on. The good people of Lordsburg saw to it that the bodies of the two unknown men who had attempted to gather information through tampering with the mail had a decent burial. Apparently, there was yet something Nella Taylor-Smith was secretly searching for. Nobody had an inkling. The woman had been convicted on so many counts. Nobody was concerned about her welfare. But this case could not be closed until the mystery was solved. The city would not be safe. And somehow Rachel felt in her heart that Buck was caught in the midst of it all.

The judge made a special trip to see Rachel, to reassure her. "Buck had to be cautious," he said, "but his report to me sounded as favorable to me as his messages to you. I've a hunch our city manager will be riding in here any day—and with the information we need. Maybe then we can rid ourselves of that hanger-on who is no longer needed, Steward Stonebreaker. No further business here as far as I can tell. I understand he—uh—made improper advances."

"He was forward," she admitted, and resisted making her words stronger.

The judge took out his handkerchief and polished his glasses. "It takes a lot to upset Norman—even more to disturb Patrick. But, you know, had I been on hand, I just wouldn't have had these glasses on. Blind as a bat without them. After all, 'Justice is blind.'"

They talked about small matters, but Rachel had a feeling that Judge Hathaway had his mind on another matter and was hesitating to make mention. She had nothing more to say. Finally, the judge spoke.

"Your yard looks lovely. Hyacinths and daffodils together make a good marriage. Speaking of which, we have several coming up, according to what I hear. That makes Cappy happy. Ours is a good relationship, particularly since we have the children. She has submitted her resignation from the government work, effective as soon as this is all brought to an end. That means as soon as that man of yours comes home. The whole town is just waiting."

"So is his wife!"

"I guess what I really wanted to say was that it might be wise for all of us to resume our activities, act normal, just in case—"

"There are other stragglers?"

"I'm wondering if there are. And if there are, we might as well flush them out."

Rachel agreed and found that other women felt the same. Why not continue the meetings, the quiltings, and allow Callie and Norman to get on with plans for the wedding?

It was at the first meeting at Aunt Em's that the other brides-to-be made their announcements. "All them quilts!" Aunt Em faked a sigh of desperation. "But let's us go on reportin', while doin' fancy stitches. Me 'n my Davey-Love, fer instance, was wonderin'—well, one thang in partic'lar puzzled us. I'm speakin' 'bout thet sketch uv two watches I understand Buck took—"

Callie, her skin tanned golden from working in the garden of the Hathaway cabin which she was to occupy as a bride, had been aglow with happiness. Suddenly, the light in her eyes died as she let out a sharp little gasp.

"I remember now," she cried out. "Bonaparte Bixby *did* leave something hidden in my room. That watch!"

Everybody was leaning forward. "And you didn't remember, darling?" Yolanda looked surprised.

No, no of course, Callie hadn't remembered. In fact, she had paid too little attention to the incident. It was of such small consequence that she neglected to lock the drawer where the other teacher dropped the watch. What caught her attention was his strange explanation, his mysterious manner. Of course (blushing) they, uh, worked closely.

"He told me it was a valuable watch and he was afraid to keep it on his person."

"Why?"

"He didn't tell me, Yo. I should have asked. But I just forgot, and I still do not understand why anyone would ransack my room for *that*—if that was the object of the search."

Rachel stiffened. There were *two* sketches! Obviously, the watch had been burned in the second one. Why on earth would anyone do that? She was glad nobody else asked....

Rachel was tired—bone-tired. Spring had come with a burst of glory. Surely the Oregon Country must be the most spectacular spot of beauty in the world. Solomon's "voice of the turtle" was in the land. Surely the sap was rising in Rachel's blood as well. Something was going to happen. But to save her life, Rachel was unable to determine whether the "turtle's message" was good or bad. She was too weary.

The watch lingered unresolved. Did Buck's having it put him in more danger? Was the missing Bixby stalking him, biding his time? And why *was* the loathsome Stonebreaker still here, managing to be ever at her elbow, a sickeningly hungry look in his owlish eyes? He, like the rest of the city, was obviously "just waiting." But the thing which stopped her heart was that—*Oh, dear God, no!*—Steward Stonebreaker was waiting, like a beady-eyed vulture watched, for *death—the death of her husband....*

33

Beloved Stranger

The brilliant morning when Star announced that Patrick would be meeting with several of the betrothed couples in order to know what type ceremonies they planned, she confided to Rachel that she felt restless. Wouldn't it be nice if she made a trip to the cemetery and carved a marker for the recent graves?

"Perhaps the two went through their brief lives searching only for earthly treasure, never having seen or known a thing of beauty because their souls were blind, preferring darkness rather than light because their deeds were evil. Isn't that how the Bible expresses it? And now their sightless eyes are unable to see the glorious stars at night or the gossamer webs of the morning. We will all be held accountable, won't we, Mother Mine—not just the simpleminded ecclesiastics wishing to keep clean their hands? Would it not be a nice gesture that I should carve in old English printing: 'Known Only to God'?"

"Oh yes, darling, yes," Rachel breathed, reaching out to hold her daughter close. "How desperately the world needs people like you and your Patrick."

"How desperately *God* needs us, my precious mother—laborers and builders, who follow in the footsteps of the carpenter of Nazareth."

Once her heaven-sent daughter was gone, Rachel gave way to a tidal wave of tears. Exhausted, at length she rose, drew a sunrise-pink gossamer fascinator around her shoulders, and began walking. She found herself heading toward the little rise just beyond

Main Street, close to town while feeling like a private world, surrounded as it was by sky-brushing pines—a private world in which she and Buck had walked together so many times. Others would have advised against it, telling her it would only make her more lonely, perhaps even that it was dangerous. But it was as if she had no control. Her heart was tumbling, racing, school-hopping, sending blood rushing through her veins like a mighty tide. And she had no power over the direction of her feet. But why should she sense a need to run?

And then ahead she saw a startling figure. Here she was all alone, unable to make anybody hear should she call for help. Her feet should be taking her the other direction to safety. Why was she here?

Rachel felt herself shaking from head to foot, and unable to move.

The ragged figure was that of a bearded man. He was on foot and limped slightly, necessitating the use of a cane. The face, beyond the beard, looked deadly pale as if—as if this person had been working underground. She stared in fascination when common sense told her that she should be getting way. There was something magnetic—something which said without words that the face should be a healthy tan, that this was a man of the great outdoors. It was even a ruggedly handsome face beneath the gruesome beard. And familiar!

"Rachel—Rachel!" The dearly familiar voice echoed and re-echoed from canyon to canyon. Echoes should grow fainter. This one grew stronger, stronger, stronger until it was overpowering.

She took a hesitant step forward. Then blindly she ran forward to him, ignoring the thorns, the thistles, the low-hanging branches which would have held her from her mate.

Laughter bubbled up inside her. "Oh darling, darling, darling—you look like a cocklebur. Oh, forgive me! You look so hungry—"

"I am! I'm starving for you!" Buck broke into laughter. "May I tell you, Mrs. Jones, that you don't look much better? Come save my life!"

Then they were in each other's arms . . . one flesh—the way it was intended . . . unable to breathe, and not caring. What a wonderful way to go into eternity. . . .

It was he who spoke first. There was no laughter left in his deep, gravelly voice. "I should kneel before you, little sweetheart of mine, beg for your forgiveness for all I've left untold. I beg you from the bottom of my heart to forgive me, and for doubting for a moment that you had no need of me. There is so much to say, to explain—"

"Oh my darling, I, too, had so much to say. But let's don't say it—at least not now. Deep down we never lost faith, and now that God has answered my prayers and brought you home, does it matter? We will start anew. What matters is from this time forth."

"Yes, Rachel," Buck said with a tremor in his voice. "I have come home."

At length he released her with a reluctant little sigh.

"But a man has some pride. We have the rest of our lives, and God grant that they be long. For Rachel, the horrible nightmare is over—for me, at least. I know you, Yolanda, *all* Lordsburg have been through your own private Hades. And you, Miss Close-Mouth, are going to share yours, if I have to squeeze it out of you! But first I must shave, have a bath, get rid of this disguise—"

Disguise! Something she would never have thought of. "So that's it—you were traveling incognito. That accounts for Patrick's being unable to find you."

Buck nodded. "He was within 50 feet of me. Once I could have reached out and touched him, but it would have endangered us both. Now to make myself presentable and then get an immediate report to the judge. You will know all soon enough. But first, while I am attending to absolute essentials, there is an essential I want *you* to attend to. Isn't it time you and Yolanda had a heart-to-heart talk?"

Rachel understood. "It is," she said with tears in her eyes. She wondered if she would ever tell the entire story. Was it necessary to dwell on her own suffering? Having her husband away had been the worst of all. And now he was home. *Oh, God be praised!* And, as always, Buck understood anyway. Else he would not have suggested that she and her best friend needed this talk.

They were on their way home now, her arm submissive to the pressure of his hand. At the door of their home, they paused, eyes adoring one another. As if she would break, he lifted her over the threshold.

"Good-bye for a short time, Buck, my darling. Look, the house is smiling. A house needs a family."

"So does this man!"

Moments later, two lifelong friends with radiant faces were embracing, smiling through their tears just as the Oregon sunshine is prone to shine through the mist. The mixture creates rainbows. And both knew rainbows are worth waiting for.

"Remember, Rachel, the qualifications we listed for a husband back when were little more than children?"

"I remember. And Yo, we have them all now—"

Rachel was unaware that her hazel eyes dreamed just as they had so long ago as Yolanda began counting off on her still-shapely fingers: "Devoutly Christian...a respectable citizen, certainly... and what did we place next in order?"

Rachel's laugh filled the Ames parlor. "We rearranged them so many times. But always our dream-man must be gentle, kind, and *loving*."

"It was you who added a sense of adventure. Well, we've had that."

"And I recall how important it was," Rachel finished, "how *very* important it was to have a husband we could trust with all our hearts. Oh Yo, I feel like a bride again. And now, I must go home to my dream-man. Also," she decided suddenly, "I want to record this. And from now on, history must unfold for itself. . . ."

And Rachel Lord Jones went home to her beloved stranger.

34

And the Truth Shall Make You Free

Hours later every available light was ablaze in waiting for the head of the Jones household. Ah, lovely dream, the thought of being alone with her husband for Mrs. Buckley Jones! Why, the entire city of Lordsburg was represented. Rachel should have known that Yolanda would rush to tell Callie, who had a very personal reason for the Bixby mystery's resolution. And it was equally natural for Callie to share the fact that Buck had returned with Cappy Hathaway in order for the lady to alert the judge, sit in on the report with her husband, and retire to being a wife and mother. All the children joined in on electing themselves to something akin to ancient town criers. "Eight o'clock and all is we-e-eell!" their young voices pealed out, going on to announce in falsetto born of excitement that their father was home. Aunt Em took over from there.

And now the house was overflowing with women-in-waiting and the tables were groaning with food. The judge had called an open meeting. Democratically, His Honor included the ladies. But for some unexplained reason, the women decided that it was their "right" to remain home should they so choose. Men were less fortunate, they decided. It was their bounden duty. Like Paul said, if women should know, let them ask of their husbands. Rachel smiled, relieved to see them take a less-militant attitude, realizing what a gift it was to be a woman.

The front door opened. Buck entered first to welcome his guests. His face lighted up when his eyes met his wife's. Rachel, tossing aside all restraint, obeyed her heart. Rushing to stand in front of him, she stood on tiptoe and brushed his cheek with a kiss, inhaling deeply the scent of shaving soap, bay rum, and the "masculine smell" which she had always attributed exclusively to Buck.

Gone was the look of sheer fatigue from the clean-shaven face. And something else was missing, something reaching back into the past they had tried so carefully to fold away. Sadness—did one ever put sadness away completely? No, but it was possible to learn to love more deeply, more completely by it. Their common grief had been one of the building stones which brought Cole's dream to fruition—and created a million more. Even before hearing the details, Rachel knew that Buck, wonderful Buck, had completed the miracle. He had made Lordsburg more than a city. He had made it safe, "Safe in the arms of Jesus."

Rachel had always served as a model for the ladies in this corner of the new world. Tonight was no exception. Following her example, they now went to their own mates or their betrothed and openly showed their affection before asking their questions or serving the gentlemen. The men hid their embarrassment with poor attempts at jokes, Brother Davey's the loudest of all.

"All right, men. Let's not let these wimmen-folks' victuals go wastin'. All in favor, dig in!"

They dug in.

For a time there was silence. Then all began talking at once, some gesturing with chicken legs, others inserting details while their mouths were filled with chocolate pie. Ladies kept replenishing the bread baskets with sourdough biscuits, causing Miss Annie to say that at this rate somebody would have to churn. But nobody complained. Excitement was too great. Soon they would know the truth....

Rachel found herself a guest in her own kitchen, which suited her immensely. She boldly pulled a ladderback chair to the table beside her husband. From then on he fed himself one-handed.

"I don't want to miss a word," she whispered from the corner of eager lips. And she didn't.

"You'll receive a medal, Buck," the judge was saying. "There wasn't a single leak while you completed the secret assignment of tracing Bixby. What a terrible way to die."

"Die?" Rachel gasped. "Bixby's dead? How—why—?"

All the other men tried to explain at once, but Rachel concentrated on Buck's words, intended only for her. A white-faced Callie was doing likewise with Norman. Yes, the truth would make them free, in all ways....

"What we'd suspected all along came out at the inquest," Buck explained rapidly. "A dentist found the jawbone was broken, and he'd set it when it was damaged. Bixby was implicated with the Dunigan gang, you know. Then there was the watch found at the site of the fire in the ashes—remember? Lots of other evidence, too. We can get to the nitty-gritty of it all later. The main thing is that we're safe."

But it was important to her why his body should have been burned. The food remaining on the table lost its appeal when Buck answered. Bonaparte Bixby had been the leader of the cult outfitting themselves in white and sacrificing live animals. There was no honor among them. Once they knew where the treasure was buried, the followers betrayed him. Killed him, yes—but did Rachel really want to know how? She did. Squeezing her hand hard, Buck hesitantly revealed that the man himself was sacrificed alive. Was she going to be sick? Rachel shook her head, even though the faces before her blurred.

"Yolanda! You've overdone," Howard's voice sounded a million miles away. "You need a doctor, so come sit beside your husband. What's upsetting you so much?"

Yolanda did as her husband invited, then lowered her voice. But Rachel overheard. "It's Rachel. You know how that terrible man behaved, and I see nothing of him."

"Nor *will* you, my darling. Stonebreaker's out of the picture, a phony, counterfeit through and through—"

"But the badge, the papers—even his knowledge of the mails?"

Dr. Ames shook his head in answer to the question. "Why?" he seemingly asked himself, "Why? Why do men reach a high rank only to succumb to thievery themselves? True, Stonebreaker handled enormous amounts of money and temptation is always there. But aren't we promised we will be given no more than we can bear?"

"Not all men know the Lord, doctor," Norman said to his colleague. "We can be so thankful for young people with persuasive powers like Patrick O'Grady and Star Jones who make use of it in spreading the gospel in their life work. And we have far too many agnostics and too few Christian physicians as well."

"*All* people—particularly those the Bible refers to as 'men in the high places'—set examples. I guess that's why it is good that the government will deal with Stonebreaker instead of *me*. He once was considered a man of honor. Then, after his conviction and dismissal—well, you know what happened. Instead of being grateful for a suspended sentence since it was his first offense, he went into crime on a full-time basis."

Miss Annie set a deep-dish apple pie before her husband. The Reverend smiled at her appreciatively, then sobered. "I guess my wife here was less surprised than I was when we discovered that Steward Stonebreaker and the Taylor-Smith woman and her hoodlums were all blackmailing one another. Seems Mrs. Shepherd knew enough to put them on guard."

"All pretty complicated," the sheriff's voice, now that his appetite was quieted, rose above all others. "Everybody ganging, betraying, blackmailing—like we had a corner on crime in these parts. But you can rest assured it won't happen again! We've learned a heap, and nobody'll be throwing dirt in faces in these parts."

"Very true," Dr. Greer said quietly. "If I may have the floor briefly, let me repeat 'I believe in the Lord Jesus Christ'—and through Him all things can be accomplished."

"And all the people shouted 'Amen'," Rachel quoted. Then with a puckish look, she added, "Even weddings—right, doctor?"

"Ask Miz Lily," he said meekly. It was unnecessary.

'Well, now, thet ain't th' only couple, is it, Emmy-Gal?" Brother Davey grinned.

Aunt Em, wiping her hands on an enormous Mother Hubbard apron, smiled broadly. "Nope—'n yuh jolly-well know it, Davey-Love," his wife said, tweaking her husband's ear playfully. "How about it Britches—yore teacher hereabouts? Should'n' yuh be tellin' th' news?"

Britches' face turned scarlet, but his reply was in perfect English. "I believe that's a proper announcement for the young lady to make."

"There's no time like the present," Callie sang out, having become a very close friend of the attractive young teacher.

"My word! It didn't take those two long," Judge J. Quentin Hathaway commented.

Rachel smiled up into the eyes of her husband. "No, falling in love doesn't take long," she said softly.

Kind eyes smiled at Rachel. All knew her life story. Her loss was their loss. They had loved Cole, just as they loved Buck. It was easy to understand how the second marriage could spring from a triangular friendship. One was the breathtaking bud of youth, the other the incomparable bloom of maturity.

What surprised them was Yolanda's loud, clear addition to her friend's words: "It just takes some of us longer than others."

Or did it? One just never knew what the Lord had in His pocket. How did that old song go? "Nobody knows what events God chooses—to bring together those He uses." Hadn't the Lord of Lordsburg always come through? Hadn't He brought them all through the swirling turbulence of its history? The Good Book told it like it was: "Nothing can separate me from the love of God."

Ahead lay loose ends to be tied together. The judge was a true-letter-of-the-law man. What's more, he was a God-fearing person. Better a hundred guilty be let go than to convict one innocent party. Not that either would happen. Buck agreed.

In the meantime, the guests in the Jones household decided as a group that this was a good time to rededicate their efforts to making this a "New Jerusalem" insofar as was earthly possible. Did not future cities need models just as individuals needed them? Lordsburg was no accident. The world had no need of another Savior, but it had a need for the just and the upright who could magnify His name, whose tracks pointed out the way to peace.

There was a soul-stirring prayer by the young Reverend Patrick O'Grady, followed by Star's bringing out a shining harp—a gift, she announced, from her father. She played like an angel, all said in parting, and for a sparkling second perhaps they themselves sounded like a band of angels as they sang "Blest Be the Tie That Binds...."

When the last guest departed, Rachel suddenly felt exhausted. She walked wearily to the table, only to have two strong arms from behind make her a prisoner. "The dishes are loyal," Buck said. "They'll wait for us."

A wee, small breeze had risen. The sky was stuck with a billion stars. And a sickle moon smiled down as they walked hand-in-hand as lovers always will.

35

The Unknown Disciple

Patrick was right. One has to have a dream to see a dream come true. Rachel and Buck dreamed with the children. They dreamed with the engaged couples, saw them married, watched them fulfill their destiny. Yes, they dreamed, and then they strengthened each dream with a prayer.

"Well, we've had an ideal marriage," Buck told her tenderly one day.

The statement was startling. "That is the first time you have ever spoken of it in past tense," she said soberly.

Buckley Jones nodded. "Does it matter? We have lived life to its richest. Does it matter so much whether God sends His Son to join us or we join Him there?"

Ultimately no, but Rachel supposed she would always wonder if she had fulfilled all God had in store for her. She frowned. Strangely, that frown caused her husband to toss back his head and fill their part of the world with laughter.

"What, may I inquire, do you find funny?"

"You! My darling, you are so transparent. Don't be hesitant to tell me what's troubling you. Telling me your concerns is like confessing your sins. You might as well. He and I know anyway."

Rachel smiled. "Yes, and I know I cannot control life from the grave—"

"You won't be there."

Rachel smiled again. "Just a figure of speech. I guess I was thinking more in terms of the tracks we leave. Our mortal span is brief, and we sometimes travel as though we had our wagons packed to journey on forever—or worse, like a herd of wild horses, cutting crescents in the tender grasses, crushing the wild flowers—"

Buck nodded. "Taking no thought of the morrow. But my darling, you have—you know you have. Your entire life has been with a loving heart in charge. Living for the day was not enough. You lived for the morrow, down to your very notes."

"My notes are my tracks," Rachel said slowly, "as are Star's sketches, besides all she and Patrick have accomplished with their hearts, their heads, and their hands. But there comes a time when the world must find its own way. That was my meaning when I left off."

"What did you say, my darling?"

"That from this time forth, those into whose hands the accounts of unspeakable suffering and sorrow fell, they must find the path to everlasting peace by realizing all things are temporary—that temporal joys of life are not enough—and be thankful that God offers us more for the taking."

"And I would add that we make a plea that all eyes turn from adversities and look to the world of foreverness." His face lighted with inspiration. "I see those tracks, my sweet. You did not crush the scattered wild violets. Instead, countless blue-eyed flowers sprang up in their place."

She leaned her head against the warmth of her husband's arm. The story had a familiar ring—of course, the story of their marriage. Death was a natural part of life, but not of life eternal....

—♥—♥—♥—

There was never a wealth of Oregon history. Old Oregon was apparently not the howling wilderness some imaginative writers described it. There were areas of wilderness, patches of vine-bound forests and waterless plains which Indians shied away from. What was known pertained more to the geography than to the history.

History, such as it was, was gathered by sign language in caves and bits and pieces gathered from missionaries' records, ship logs, and diaries of emigrants and early-day settlers. Even then it was difficult to piece together. Its people did not seem to sip from the same cup. O'Grady, was it, who wrote the communion creed?

And so it was that researchers took great delight in discovering the records left behind by the inhabitants of one of its major cities, known once upon a time by the name of Lordsburg. Of particular interest were the delightfully written notes, so real that the characters might be living among them a century later. The only problem was that, although many labored for years in their dedicated effort to trace the characters, so well-described and named by families (including their friends), all led to dead ends. It was as if, at some point, the writer identified only as R.L.J. had intended it to be so. Such conclusions add to the Oregon mystique.

The name Lord was prominent, but the details were missing. Equally prominent was Jones, of which there surely must have been thousands—all it seemed, unrelated. There was a professor at Willamette by the name of Jones. But the university's records made no use of Christian names. One Jones was elected to serve Oregon as a state representative, but records were yellowed and the given name had faded. Nowhere was there a Mary Cole. Of course, she undoubtedly married, perhaps moved away. Ames & Ames were only a footnote in medical journals.

Among the circuit riders was one Galloway, but there was no marker in any of the cemeteries under "Galloway." There were no church records because, unfortunately, the main church was destroyed by fire, and with it all its records. The other churches were smaller and, strangely, their records less complete than word had it that the great church had kept for posterity. If so, time must have traveled backward.

There was an abundance of artwork. As to whether it was all done by one artist was a moot question. Legend declared that the works were all completed by the same talented hand. The same person who vouched for that told of the states' most beautiful wedding between a devout young minister and a spiritual creature sent from above—too pure for this world and yet unable to return to her heavenly abode without her love. And so, legend went on, rulers from above and below took mercy on the young lovers and swept them both away in a whirlwind. Such stories, of course, never found their way into history books—or into church dogma for that matter. It would be a sacrilege.

So, scratching collective heads, the fact finders agreed to dismiss it all as fantasy—fantasy art, a subject which actually was centuries old and was no longer recognized in the art world. Little did they know that there would be a renewal one day of works rich in research and symbolism. Admittedly, however, the person or persons must have been highly educated, real scholars. The works were oft discovered in the strangest places. How could people of their wisdom, the learned researchers pondered, put stock in paintings based on Shakespeare, Mother Goose nursery rhymes, Latin scrolls, and the Bible back in that "howling wilderness"? Best dismiss it all as a hoax. People would laugh otherwise.

One note by the mysterious R.L.J. was a bit more difficult to pooh-pooh away—a plaque mounted on a magnificently shaped fir tree: Christmas Began the Night Someone Gave Shelter to a Homeless Family—*Keep That Tradition Alive*. Well now, there was real neighborliness. But nobody removed the thoughtful words, and it is supposed that the tree was felled along with its neighbors when the timber industry reached its peak. Supposedly, a Jones would never allow it to be cut.

But there was one which nobody could deny! And of all the common places, this took the prize. Worth preserving, the researchers agreed and built a low picket fence around the site. That gesture may have been their most worthwhile achievement, at least had they taken into consideration that the peaceful little cemetery was situated so near the equally peaceful appearing river. There was no way of foreseeing that a rain-swollen river can become vindictive, rise above its banks, and take away a work of art which the world does not appreciate. And with it went the secret of the sheen to the printing which shone like a fallen star in the darkest hour of night. It has never been duplicated. And few know that the soul-stirring words came from the ancient quill which penned *The Unknown Disciple*:

> The Carpenter of Galilee
>   Comes down the street again,
> In every land, in every age,
>   He still is building men.
> On Christmas Eve we hear Him knock;
>   He goes from door to door.
> "Are any workmen out of work?"
>   The Carpenter needs more.

Beneath it was the single word: Star.

MEMORABLE BOOKS
by June Masters Bacher

The Love Is a Gentle Stranger Series

An adventurous saga of the American frontier and a young woman's quest to find a new beginning.

Book 1	*Love Is a Gentle Stranger*
Book 2	*Love's Silent Song*
Book 3	*Diary of a Loving Heart*
Book 4	*Love Leads Home*
Book 5	*Love Follows the Heart*
Book 6	*Love's Enduring Hope*

The Journey To Love Series

The continuing story of Rachel Buchanan and Colby Lord along the Frontier Trail to Oregon.

Book 1	*Journey To Love*
Book 2	*Dreams Beyond Tomorrow*
Book 3	*Seasons of Love*
Book 4	*My Heart's Desire*
Book 5	*The Heart Remembers*

The Love's Soft Whisper Series

Courtney Glamora is sent to the rugged Columbia Territory where she becomes a pawn in a family feud.

Book 1	*Love's Soft Whisper*
Book 2	*Love's Beautiful Dream*
Book 3	*When Hearts Awaken*
Book 4	*Another Spring*
Book 5	*When Morning Comes Again*
Book 6	*Gently Love Beckons*

Quiet Moments—A Daily Devotional for Women
The Quiet Heart—A Daily Devotional for Women

Contact your local bookstore or Harvest House Publishers for more information about books by June Masters Bacher:

Customer Service
Harvest House Publishers
1075 Arrowsmith
Eugene, Oregon 97402

Dear Reader:

We would appreciate hearing from you regarding this Harvest House fiction book. It will enable us to continue to give you the best in Christian publishing.

1. What most influenced you to purchase *From This Time Forth*?
   ☐ Author   ☐ Recommendations
   ☐ Subject matter   ☐ Cover/Title
   ☐ Backcover copy   ☐ _____

2. Where did you purchase this book?
   ☐ Christian bookstore   ☐ Grocery store
   ☐ General bookstore   ☐ Other
   ☐ Department store

3. Your overall rating of this book:
   ☐ Excellent   ☐ Very good   ☐ Good   ☐ Fair   ☐ Poor

4. How likely would you be to purchase other books by this author?
   ☐ Very likely   ☐ Not very likely
   ☐ Somewhat likely   ☐ Not at all

5. What types of books most interest you?
   (check all that apply)
   ☐ Women's Books   ☐ Fiction
   ☐ Marriage Books   ☐ Biographies
   ☐ Current Issues   ☐ Children's Books
   ☐ Self Help/Psychology ☐ Youth Books
   ☐ Bible Studies   ☐ Other _____

6. Please check the box next to your age group.
   ☐ Under 18   ☐ 25-34   ☐ 45-54
   ☐ 18-24   ☐ 35-44   ☐ 55 and over

Mail to: Editorial Director
Harvest House Publishers
1075 Arrowsmith
Eugene, OR 97402

Name _____

Address _____

City _____ State _____ Zip _____

Thank you for helping us to help you in future publications!